HARREN PRESS PRESENTS

A SCARLETT NIGHTMARE:

DEATH AWAITS

HORROR ANTHOLOGY

Edited by: Samantha Lafantasie, Audrey Grover, Mike Gasparovic
Cover Art/Design by Sean Spinks

Table of Contents

Dedications:

To everyone who helped make this possible. We at Harren Press Salute you!

Forward

Death Awaits. A fitting title, for that is what awaits you within its pages. Like a blanket sewn from severed flesh, it embraces you with the comfort of congealed blood. Exactly what you would expect from a volume bound in human skin. I remember the symphony of screams as I flayed my victims. My blades are still covered with their gore, but don't worry, I promise they will be clean enough for you to see your own blood decorating them.

In the meantime, why don't you begin reading? I promise that death will be waiting for you when the last page is turned…

-Mr Empty

Dead Air
By
Jessica Freeburg

"Look, if I see a big, black, shadow-man standing at the foot of my bed, I'm pulling the covers over my head."

The punch of the airbag knocked every bit of breath out of him. His ears still rang with the sound of twisting metal. The voices streamed through the radio, muffled by steam hissing through the crumpled hood of his sedan.

"Not me! I'm getting out of bed and channeling my inner Ralph Machio!"

He opened his eyes to darkness. At least he thought his eyes were open. The last thing he had seen was the tree a second before his vehicle smacked head-on into it. Before that he had seen something else – something even more terrifying. Or had he?

"Right! And how exactly do you plan to beat up a shadow figure? It's a shadow!"

Pain pierced his abdomen. He slipped his hand under the inflated airbag to the sticky, wetness of blood.

His eyes finally adjusted to the night sky. Moonlight glimmered off shards of glass clinging to the frame of the windshield as the airbag wheezed and shrunk in front of him. Blood trickled from his nose, mangled by the impact of the bag.

"Have you ever seen Karate Kid, Shane? Pretty sure those moves can take down any opponent."

A hanging cluster of glass quivered, then crashed against the dashboard. He squeezed his eyes shut against the sound, and swallowed thick, salty fluid down the back of his throat.

"That shadow-man doesn't stand a chance once I get my wax-on-wax-off motion going."
"That mental picture may be scarier than the shadow man."

Warm air rushed against his cheek. He squeezed his eyes tighter as if not seeing the thing again would make it not be there. The smell of rotten meat, like last week's chicken dinner festering in the summer sun, rose into his broken and bloodied nose.

"I think my plan is better than hiding under a blanket. Just 'cause you can't see it, doesn't mean it isn't there."

The rush of air might have been the breeze flowing through the broken windows, but it felt warm – like breath – and then it stopped. That thing he had seen in his rearview mirror, it wasn't real. It couldn't be real. But he had stared at it so long that he didn't see the tree until it was too late. He opened his eyes, now nearly convinced the smell had been his imagination.

A bloodied face resembling a man stared back at him. The beast was perched in the passenger's seat, leaning toward him over the console. The only thing wider than the creature's yellow eyes was the smile that seemed to split its fleshless face. Blood pulsed across the white skull that encased the eyes. Bits of flesh clung to its temples and mandible. Lip tissue framed a garish smile of needle-sharp teeth.

"It's you." The driver's voice slipped past his lips in a ragged whisper. "I didn't believe him … you're real…"

The creature's chest fell as it exhaled, the charred bits of flesh clinging to its rib cage swayed with the motion. Rancid breath rushed against the injured man's face again. The smell of rot caused bile to rise in his throat as he choked on his own blood.

"We'll have to leave you with those mental images of Jolie attacking a shadow man, kung foo style, while we break for the news. Stay tuned for more Paranormal Talk after the break."

He tried to move, but he was pinned into the seat by the twisted frame of his vehicle. What had once been his car might now become his tomb. With every strained movement, blood rushed from the pierced flesh of his abdomen. The bloodied creature sat. Breathing. Waiting. Watching each labored breath.

***

"We're back with more of our listener's creepy tales on Paranormal Talk. I'm your host, Shane Baker along with kung foo master, Jolie Reid. We have Jonathan on the line. Jonathan, thanks for calling in tonight. What's your story?"

A light static came over the telephone.

"Did we lose him?" Jolie asked. She adjusted her headphones, causing her long, black hair to bunch up on top her head.

"Jonathan, are ya' still with us?" Shane glanced at the phone where the red light indicated that the line was still in use.

More static came across the audio, followed by the light clearing of a throat.

"I'm here," said the quiet voice of a young boy.

"Hey, buddy, you sound a little young to be a fan of Paranormal Talk. Do your mom and dad know you're listening?"

"I listen with my dad every night."

"Dude, you have some pretty cool parents," Jolie said.

A small laugh cut through the steady static on the other line.

"What's your story, Jonathan?" Shane peered over his microphone and raised an eyebrow at Jolie who sat behind the soundproof glass of the control room.

Jolie scribbled on a sheet of paper and held it up. It read, "Kids are CREEPY!" Shane smiled and nodded before ruffling his hands through his light-brown, wavy mop and pointing at Jolie. She adjusted her headset and smoothed her hair down.

"The man comes in my room at night," the boy whispered.

"What man?" Jolie asked.

"I don't know," Jonathan said. "He just stares at me and smiles."

"Is he human or is he more of a shadow figure like we were talking about earlier?" Shane asked, leaning back against the gray fabric of his chair. He laced his hands behind his head, the thick muscles of his biceps flexed. His eyebrows furrowed in con-templation.

There was a long pause. The boy cleared his throat again, then took a slow, deep breath before speaking.

"He's a man, only he doesn't have any skin. Well, he has a little skin, but it's all burnt and hanging."

Jolie shuddered. "You actually see this thing in your room?"

"Every night," the boy said in a hushed tone.

Hinges squeaked as a door opened on the boy's end of the line.

"I have to go," he whispered urgently before the phone clicked and the line went silent.

Jolie and Shane exchanged worried looks.

"Well, folks, you wanted freaky. I'd say you got it tonight." Shane's voice boomed with the vibrato of a showman into the microphone.

"That was a little extra creepy," Jolie said. "We hear a lot of strange things on this program, but hearing the description of that guy from the voice of a child upped the creep factor a thousand percent."

"You do know that one hundred is the highest mathematical percentage, right?" Shane teased, not missing a beat.

"What do you suppose he's talking about?" Jolie asked. "You don't think he actually sees a fleshless guy hanging out in his room every night, do you?" Her face was tight with genuine concern.

The station had been thrilled when Jolie, fresh out of college, had applied for the position with Paranormal Talk five years ago. Many fans first tuned in after meeting the uncommonly beautiful co-host at conventions or seeing her on the show's banner. Shane pulled in some female followers with his boyish good looks. But it was the pair's comfortable banter, and Shane's perspective on all things paranormal, that solidified their devoted fan-base.

"There's a legend of a creature called Raw Head. It tends to visit children mostly, and is said to watch them with this awful grin," Shane replied. "Based on his description, that would be my first guess."

"That's truly horrifying," Jolie said. "What do these creatures do?"

"Typically, they just remain motionless and stare – sometimes all night long. It's a pretty creepy phenomenon." Shane shrugged his shoulders. "Let's see what our next caller's creepy tale is."

"We have Tina on line one."

"Tina, what's your story?"

"Well, I was going to tell you guys about this time I saw a shadow figure in my closet, but honestly, I'm a little worried about that kid. Can that Raw Head thing hurt him?"

"I've never heard anything to indicate that they are dangerous, but they sure are creepy as hell. I'm sure our friend Jonathan is going to be alright."

"Gosh, I hope so. I'm a mother," the woman said. "I can't imagine if something like that was happening to one of…"

"Actually, Tina," Jolie cut into the conversation. "Jonathan has called back, would you mind if we put him back on for a moment."

"Of course, please do!" The caller sounded relieved.

"Jonathan, you're on the air again. Is everything okay, buddy?" Shane asked.

"I'm scared." The boy's voice was a whisper.

"Is the man in the room with you now?" Jolie's voice cracked with tension.

"Yes."

"Hey, buddy, is your mom or dad home?" Shane asked.

"My mom is."

"Go get your mom, Jonathan," Shane urged.

"I can't…"

The phone went dead. Jolie stared at Shane. The theme music began to roll in the background, and Shane glanced at the clock. It was midnight.

"I'm afraid that's all we have time for tonight, folks. I'm sure most of our listeners are a little worried about our last caller. I want to assure you that we will be calling Jonathan back immediately and speaking to his parents. For now, we need to say goodnight.

We appreciate all your phone calls this evening. Sleep well, and we'll be back tomorrow night with more Paranormal Talk."

Shane pointed a finger at Jolie in the control room. Then he held his thumb and pinky to his ear like a phone. The theme music faded as Jolie pressed the talkback button.

"Holy crap!" Jolie said. "That is by far the creepiest thing I've heard in the five years I've been doing this show."

"Honestly, I'm a little freaked out, and nothing freaks me out anymore," Shane said.

"Okay, I just dialed the number that Jonathan's call came from," Jolie said.

Picking up the receiver of the desktop phone, Shane pressed the blinking button on the dial pad and waited as the phone rang. On the fifth ring, the phone on the other end clicked.

"Hello?" A woman mumbled, her voice thick with sleep.

"Hello, ma'am. I'm sorry to be calling this late. My name is Shane Baker. I'm the host of Paranormal Talk, and we received a call from your son tonight that has us a little worried."

"Is this a joke?" she asked, her voice bubbling with anger.

"No, ma'am, not at all," Shane replied. "I don't want to alarm you, but your son, Jonathan, seemed very afraid that there was a creature of some kind in his room."

"You're sick! How dare you call me in the middle of the night saying something like that!" The woman's voice shook with rage.

Shane, usually unflappable, stumbled over his words. "I'm not trying to frighten you. I'm really not, but your son seemed so terrified, and before we could get to the bottom of it, the call dropped."

The woman's trembling breath was the only thing that permeated the silence.

"Could you just check on Jonathan before I let you go? We want to make sure he's alright."

"Jonathan has been dead for seven months." The woman choked back a sob. "You are a sick son of a bitch. If you call here again, I'll call the police."

The phone clicked before the buzz of the dial tone filled Shane's ears. He held the phone in front of him, staring at it, as Jolie heaved the metal door open and stepped into the room.

"What'd she say?" Jolie eyed him expectantly. "Is the kid okay?"

Shane continued to gaze at the phone in his hand. Slowly, he set the phone on the cradle and turned his attention to his co-host.

"He's dead."

Jolie shook her head in disbelief. "What … how?"

"The woman said he's been dead for seven months." Shane ran his hand through his hair and leaned back in his chair. "It had to be a crank call from someone. Maybe she has another kid in the house."

"That's messed up," Jolie said. She took a deep breath. "For a second, I thought you meant she *just* found him dead. I was freaking out!"

"Just when you think this job can't get any weirder…" Shane shook his head and grabbed his jacket off the back of his chair. "Shall we call it a night?"

"Yes, please." Jolie slipped the strap of her purse over her shoulder.

***

Shane dropped into the chair and spun himself around until his knees were under the desk. Resting his elbows on either side of the keyboard, he rubbed the palms of his hands into his eyes. Sleep had not come easily the previous night. In the half-decade he'd been hosting Paranormal Talk, nothing had rattled him as much as last night's phone call from the little boy.

"You couldn't sleep either, huh?" Jolie set a cup on Shane's desk. Steam from the coffee rose above the white Styrofoam.

"Thanks," he said, lifting the cup to his lips. "That kid last night…"

"…was totally freaky," Jolie interrupted.

"I can't stop thinking about him."

"That's why you're calling his mom back today."

"No way! She was furious with me last night." Shane took another sip from the cup.

"Fine. Then I'll call." She pulled a slip of paper with a phone number from her pocket and smoothed it out in front of Shane's phone. Her fingers bounced over the numbers on the keypad before she raised the receiver to her ear and hoisted herself up to sit on the edge of the desk.

"This is a bad idea," Shane said shaking his head.

"Shh!" Jolie held a finger to her mouth. "It's ringing."

"Hello, you've reached the Fairbanks residence," the happy voice of a woman welcomed the call. "Tim, Colleen, and Jonathan can't take your call right now. Please leave us a message, and we'll call you back."

"Mrs. Fairbanks, this is Jolie Reid from Paranormal Talk." Jolie scribbled the names on the slip of paper as she spoke. "We were concerned about the phone calls we received from your home last night. We're just calling to check in and make sure you're doing alright. Hope everything is okay. Have a good night."

Jolie replaced the receiver in the cradle. Her eyes narrowed as she gazed at the slip of paper she'd written on.

"Oh, no. You're doing the 'it's-about-to-get-serious' stare-down with that piece of paper," Shane teased.

Jolie jumped off the desk. "Well, I've got a few names to work with. I'm going to do a little digging."

"You live for research."

"Then I can tell my mom that degree in journalism wasn't a total waste," Jolie said as she walked away.

"Wait, your mom thinks you're wasting your education working here?" Shane called after her.

***

"Dinner time," Jolie announced when she returned to Shane's desk with a notebook in one hand and a bag from Jo-Jo's Diner in the other.

Shane groaned. "Is it seriously late enough for dinner already?"

"You've had your ass in that seat for a good nine hours. And if I know you, you skipped out on lunch," she said. She placed the sack between Shane and the computer screen. "Your usual. Hands off my French fries."

Shane reached into the white paper package that steamed when he unrolled the folded top. "One isn't going to kill me."

"One, and no more! I won't be held responsible for your high cholesterol."

Shane unwrapped his turkey-avacado roll and popped the lid on a side salad. The smell of Jolie's bacon cheeseburger and fries at the bottom of the bag taunted him. He snatched a fry before pushing the bag toward the end of his desk.

"Here's what I dug up on the Fairbanks family." Jolie rolled her chair over from her desk a few feet away and opened the notebook on her lap.

"Jonathan Fairbanks, age 10, died exactly seven months ago yesterday."

"The timing of that is a little creepy."

"Even creepier is how the kid died. He fell out of the top bunk of his bed and broke his neck. His dad found him dead on his bedroom floor in the morning."

Shane used a napkin to wipe a drip of dressing from his chin that had slipped from his turkey-roll.

"That is an unusual way for a kid to die," he said as he chewed.

"Now, if that was all we knew, we could brush it off as a freak accident. But given what Jonathan told us last night about the fleshless man who visits him every evening, I'm inclined to wonder if there's more to it."

"*He* didn't tell us. He's dead. One of his brothers must have been crank calling."

"Interestingly," Jolie continued, "it doesn't appear that he has any brothers – or sisters for that matter. Based on all the info I could find, Jonathan was an only child."

Shane took another bite from his sandwich. "How the heck did you scrounge up all this information?"

"I have a friend who's an EMT for Fairview hospital. And a little thing called Google. David, the father, is a financial analyst. Mom was a teacher at West Oaks Elementary in Albertville, fourth grade, until the end of the last school year. I couldn't find any record of employment after that."

As Shane stabbed at a tomato wedge in his salad, the phone rang. He grabbed a French fry before answering the phone.

"Shane Baker speaking." Even off-air, his voice carried a vibrato that gave it a musical quality. He snatched another fry from Jolie's pile.

"My name is Colleen Fairbanks." The woman's voice spoke quietly. She cleared her throat before continuing. "You called me last night about my son."

Shane froze, the fry he'd swiped resting against his lower lip. Setting it down, he took a turn clearing his throat.

"Yes, ma'am." The usual showman tone of his voice was replaced by sympathy. "I'm terribly sorry about upsetting you." Making eye contact with Jolie, he mouthed, "It's his mom."

Jolie set her burger down and watched Shane intensely while he spoke to the woman.

"I didn't believe you. I was home alone. My husband was away for work…" Her voice trailed off. Shane heard a sniffle before she continued. "He died in a car accident last night." Her voice cracked on the last word.

"I'm so sorry," Shane said solemnly.

"I've been in shock all day." She sniffled again before continuing. "But I couldn't stop thinking about your call."

"I can understand how my call upset you, and I want to apologize…"

"I checked the phone records," the woman cut in. "Two calls came from my house last night after I had gone to sleep. One at 11:50, the other at 11:55. Both calls were to your show." She took a deep breath. "Someone was here … in my home … while I slept, and they called you."

"I'm not sure what to make of that, Mrs. Fairbanks. The caller sounded like a young boy. He told us his name was Jonathan."

"How is that possible?" She paused. "He told you about the man, didn't he?"

Shane was too stunned to answer.

"He told my husband about the man, too, but we didn't believe him. I believe him now." Her voice trembled as she spoke. "Can you help me?"

"I can try."

"Can you come to my house? I want you to help me find out who the man is and what he wanted with my son. And if Jonathan's spirit called you, maybe you can help me speak to him."

"Yes, Jolie and I could come over."

Jolie put her hand over her mouth

"Tonight," the woman said.

"Tonight?" Shane looked at Jolie as he spoke. She nodded her head. "Can you give me your address?"

Shane scribbled the information on a sticky note before hanging up.

"Eat up," he said to Jolie. "We're going to do a little paranormal investigating."

***

Shane rang the doorbell and then stuffed his hands into his jean pockets. They had driven from the city through two suburbs to get to Albertville, and then drove another ten minutes through town until they found the address. The home was dark, except for a dim light that appeared to be on in the far, back corner. Craning his neck, he looked through a front window.

A woman stood in the center of what appeared to be a living room, the moonlight through the window was just bright enough to make her visible. A long bathrobe covered her from neck to mid-calf. Although the details of her face were shrouded in shadows, it was clear that she was looking back at Shane.

Raising a hand from his pocket, he waved. The woman remained still. Goose bumps rose on the back of his neck.

"Is she going to let us in or just stand there staring at us?" Jolie asked as she rubbed her hands together to warm them. The autumn chill had begun to make local residents break out their light jackets, but Jolie hadn't quite given in to the need for an extra layer. She shivered in a cotton sweater and jeans.

Shane looked at Jolie. "Should we ring the bell again? I mean, I think she sees us, but…"

Before he finished the thought, the door began to slowly open. The pale woman peered at them around the edge of the oak frame. Her face was framed by strands of blonde hair that had slipped out of a loose braid.

"Come in," she said, her voice just above a whisper.

Jolie hurried into the warm house. Shane hesitated just beyond the threshold. The woman's gaunt appearance gave Shane a feeling of unease. She reminded him of a cancer patient entering the final stages of a losing battle. In the pale light of the moon, her skin had a gray-blue tone that made her look as if the battle had already been lost.

She had lost her son and now her husband, Shane reasoned. Of course she looked worn-out and haggard by grief.

He stepped in further. The goose bumps spread across his body as the door closed behind him.

Mrs. Fairbanks thanked them for coming. Shane offered his hand in greeting. The woman shook his hand limply, her flesh as chilled as the breeze outside.

Pointing toward the hallway, she said, "Jonathan's room is down there."

Jolie began to walk, but paused before leaving the living room. She glanced back at Shane who still lingered near the front door.

"It's the room with the light on at the end of the hall," Mrs. Fairbanks said. She waited for Shane to move toward Jolie, and then she followed behind him.

Shane couldn't stop thinking that the house felt dark. Not just a physical darkness that comes from the night or a lack of artificial light, but the kind of dark that penetrates the soul – the kind that makes your intuition scream for you to run. Shane pushed down his worry. Sometimes, the story of a place breaks into his rational thought. The fear in the boy's voice on the phone last night, and the realization that he may have been speaking to a dead child was more than even he could process without being freaked out.

The house was quiet. Even their footsteps seemed hushed against the carpet. Images of a happy family hung in frames on either side of the hallway. A row of photos featuring a little boy from the time he was a bald-headed baby to several school headshots, highlighted by a playful grin often missing a tooth or two, nearly filled an entire wall. Across from the bedroom door was a bathroom. A nightlight illuminated the space in a dull yellow glow. Shane glanced into the room and noticed the bathtub just beyond the entrance, curtained by black fabric speckled with screen-printed stars. It was like looking at a clear, night sky.

Turning toward the bedroom doorway, the bright blue paint on the walls created a glow that leaked into the hall. Jolie stepped into the room with Shane following closely behind. Mrs. Fairbanks stood a step beyond the doorframe, her hands tugging at the sleeves of her robe, pulling them down until only the tips of her bone-white fingers peeked below the fabric.

Shane walked slowly around the room, from one corner to the next, looking under the bed, in the closet, and behind the floor-length curtains made of the same fabric as the curtain in front of the bathtub. He wasn't looking for anything specific. He was letting the details of the space sink in. He could imagine the young boy in the pictures curled up in the top bunk, shaking with fear as some creature smiled at him from the doorway where his mother now stood.

Jolie pulled out a small, silver, digital recorder and pressed Record.

"This is Jolie, Shane and Colleen Fairbanks in Jonathan's bedroom. EVP session one."

She sat the device on the top of the dresser before continuing.

"Jonathan, are you with us tonight?" She waited, allowing enough time for an answer before moving on to the next question. "Did you call Paranormal Talk last night?" Wait. "Do you need our help, Jonathan?" Wait. "Do you need us to protect you from that man?"

Jolie picked up the recorder and pressed Stop. She glanced at Mrs. Fairbanks, still outside the doorway, before pressing play. Her own voice came through the speaker with a tinny sound that comes from the volume being too high. Each question was followed by silence, until the last.

Before the recording ended, a voice whispered, "He's here." It was enough to recognize the same, small, frightened voice they had heard on the phone the night before.

Shane nodded at Jolie. "That was very clear."

Mrs. Fairbanks slowly nodded. "That was Jonathan."

Jolie pressed Record again and set the device back on the dresser.

"EVP session 2. We heard you, Jonathan. We're here to help you, but you have to tell us what you need us to do. How can we protect you from the man?"

She reached for the recorder, but before she could press Stop, a young voice called out from the corner of the room.

"I'm scared."

Jolie and Shane spun to see the full-body apparition of a boy, around ten-years-old. He was solid as any human, huddled with his arms around his knees in the corner of the bedroom. The checkered print of his pajamas swayed as he rocked back and forth.

"Jonathan?" Shane's voice trembled as the name passed his lips. He had never seen a spirit take on such a fully human appearance, yet it was obvious this child was not among the living. His eyes were sunken into dark-rimmed sockets. His pale skin possessed an unnatural bluish-gray tint.

Shane turned to Mrs. Fairbanks who had stepped just barely over the threshold of the room. She peered around frantically as if searching.

"What is it? Do you see him?" she asked.

"You don't?" Jolie asked.

"No! Where is he?" she asked, her voice becoming shrill.

The goose bumps returned to Shane as he watched her – her eyes – her skin. She looked almost as dead as the boy.

"He's here!" Jonathan said.

Jolie scanned the room. "Where? I don't see anything."

"I'm scared," Jonathan said again.

Shane stepped closer. He crouched down so he could speak directly to him. The color of the boy's face and the blank, fogged-glass look of his eyes made Shane's heart race. He was staring into the face of a dead child. For the first time in many years, he was frightened.

"We want to help you, Jonathan," Shane said as calmly as possible. "We want to help your mother."

Mrs. Fairbanks moved behind Shane. She stared into the corner where Jonathan sat. "I don't see him. Why can't I see him?"

"You can't help her," Jonathan said sadly.

"Why not?" Jolie asked.

The boy began to rock faster, his eyes wide in terror as he stared at his mother.

"My mother's dead," he whispered.

Jolie shook her head. "Your mom is right here." She looked at Shane. "Maybe he can't see her either."

"The man won't let me go to her." Jonathan began to cry.

"Where is the man, Jonathan?" Shane asked.

Jonathan raised a trembling finger and pointed over Shane's shoulder. Shane rose to his feet and spun around expecting to see the ghastly Raw Head. Instead he stared into the face of the boy's mother who continued to look into the space where Jonathan's spirit sat.

"Where, Jonathan?" He looked at the boy who had backed further into the corner.

He looked up at Shane with the terror of a trapped animal facing their predator moments before being consumed. He pointed again behind Shane.

Jolie looked frantically between the door and Shane. "There's nothing there!"

Shane again looked closely at Jonathan's mother. She stopped searching the corner of the room with her eyes, and returned his stare. The dark skin around her eyes seemed darker than before, and just below her lower lip, a gash about an inch long trickled blood down her chin.

"Mrs. Fairbanks?" His voice was unsteady. "You're bleeding."

She reached up and touched the wound. As she ran her fingers across the skin, her pale flesh began to peel, and more blood oozed from the tear. The white of her jawbone glistened through the blood. Her eyes remained locked on Shane's eyes.

Shane's breath caught in his throat.

"He's here," Jonathan said.

Mrs. Fairbanks smiled, still staring into Shane's eyes. Her smile grew bigger as Shane's eyes widened. The skin around her lips and on her cheeks began to split and then drop to the floor near her feet.

Jolie screamed as the woman's scalp slowly slid off the back of her skull, leaving just a few tufts of hair attached to bits of skin that remained. Blood oozed over the bone like water over a rock.

The creature cocked its head at Shane before stepping closer. The garishly large smile took up most of the nearly fleshless face.

Shane moved protectively toward the boy. As he stared into the face of the creature, he realized the horror Jonathan must have felt, alone in his room with this beast.

"Jonathan, do you know what it wants?"

"My soul," he whimpered. "He took my mom and now he wants me."

"How did he take your mom?"

"She was sad … all the time. She cried a lot. Sometimes she wouldn't get out of her bed for days."

The creature stood perfectly still. The robe that had covered its body now lay in a heap at its feet, amidst a pile of flesh that seemed to melt off its body leaving charred remains to dangle from the rib, pelvic and clavicle bones.

"One day, when I came home from school, I found her in the bathtub … the water was red and her eyes were open, but they didn't see anything anymore." Jonathan began to cry. "He was there, staring at her."

Jolie inched backward toward the door, staring at the creature as it watched Shane. It still seemed to be searching for Jonathan as it peered around Shane's body.

"I don't think it can see you, Jonathan." Jolie's voice squeaked.

"He can't see him." The gentle voice of a woman came from the hallway.

Jolie jumped as she looked over her shoulder. Mrs. Fairbanks stood inside the bathroom door, a soft glow surrounded her. She wore the same robe and long nightgown that the creature had been wearing before. Her face was bright, her flesh pale, but not sickly like the skin the beast had worn.

"He's from Hell," she continued. "He was my demon before I listened to his words and took my life. When Jonathan's spirit left his body, this demon kept him here – trapped in his death – too frightened to move toward the light because this monster blocks his path."

"Why did you call us here!?" Jolie said.

"I had to. He needed you to help him."

"But when we called back last night…" Shane began.

"That was the creature, not me. It knew Jonathan was reaching for help and it did not want him to succeed."

"How can we help him?" Jolie asked.

"He needs to come to me," she replied. "The demon can't see his soul because he belongs to the light, but Jonathan has been too terrified to move from this room because that beast has stayed watch over this door since my son's soul left his body."

Jonathan looked up at Shane, his eyes wet with tears.

"Go to your mother, Jonathan," Shane encouraged.

Jonathan shook his head. He pressed against the wall.

"I will stay between you and the monster," Shane said. "I won't let him get you."

Shane reached his hand toward the frightened boy. Jonathan hesitated and looked from the beast back to Shane, before putting his small, cold hand into the trembling palm of the radio host he had listened to with his dad.

Taking a step forward, Shane kept his body between Jonathan and the creature. The only sound it made was the wheeze of the air that flapped the flesh on its chest as it breathed. It watched Shane intently with a perpetual grisly smile as the pair slowly inched along the wall toward the door. The boy's cold body pressed against Shane's thigh like a plank of ice, sending shivers through him.

The beast turned its head and reached a gnarled hand toward them as they made their way around the room. When they were safely out of the monster's reach, Shane ran toward the door, holding Jonathan's hand. He pushed the boy toward his mother.

The moment the boy fell into his mother's arms a bright light exploded around them. Jolie and Shane shielded their eyes. In an instant, the pair vanished. The demonic beast rose on its toes. It reared back its head, splattering blood through the air and screeched.

"Run!" Shane grabbed Jolie's hand and pulled her through the doorway.

They rushed down the narrow hall. Jolie tripped, bumping hard against the wall. A portrait of the Fairbanks family fell to the floor, and the glass shattered in the frame. Shane, still holding Jolie's hand, pulled her to her feet and nearly dragged her through the living room.

They could hear the sound of the beast's feet pound against the carpet as it followed them down the hallway. Shane's hand slipped on the doorknob before finally twisting it open. He nearly flung Jolie through the doorway before looking back to see the monster crashing into the walls of the hall as it ran. The pictures crashed around him as he stumbled toward Shane.

"Get in the car!" he screamed, his voice cutting through the night like a saw through metal. He fumbled for the keys in his pocket as he raced toward the vehicle.

Slamming the door shut, he jammed the keys into the ignition and stepped on the gas while shifting into reverse.

"Go! Go! Go!" Jolie's shriek was barely audible over the rev of the engine.

The creature stood in the doorway of the house, head thrown back, blood dripping from bits of flesh that clung to its bones as it screamed at the sky.

Shane backed toward the street. Missing the last half of the driveway, his tires tore up the grass in the yard. The car bounced over the curb and onto the street before he shifted into drive and sped away. Jolie turned to watch through the back window.

"Is it following us?" Shane asked.

"It's still standing in the door."

She watched as they turned a corner, and she continued staring back all the way through town. She finally turned to face the front of the vehicle when they were a few miles from the radio station.

"It can't hurt us," Shane said. "Spirits can't hurt people." He spoke to comfort himself as much as to comfort her.

"Then why did we run?"

"Because that was the scariest damn thing I've seen in my entire life."

Silence hung between them for several blocks before she spoke. "How do you know it can't hurt us? What if it comes after us?"

"It can't, and it won't." Shane said. "That's according to everything I've read."

Neither of them spoke for the remainder of the drive because the truth was, and they both knew, that Shane didn't know that for sure. There were no hard facts on paranormal creatures. There were theories and guesses, but no one knew for sure. Years of radio calls had proven that. So they let the fear settle within them and accepted the uncertainty that would always be a part of them. The beast would chase them for the rest of their lives – if only in their minds.

Prey Upon the Wicked
By
Naching T. Kassa

Komen Daru awoke in the darkness of his sleep chamber. The engines of the ship thrummed softly, providing the only sound within the room. Daru wondered what woke him. He had the vague notion that it had been a scream. A strong, psychic scream.

A soft tone sounded, and he knew that a subordinate waited outside his door. He slid a grey, three-fingered hand over a panel in the wall. The door slid open.

"Komen Daru?" A tentative voice said. "I apologize for awakening you during your rest period, but a situation has arisen."

"What is it, Omen Mu?" Daru replied wearily and blinked his large, black eyes.

"It is Omen Plattu … his life force has been terminated."

"What?" Daru cried. He rose off the long, silver dais that served as his rest altar. "Show me."

"The body has not been moved," Omen Mu explained, as they hurried down the curved corridor of the saucer-ship. "I have taken the precaution of assembling the crew at the scene as well."

Six pairs of onyx eyes turned upon Komen Daru as he arrived. Their grey faces were expressionless, but Daru could sense their surprise and fear.

The body of Omen Plattu lay upon the silver floor. His long arms bent behind him in an unnatural manner. The eyes were dull, having lost the gleam of life some time ago.

The strangest aspect of the body was the color. Even in death, Daru's people retained their grey pallor. Plattu's body was blanched white.

Komen Daru knelt beside the body and studied it, a gnawing fear growing within him. He carefully shielded his feelings from the others, afraid to send them into a panic. His mind screamed "disease" as his eyes scanned Plattu's skin.

Omen Plattu had been part of the specimen gathering mission on the water planet they now orbited. He and two others, Omen Lan and Omen Dei, had returned to the ship only an hour previously. They had brought back several specimens and Daru feared that an undiscovered virus might have been among them.

"Have the body taken to the laboratory, Mu." He said. "I will perform the autopsy myself."

Omen Mu beckoned two of the crewmen forward. Omen Lan and Omen Ko stepped up to take charge. They lifted the body easily and hurried away.

Daru pulled Omen Mu aside. "See that everyone on board is sanitized."

"You fear disease?" Mu asked, fear spiking within him.

"Calm yourself," Daru commanded. "I only take precautions." He watched as the body disappeared around a curve in the corridor.

"And as another precaution, Mu," he continued, "leave the orbit of this strange planet at once."

Mu nodded in assent.

There was no need to enter the decontamination chamber following the autopsy, but Komen Daru did anyway. He walked, sans spacesuit, into the small room and allowed the sanitizing gasses to flow over him. His thoughts were elsewhere.

Omen Plattu's life force had not been terminated by any virus. The true reason for his death was extreme loss of blood. His entire body had been drained, drained through the two small puncture wounds on Plattu's neck.

Plattu's arms were broken prior to his death. Apparently, he had been attacked from behind.

All of Komen Daru's people possessed the strength necessary to inflict such a grievous injury. They did not possess a means to drain a body of blood. Nor did they harbor any such inclination. At least Daru hoped they harbored none.

Daru had heard of a psychological illness, which affected about twenty-five-percent of those who traveled in deep space. For no reason at all, and without any warning, the victim of such sickness would go completely mad. Violence was often a part of such a fit. Daru wondered whether a member of his crew had become "Space Sick".

As Daru left the decontamination chamber, he resolved to question each member of the crew with their psychic shields down.

He entered the corridor and slid a hand over a communication panel in the wall. Omen Mu answered immediately, and Daru gave his orders.

A psychic-scream ripped through Daru's mind. The fear paralyzed him for several seconds, forcing him to run through every emotion the scream expressed. Aside from the fear, he felt hopelessness and despair. All of which culminated in the awe of death.

When the paralysis subsided, Daru ordered every crewman to assemble in the Control Chamber, then hurried to that location himself.

Within moments five crewmen stood before him. He waited another minute for the arrival of Omen Tartu, though he knew there was no chance he would arrive. Tartu was the victim of this latest attack.

They found the body over twenty minutes later. It had been folded in half and placed in a refuse tube. Like the body of Omen Plattu, the skin was a strange, chalky white.

Another autopsy was performed. Daru arrived at the same conclusion as before. Cause of death was complete blood loss.

Daru wasted no time in interrogating the remaining members of the crew. They submitted to his queries willingly, with no shields. All crewmen showed no sign of guile. None of them could have committed the crimes.

After the interrogations, Komen Daru arranged a meeting with Omen Mu in the Command Chamber. His plan was to report the current set of circumstances to Domen Rar, leader of High

Command. When he entered the Chamber, he discovered that Omen Mu waited for him.

"Communication with High Command will be impossible, Komen." Mu announced as Daru entered. "The Communications Uplink has been destroyed."

Daru stared at the instrument panel. It had been smashed beyond repair. Electromagnetic gel oozed from the machinery.

"It appears our assailant wishes to disable us." Omen said, pointing to another instrument panel. "He has also destroyed our navigation system."

"Go to the armory." Daru said. "Collect weapons for yourself and for me. Confine the crew to their Sleep Chambers. We shall search the ship."

Daru began his search in the Holding Cells of the ship. This area housed the specimens gathered from the various planets visited by Daru's people. These specimens were harvested for their ability to carry certain genetically engineered viruses.

The scientists on Home World would extract DNA from the specimens. Then, they would use the genetic material to create viruses capable of destroying all life on the specimen's planet. Once this had been accomplished, the infected specimen was reintroduced into its environment.

Within two days, the plague would take hold and most of the planet's population would be decimated. By the end of the week, the plague would have ran its course and the planet would then be ripe for colonization.

Occasionally a specimen, which was already infected with a disease common to that planet, was brought on board. When such an event took place, the Komen was ordered to program the ship for self-destruction. No infection was ever been brought back to Home World.

The Holding Cells were plastiglass enclosures filled with cryogenic gel and organized in groups of ten. The specimens were placed inside the gel and frozen for travel. Daru made his way to the group, which held the newest acquisitions. These specimens had been taken from the water planet.

Creatures, frozen in cryogenic stasis, watched him as he entered. His laser weapon— a long, fluorescent, azure tube—held at the ready, he moved slow, filled with great discomfort.

He paused as his foot encountered a strange, oily puddle on the floor. Following the slick, he discovered it to be cryogenic gel, leading to a large enclosure, one which had been utterly destroyed.

A communication panel on the left lit up. Omen Mu's voice filled the room.

"Komen Daru, I have found something of great interest in the Morgue. Please, come at once."

Daru passed a hand over the glowing panel and said, "I too have made a discovery. I think you should come here first, for I believe I have found the source of our misfortune."

"Very well, Komen." Mu said. The panel dimmed.

While Daru waited for Mu's arrival, he investigated the remains of the enclosure. The name plate was nowhere to be found, so he was uncertain as to what the enclosure had contained. The only thing he found was a gold time piece. Inside was a small image imprinted upon a slick piece of paper. He recognized it as what the inhabitants of the water planet called a photograph.

The image was of a human female's face. Daru winced at the extreme ugliness of the image. The animal possessed long, red hair, small green eyes and a large mouth. Daru was glad that his people would soon be eradicating these creatures from the water world. They were too ugly to live. He closed the piece and placed it in his top pocket.

Omen Mu's arrival was less than encouraging. He paused when he caught sight of the damaged enclosure, waves of fear washing over him. Daru's senses were assailed by Mu's fear.

"What is it?" Daru asked impatiently, unnerved by Mu's terror.

"It is as I had feared." Mu said. "The animal that was inside, was one of the most dangerous we have ever encountered."

"What was it?"

"It was once human-"

"Human!" Daru scoffed. "Humans are weak, fragile beings! They do not possess the strength necessary to perpetrate these crimes. How can they be considered dangerous?"

"This is no mere human," Mu replied solemnly. "It is an off-shoot of the human species, something more than mortal. We had been studying Subject 66 for quite some time and have discovered it to be the perfect killing machine. It is a creature capable of spreading disease over an entire planet, if properly conditioned to do so. In fact, it carries its own disease."

Daru was alarmed by this last statement. "How can this be? I tested the bodies of Plattu and Tartu myself. They showed no sign of disease."

"That is because they show no sign of infection until *after* death. Once death has passed; they will rise again, possessing greater strength and mental capacity. Or … at least, they would have."

"What do you mean?" Daru asked.

"It would be best if I showed you. The Morgue computer could also be accessed and I could explain further."

Moments later, Daru stood before the altars, which housed the bodies of Plattu and Tartu. Both had been destroyed. The heads of both bodies were missing.

"What have you brought upon this ship, Mu?" Daru asked, his voice uncharacteristically hushed.

"The humans call them vampires," Mu replied.

Daru accessed the Morgue computer in order to view all research material concerning Subject 66. The information chilled him.

"We have none of these things." Daru said, as he read the list of objects used to deter and kill a vampire. "What is 'garlic'? What is a 'crucifix'?"

"Garlic is a malodorous plant grown on the water planet. Unfortunately, we have none of them on board. A Crucifix is the symbol of a certain deity worshipped there. It looks like this…" Mu used his fingers to form a cross. "We can manufacture those."

"How did you capture it?" Daru asked.

"We took it while it slept and froze it cryogenically."

"I see. It is unlikely that such a plan will work again. Still, it seems that crucifixes only keep the creature at bay. They will not kill it. The report states that only a steak through the heart or sunlight can destroy such a beast. Since we cannot return to the system of the water planet, we cannot use the sun. That leaves us only the steak. We have that, I trust. We took enough from the Bovine creatures."

"We do." Mu replied. "The steak we use for sustenance will be a satisfactory weapon should it remain frozen. I am afraid that in its natural state it will be of little use to us. Shall I arm the crew?"

Daru did not answer. Something nagged him in the back of his mind, something about the headless bodies of Plattu and Tartu. He sighed. Perhaps it would come to him later. He ordered Mu to arm the crew with steaks and crucifixes. Mu nodded in salute.

Daru crept down the corridor toward the Control Chamber alone. He and the others had spread throughout the ship, searching for their erstwhile prisoner. Daru had just seen a shadow enter the Chamber. A shadow seemingly without a source. He moved forward to investigate.

The frozen meat of the Bovine creature had been cut into shards and he carried it in a gloved hand to avoid frostbite. He gripped it and the crucifix with grim determination.

Daru entered the Chamber, stumbling upon the creature. It was facing away from him, its back exposed.

Daru crept toward the beast as quietly as he could. If he could catch the thing unawares, all of their problems would be solved.

Luck was not with Komen Daru. He was but inches away, when the beast faced him.

The thing appeared disgustingly human, save for the crimson-colored eyes and the strange teeth. Its hair was as dark as the attire it wore and the color accentuated the paleness of its frightful visage.

Daru thrust the crucifix before him. The creature's reaction was not as expected.

The thing did not quail before him in abject terror as the report stated it would. Instead, it stood straight. Daru sensed its puzzlement and the slight transition to merriment. It began to laugh. The sound chilled Daru's blood.

"Even humans know that you must believe in order for *that* to work," he said.

Daru threw the cross aside. He raised the steak next.

"What is that?" The Vampire asked, his voice curious.

"A steak." Daru replied. He was confused as to why the Vampire was not afraid.

The vampire laughed, harder than before. Daru decided to use this moment of helplessness to his advantage. He rushed the Vampire and drove the steak into its heart. The vampire looked down and fell against the instrument panel. He did not burst into flame, nor did he crumble into dust. He simply leaned against the panel, overcome with mirth.

"Where did you get your information?" The vampire chuckled. Daru watched in dismay as the vampire pulled the frozen meat from his breast.

"From the ship's computer," Daru answered. He was quite perturbed by this turn of events.

The vampire's laugh slowly subsided. "I hope it is more accurate when describing your people and culture, than it is in describing mine. It told me your people are conquerors."

"We are," Daru said, proud. His eyes strayed to the communication panel on the wall opposite of him, about twelve feet away. If he could alert the others, perhaps all of them together could overcome the creature. That is, if he could survive until their arrival.

"I was a conqueror … once." The vampire said, a tinge of nostalgia in his voice.

Daru decided to distract the creature. Perhaps, if he could immerse it in conversation, he could make his way to the communication panel.

"You were?" Daru asked politely.

"In a time long past, I warred and waded in blood. I thirsted for it. Now, as I enslaved others, the thirst has enslaved me."

Daru congratulated himself on his plan. The vampire seemed completely unaware of his movement toward the wall. Even though the creature was more than human, it was still just as stupid as one.

"The world grew tame, as have I. I have grown weary of it. There is little left to conquer there." A grin spread over the vampire's pale face. The fangs gleamed.

Daru was only two feet from the wall.

"A wide horizon now spreads before me. I have left the tedium of Earth, there are new worlds to conquer … At last."

One foot from the wall.

The vampire's crimson eyes locked with Daru and bored into him. The orbs gripped his mind, he felt his will ebb, and he closed his eyes to cut the contact.

To his horror, the contact did not cease. He felt a strange paralysis sweep over his body and his eyes flew open much against his will. It seemed that by speaking, the vampire had hypnotized him and gained entrance to his mind. This fact was proven, when Daru began to hear the soft susurration of a whispering voice within his head.

Strange pictures filled Daru's mind. He saw strange, metal men astride great snorting beasts. They held brutal weapons in their hands and they used these to beat and cleave at one another. The blood was copious. It soaked into the ground, becoming a flood as the battle progressed.

The blood morphed into the hair of a woman. Her emerald eyes gazed sadly into his own. Daru saw great beauty in those eyes, and in everything about her. He knew these feelings were not his own.

The battle began again and when it was finally won, those taken prisoner were impaled upon great wooden spikes. They died slowly, agonizingly.

The woman's eyes appeared before him. Tears streamed from them and dripped from her lips. Daru knew that he seen her before.

He saw her face within the golden time piece. That same piece that resided in his pocket.

Daru felt his will drain and drown within those eyes. The vampire advanced upon him, and the woman's eyes superimposed over him. A subtle fear coursed through Daru, unable to shake loose from his paralysis.

The pictures began again; pictures of death, blood, and carnage. The pictures changed and Daru began to see his own memories flash before his eyes. He saw disease ravaging planet after planet. He witnessed plague after plague, as though the vampire was privy to his thoughts, reading each memory as it appeared.

At last, the pictures ceased. The vampire stood before him, pulling the time piece from Daru's pocket. Daru watched as he opened it.

A faint, tender smile pulled the vampire's lips. He touched the photograph with one long finger, then closed it.

"You should have used the laser on me," the vampire said, looking into Daru's face again. "If you had, and had detached my head from my body, I would be dead."

Daru groaned inwardly. That had been the solution to the riddle of the headless corpses. They could not be reborn without their heads.

"Mu … was … right." Daru managed to croak out. "You … are … dangerous."

"More than you will ever know," the vampire replied. He snarled and sank his teeth into Daru's throat.

Daru saw only blackness.

He had once been known as "The Impaler," striking fear into mortals even after his death. Now, he stood on a spaceship draining the last drop of blood from an alien body.

Once the blood was gone, the vampire tore the head from Daru's shoulders and tossed it aside, then turned to the instrument panel. It would be difficult to repair the navigation controls, but not impossible. After he had dealt with Mu and the others, he would tend to them.

He opened the watch again, and gazed upon the face of the woman within. Still on the Earth, a planet he could no longer see upon the view screen, she was a minister's daughter. It was she who had given him the malady from which he could never recover.

He remembered the words that infected him. She had said that he was a "denizen of Hell," one who preyed equally upon the innocent and the wicked. Her disappointment in him was complete, but she would never cease to pray for his salvation…and, she would never cease to love him.

He would protect her future on that blue marble out in space. And though he longed to share in it, he knew his future lie elsewhere. He had a people to conquer and, perhaps, to end. They would never visit her planet again.

The Impaler closed the watch and hurried from the Chamber.

It was time to prey upon the wicked.

The Most Wonderful
Undead Time of the Year
by
Roy C. Booth and Axel Kohagen

Nothing in the following story can be truly understood unless it is clear that Phil Dexter was, first and foremost, initially a good human being. His family would not argue with that. His wife loved him unconditionally, his daughter perhaps even more so. Even Ralph the dog adored him.

Phil blinked when he saw the limbs of his evergreen trees shake, dumping snow in the process. He dried the last dish, then checked the living room. Ralph was curled up on his doggie bed. He put the dish on the column with the rest of them.

"Ralph! Outside."

The Labrador obeyed his command, bounding with tail and tongue wagging, and Phil left the door open only long enough for the slim dog to sneak out. Then, he shut it, shivering in the cold. In the living room, his daughter Jessica held up one doll while it explained to a boy doll why they were boyfriend and girlfriend. Martin, his brother, who had no children of his own, watched the exchange.

Ralph stood in the copse of evergreen trees, barking. Phil heard his wife Marilyn step toward the bedroom door upstairs, ready to shout down at him about Ralph's barking. Wincing, he opened the door, then stopped outside to yell at the dog.

Ralph came running, but before Phil could get inside he noticed footprints outside the kitchen window, the tread of some kind of boot, but the sole of this shoe had long ago worn away. In places, he could see where a slender toe had made an impression in the snow. If their small Wisconsin town had been any bigger, or even contained a department store, he might've thought a homeless person was peering into his house.

"Snow's sure coming down," said Marilyn coming down the stairs, wearing a modest but attractive sweater, sipping a cup of cocoa. Low-fat. Phil was very health conscious, infecting his whole family with this spirit.

"Complete with winter time frolickers," said Martin.

Phil sat on his favorite faux-leather chair and smiled. Jessica was oblivious to everything but A Christmas Carol, which she was watching for the first time. To his daughter's right, the Christmas tree looked on approvingly. The thing almost looked a little slumped, as if glad to finally be almost done with guarding the presents.

"There are no frolickers out there," Marilyn said.

"There are, too," Martin said. Intently. He smiled at his sister-in-law. "See? There's at least one there. By the trees."

"I see nothing." Marilyn folded her arms over her chest.

"You can just see the hood. The little ... the peak of the hood, there. From a woman's snowsuit or something."

"Martin, that's a tree."

Martin sighed, throwing up his hands in mock disgust. Phil didn't tell his family about the movement he'd seen out by the trees, or the footprints he'd found. Instead, he rapped his remote control on the wood of his armrests. Marilyn heard the noise and furrowed her eyebrows. Without her saying a word, he knew it was time to stop fidgeting.

Phil put his first paper of the evening down and picked up the second. He liked to read a variety of different newspapers, to keep from getting a biased view on anything. They had the money for the subscriptions, and they could always recycle them. Usually the things he read about became the household changes his wife groaned about. She always told him he didn't have to be perfect, but he liked to come as close as possible.

"Phil, how much longer are you going to stay up?"

Phil pretended to think about this, pursing his lips and saying "Hmmmmm..." loud enough so Jessica would turn around to watch him.

"Well, I could stay up to see Santa..."

Jessica paused the movie and turned to him in four-year-old fury.

"You said I couldn't stay up for Santa! Why can't I?"

"Maybe next year," Phil said. He felt bad about this because he and Marilyn had decided this would be their last year of pretending there was a Santa. Next year, the bitter, inevitable truth would have to come out. It seemed like a shame, but school would be starting soon. Other kids would talk. And Phil believed too much sugary unreality led to unfocused lives. He saw tons of kids living those unfocused lives at the high school he taught at, and he didn't want his daughter to grow into such a life.

Jessica accepted this and turned back to her movie. She was a good kid, and rarely complained. When she did, she often found herself reasoning with her thoughtful father for as long as it took to resolve the issue. Sometimes, when Phil looked in her eyes, he thought his daughter might rather fight it out than labor toward a compromise.

In the movie, Scrooge had just gotten a rather frightening message from Christmas Present and was about to face the dreaded Christmas Future. Phil had forgotten that the George C. Scott version had been so stark, so harrowing. He was prepared to shut it off the second it caused his daughter one moment of distress, but so far, that had not happened.

"Seriously," Marilyn said, flexing her toes into the carpet as she did whenever sleep was nearing. "How much longer?"

"Not too much, honey. Few hours, maybe. Not feeling too tired yet."

Marilyn sighed and padded across the floor. Phil had a hunch she felt lonely going to bed, even if he didn't sense any desire on her part to make love. He'd be more than happy to oblige her if she did, taking the time to make sure she found the experience more fulfilling than he did.

"Uhgk, you're still a kid. Check the locks before you come up. Martin's been forgetting again." The love wasn't stressed, but it was there. She kissed his forehead and toddled off to bed.

Christmas Future screeched onto the screen, grabbing Phil's full attention. Christmas Future, unlike Dickens's other visions, resounded in the same form every time – as Death itself. A not so subtle reminder of the future in store for everyone on the planet. This Death wailed like a banshee as it stalked toward George C. Scott, looking fluid and frightening in its black cloak. A skeletal hand peeked out from a baggy sleeve.

And yet Jessica didn't seem disturbed. Phil had already gotten the remote control up, but decided the ending of A Christmas Carol was happy enough to make up for the scary bits. Truth be told, he might have been worried about his own sense of serenity. Something about those footprints made him squirm, and he was beginning to think he'd heard footsteps behind him as he walked back into the house.

He turned to his brother, but found him staring out the window. "What is it?"

"Thought I saw someone," Martin replied. "Just a shadow."

Phil nodded.

"Need anything?"

"No," came the reply. "Hey, Phil. Thanks."

"Don't mention it." Phil tried to get back to his newspaper, knowing praise was about to be bestowed upon him, and he felt that cheapened any act of charity. That's why he always made his donations anonymously and, when he did volunteer work, tried to avoid giving a last name.

"I know I've never been good to you, and I've said some things I regret. But you trusted that I could quit drinking before anyone else did," Martin said.

Phil nodded. The trust hadn't come easy. It had been a forced trust, and they had dumped all of the alcohol in the house down the drain before Martin came to stay with them, including the medicinal kind.

"We both started down the wrong path in high school. The way dad drank, I'm not sure we had much of a choice," Phil said.

"But you sobered up," Martin said. "Before we were even out of high school, you sobered up. You tried to help me, but I just couldn't do it. I really tried, but I couldn't keep up with you. I don't know why you ever believed in me."

Marilyn hadn't believed in him. She remembered when Martin broke into a house because he was trying to get home and was too intoxicated to tell it wasn't his -- even though it was in a city thirty miles away from his house. Marilyn hadn't been sure, but Phil had insisted that it was the right thing to do, especially considering the season. Martin was family. And so, on the first of December, Uncle Martin came to stay.

It had been a success. Even Marilyn had been pleased. Things were a little tense when someone broke into their shed, leaving behind the foulest smell imaginable. Marilyn was convinced Martin was responsible for this, and would not be talked out of kicking him out until three people swore Phil's brother was working at the local gas station at the time of the crime.

"Nobody else would've taken me in. I mean, when Susie divorced me for being a drunk... I took that as a pretty big sign."

"It's what brothers do," said Phil.

"No one else would have. Also, hate to say it, your dog tracked something in."

Martin pointed to a clot of...something on their tan carpet. He may have turned his life around, but he was still far from the ideal houseguest. Phil still cleaned up his soda cans about half the time, and he had yet to see his brother holding a rag or anything resembling a cleaning product inside their house. He didn't mind; loving his house was just another way of loving his family.

The crud on his floor came from some animal, which was nothing new. Ralph had been to every training class the pet store a town over offered, but he still loved chewing on any dead squirrel or bird he could get his mouth on. This piece smelled worse than usual, like the smell in the shed. He felt something hard on the dead flesh, even through the paper towel he was using to pick it up.

When it started to feel like a toenail, he closed his eyes and tried not to think about a time, long ago, when his car started sliding toward and–

"I love this story," Martin said, turning to the end of A Christmas Carol. "There's a whole genre of Victorian era Christmas ghost stories. Did you know that?"

"No. I didn't," Phil said, blinking. He wished they saved a few beers for moments like this. The back of his neck was sweating. Ralph sat up from his sleep and walked over, licking his master's hand.

"Yeah. A lot of them are like this. Second chances. Warnings. Signs to repent. The ghosts come, people change, and then Christmas comes and all is better. I got obsessed with them in college on Christmas, being off on my own and all. Pretty good reads."

The three finished up the film. Phil used the deep breathing advice he'd gotten from a yoga instructor at the local Y to keep his heart rate down. Eventually, images of snow flying and legs kicking through the air were replaced with the movie and the living room before him.

When it was done, little Jessica nodded to herself and stood up.

"Will you be okay getting up to sleep?"

"Yeah. I saw the scary bone one before."

Phil blinked again. "When?"

"Sledding. Just standing there, behind our trees. Didn't say nothing."

Martin politely smirked behind his niece.

"If he's out there, shouldn't you let your Uncle Martin tuck you in?"

Jessica nodded. "I guess," she said. She was a very serious girl.

"You're turning in, too, Martin?" Phil asked.

"Yeah. Big day tomorrow, isn't it? Christmas morning. Everything good happens."

"Sleep well you two."

"Say 'hi' to Santa for me," Martin replied with a wink, and then managed to whisk a giggling Jessica upstairs before she could ask to stay up late again. Everyone knew she'd be asleep in two minutes anyway; everyone except Jessica herself, of course. Martin might even be asleep before his niece. Healthy, decent living had done wonders for him.

As the night settled in, Phil finished up his paper but kept getting more and more distracted, realizing the quiet of the winter eve. Even with inches of snow dumping all around his house, it was completely still inside. Even the dog wasn't up and about. Ralph must have left me to crawl in bed with Marilyn.

Then he heard a clacking noise on the kitchen linoleum. The kitchen. Where the basement connected to the house. There was a door from the basement to the garage, and that went outside. Something could get in that way.

The clacking and sliding grew closer and closer. Phil put down his paper and folded his hands in his lap.

There was the shadow of a person, illuminated by the suburban streetlight outside, clearly visible on the living room carpet. Phil smelled cold, rotting meat.

"I thought I saw you, you know."

Silence.

"When I parked the car tonight. I thought I saw you by the garage. Right before I shut off the headlights. I think that's why I wanted to show Jessica that movie tonight."

She shuffled out from the kitchen, her pace slow and deliberate. Her black hooded coat was out of style now; in fact, it had gone out of style six months after he ran her over and killed her. He'd been hurrying home from Marilyn's house after a high school date, trying to avoid his dad's drunken wrath. Maybe drank a little too much himself at the homecoming kegger before that, he didn't know, he only had one red plastic cup of beer.

She wasn't dead when he dragged her into the woods, but she was dying.

"I never forgot about you," Phil said, forcing himself to face her. When his face turned toward hers, her jaw dropped open, a soft hissing noise escaped from her throat.

She was dead, but she was still shuffling toward him. Her mouth slackened, and the one shrunken eye remaining in its socket looked lazy and tired. Her fingers hung below their bones like a broken glove.

He had moved halfway across the country for college and never gone back home. She had followed him slowly, tearing all the flesh off her dead feet in the process, her dead body flaked away, bit by bit; but her rage at being murdered too soon powered her ever forward. Mostly bone now, inside her big black coat, she looked exactly like the Ghost of Christmas Future.

"You're here for revenge."

There was no response from the revenant other than a slight swaying.

"But I've been thinking about it. I do my part. I take care of my family. I give. I share. After I did what I did to you, I was a much better man. I was even a good man."

A skeletal hand clamped down on his. A pointy finger bone found the soft flesh of his inner palm and pushed, bidding Phil to come with the apparition.

"I have a wife. A good kid. A brother. Dog, too. In this house. I do right by them."

Still, the hand tugged at him.

"What more can I give? What more can I do? What could I still owe you?"

The tugging grew more insistent, and Phil thought he saw something light up in her remaining eye, under the hood of the heavy black cloak. As he looked into it, he realized it didn't matter what he said or how much he pleaded. He had to go.

She led him outside into the snow. He tried to shut the door behind him because he knew the cold would fill the house quickly, but she kept tugging at his arm. She moved quickly for a thing that shuffled on broken bones. His feet felt cold, and he realized he was barefoot. He turned back one last time to the house, and then realized he'd never be going back inside.

When they reached the cover of his evergreen trees, she stopped. She plopped into the snow and motioned for him to do the same. He did, instantly aware of how cold the snow and ice felt through his pajama pants. He crossed his legs and folded his arms in front of him.

The revenant sat close to him, her jaw working up and down. She reached out and took both of his hands, and he feared she was going to devour him. He started to stand again, but her grip was strong. She nodded when he grew still.

"I'm sorry I just drove off," he said. "I was too scared. Believe me, if I could do it again, I would have stayed and took my chances. I know there's forgiveness in the world. Now. I didn't know then. I didn't know any better."

Her face, now a collection of frayed tendons and leathered bits of skin, tightened. She may have smiled.

He realized he was going to freeze to death. The revenant's cold, bony hands rubbed his arms, comforting him as he sobbed. Then the hands released him. The dead thing shrugged off its hooded coat. She had to pull more forcefully to free the fabric from the places it grew into her skin, but she got it free. With a shaking hand, she held the coat out for him to wear.

"Thanks," he said. He slipped it over his shoulders because it was too small for him to wear. The dead girl nodded. Her hair fell in front of her face. It was dead, black, and bloody. He could not remember what color it had been when he killed her.

"I am sorry," he said. The cold made his voice shake. He glanced up to see his house, his wonderful house, and he could almost see the warmth escaping from it.

He thought about kicking the revenant in front of him and running back inside.

But he didn't.

The dead girl squeezed his hand.

THE END

60

Where the Wind Blows
by
Rose Blackthorn

The wind was blowing again. Sometimes he wondered if it ever stopped, or would just blow on and on forever. He couldn't remember it blowing this much before the end of the world, but before then he'd had a lot more on his mind.

He had his job. It wasn't anything spectacular or fancy. He worked at the local auto parts store, mostly stocking and cleaning up at the end of the day. But he also did the occasional delivery in the company truck, and that was okay. Getting out of the store and spending a little time out on the streets was a nice change of pace. The money wasn't great, but it was steady. It allowed him to have his own little apartment, and buy the food he liked rather than the food his Mom had always tried to feed him.

"Broccoli is good for you, Nathan," she would say. She'd had a bland mid-western accent, but in his memory she always sounded like a Jewish mother. "It's good for the blood."

He had his family. His mother Barbara and father Randall, both living the middle-class American dream. Three-bedroom house, two car garage, fenced in yard for the dog, Max, and a lawn that refused to stay green and weed-free no matter how much time or what fancy chemical Dad put on it. There had also been his sister, Sharon, ginger-haired and freckled like Nate, but much prettier. She was four years younger than he and still in high school when the world ended.

For the last little while, Nate even had a girlfriend. She had been on his mind the most. Her name was Calleigh, and she had long, dark blond hair and grey-green eyes. She was the same age as Nate, and liked a lot of the same things. Pizza with a thick pan crust, drowning in pepperoni and cheese (no vegetables thank you very much!). Horror movies of any kind, even (or maybe especially) the corny zombie flicks with the really bad special effects and even worse acting. Sleeping in late on Saturday mornings and eating cereal out of the box while watching kiddie cartoons. Best of all, she hadn't been worried about getting flowers (at least from the florists), or jewelry (she was okay with the plastic ring from the gumball machine).

She was laid-back and unworried, and just as quick to pick a t-shirt up from off the floor and sniff it to see if it was still clean enough to wear. Added to the fact that she was beautiful and she was pretty much the perfect girl. Definitely the perfect girl for Nate.

So yeah, he hadn't spent a lot of time paying attention to the wind. But now he didn't have so much going on in his life. There was no more pan pizza, no more Saturday morning cartoons, and the cereal was always dry because there was no more going to the store for milk. Dad didn't have to worry about his yellowing, weedy lawn anymore, and Mom didn't have to worry about Nate's diet. In fact, except for Nate, no one had to worry about anything anymore.

Time was strange; it warped, like memories. He hadn't kept track of the days, so he wasn't exactly sure how long he'd been alone. Part of the problem was he wasn't sure if day and night were progressing the way they should be. He remembered movies and Twilight Zone episodes were aliens came and kidnapped whole towns for scientific experiments or where electro-magnetic storms from the sun, or even passing comets could reduce everyone to small piles of ash and unburnt clothing. But even if any of these theories might be true, it still didn't explain how he came to be here, alone but uninjured.

He sat on the porch at his parents' house, eating pre-popped popcorn from a bag he'd scavenged at the corner market. He tipped back in one of his mom's wooden chairs, feet propped on the railing in a way that would have had her getting after him to sit down properly and not ruin her furniture. For a moment, he imagined the sound of her voice.

"Nathan, you get your dirty feet off the railing, and stop trying to break my chair!"

She would be standing in the doorway with her hands on her hips, salon-styled hair perfectly coiffed, and wearing the jeans she thought made her look cool—although they only emphasized her modest muffin-top.

Dad would call from the living room, "Barb, you're going to give yourself a stroke. It's just a chair. And I put my feet on the railing all the time."

Nate smiled to himself, envisioning every detail. The lawn stretching out to the sidewalk with a few hardy dandelions raising their yellow heads. Max, his dad's seven year old lab mix, would be laying on the top step of the porch, soaking up the last rays of sunlight. Cars passing on the residential street, or kids on bicycles enjoying the last golden days before the weather turned cold. But the wind was blowing, pushing dead leaves and trash down the deserted street, and it pulled him from his pleasant reverie.

He looked at the book on his lap, which he'd found in Sharon's room, surprised that she had anything like this. It was an old book, the cover soft and tattered, the spine broken in a couple of places. There was no artwork on the cover, just words printed in faded gold-leaf. *A Book of Shadows* it stated in large letters at the top, then beneath, in smaller font, *Celebrations of the Great Rites*. At the very bottom of the cover, in tiny dark print was *Knowledge is good, be the price what it may.*

He shoved another handful of slightly stale popcorn into his mouth, wiped his palm on his jeans, and opened the book. It fell open to the page titled *Samhain – Celtic New Year* but it was the ink drawings of carved pumpkins and cemetery headstones that caught his eye. Halloween had always been his favorite holiday, and it was coming up.

He started reading the chapter, still wondering why his sister had had the book in her possession, when what he read struck a chord. Samhain, also known as All Hallows Eve and later Halloween, was believed to be the day of the year when the veil between living and dead was the thinnest. The old pagans, according to the book, believed this to be the best time to communicate with loved ones who had passed over. Back before the end of the world, he would have laughed at the thought and tossed the book aside, not that he'd have picked it up to read in the first place. But now, it wasn't like he had anything to lose. And even communing with the dead would be better than being all alone.

He read through the chapter and the outlined rituals several times. He wasn't interested in getting "skyclad" whatever that was, or becoming one with nature. But if there was any chance at all he could communicate with his parents, his sister, or with Calleigh— if for no other reason than to find out what had happened to them—he didn't see any reason not to try.

The book stressed that this would only work on the correct day, so he had to find out what the current date was. Looking at a calendar did him no good, and he no longer had the option to check his laptop or cell phone for the current time and date. But now that the date was important to him again, he knew just how to find out.

Upstairs in his parents' bedroom, on the table next to Dad's side of the bed, was a clock. It was small, with a white face surrounded in brass and set in a wooden base. It had been a gift from Nate and Sharon last year at Christmas, and had a small brass plaque on the back with their names on it. The clock was battery operated, and still running. But what made Nate think of it was the tiny inset squares in the clock face. One showed letters, the other numbers; the letters said 'Oct', and the numbers said '25'.

"October 25th," Nate said to himself, holding the small but heavy clock almost reverently. "Six days."

One of the things the book stated was to surround the "circle" with mementos of the passed loved ones he wanted to summon. The circle was apparently some kind of sacred ground, which immediately made him think of the cemetery. Halloween night at the cemetery might appeal to him if he had a couple of friends and electric street lights. But by himself in a deserted world, he really wasn't interested. He flipped back to the table of contents, found a listing for "circle" and read that section. According to that, all it had to be was a space set aside specifically for the ritual. Since everything that reminded him of his family was in his parents' house, he would do it there.

The other thing the ritual said was to decorate the circle with objects or images that put the practitioner in the proper state of mind. What would put him in the right mindset for Halloween? Nate grinned, and headed for the closest store.

Over the next few days he prepared for the ritual, slightly altered to fit his own needs. He brought back loads of Halloween decorations, which he put up both inside the house and throughout the yard. No electricity meant no strings of lights, and no air-blown inflatable decorations. But he strung yards of black and orange crepe paper, long lines of dangling vinyl bats and spiders, and arranged huge artificial spider webs over all the bushes and most of the front of the house. He hadn't wanted to spend Halloween night at the cemetery, but he didn't mind bringing a fake one home. So he set up painted foam and resin headstones in the front yard, with names like Hugh R. Next, Ima Goner, Myra Mains, and Ted N. Buried. Because it reminded him of nights spent watching low-budget horror flicks with Calleigh he also put out various plastic body parts or full sculpted zombies that looked like they were dragging themselves out of the "graves."

He brought one of his mom's small wooden tables out to set on the porch and draped it with a black lace tablecloth. On top he arranged pictures of Mom and Dad, Sharon, and Calleigh. Per the instructions in the book he added a bowl of clean water and another of sea salt, tall candles to represent the four directions and spice-scented votives that he placed with each photograph. There was a small brass censor with a cone of vanilla incense ready to be lit, and a small metal pot with some sand in the bottom. When he was sure he had everything ready, he checked the book again. After all his preparations, he had one more day to wait. Tired but hopeful, he went into his old bedroom and fell asleep on his bed.

The wind blew; it was always blowing since the world ended. Nate lay in bed, asleep and dreaming; but in his dream he stood on the sidewalk in front of his parents' house. The wind gusted, and dead leaves raced each other past his sneakered feet. The sky was covered in heavy roiling clouds, and as Nate looked up he saw a murder of crows—or perhaps it was an unkindness of ravens, he couldn't be sure—coursing across the stormy sky. They traveled in the direction of the wind, gusts hurrying them on their way. Their raucous calls filtered back to him, ripped apart by the tumultuous air.

Movement on the ground caught his eye, and he looked back at the house. In the wind his shabby decorations flapped and flew, threatening to join the fleeing birds. The cheap headstones leaned on their shallow stakes, and the fake body parts were slowly tumbling toward the far fence, nudged by the insistent breeze. On the porch, half-hidden by the waving shredded cloth of a dime-store ghost, someone stood behind the table—*altar* his mind whispered—he'd set up with photos and props.

"Hello?" he called, wondering if the figure on the porch could hear him through the ever-present wind. "Hello, who's there?"

"Nate, I miss you," a soft voice replied, and the wind dropped for a moment, letting him see that the shadow on the porch was his girlfriend Calleigh.

"Calleigh!" he yelled, trying to open the gate so he could cross the yard to her.

"I miss you," she said again with tears sparkling on her face, and the wind howled as it bowled all his tacky decorations across the yard and pinned them to the fence. He pulled his eyes from the carnage and looked back at the porch. There was no one there.

Nate opened his eyes, tears stinging. He knew he'd been dreaming, and that Calleigh hadn't been there. But he couldn't help the welling emotion. "I miss you too, Calleigh."

***

Nate woke late on Halloween day. "Samhain," he told himself.

After his dream, he was less hopeful of getting any kind of positive outcome from his intended ritual. But he'd worked on it all week, and if he didn't go through with it now, he'd have a whole year to wonder if it might have succeeded before he could try again.

"Halloween has always been the best day of the year for me," he said, going out to check his decorations. "No reason for that to change now, right?"

All he had to do was wait until the sun set, and the magic hour of midnight to arrive. He ate some crackers with canned cheese, and drank slightly warm soda out of the can. The yard decorations were still up, regardless of his dream during the night. Everything was ready on the altar. Nate made sure he had a back-up lighter, and matches as well; the Book of Shadows waited in the seat of his chair. While he waited, his mind wandered.

He remembered going out to eat with Calleigh, at the little-hole-in-the-wall pizza place they loved. The cafe was filled with people, mostly Nate and Calleigh's age, but some were older and some were younger. The jukebox played the Eagles 'Hotel California', and Calleigh laughed as Nate sang along.

After dinner, they'd walked back to the apartment hand in hand, Nate still singing, and Calleigh in tears from laughing at his toneless but good-natured attempt to carry the tune. They'd crossed the street to reach their building…

Then Nate had opened his eyes in bed, wondering where Calleigh was. Had she drawn the early shift? He couldn't remember. Everything was quiet, even the old refrigerator wasn't humming the way it always had.

That was when he'd realized the world had ended. Everyone was gone, not just Calleigh. No power, no radio transmissions, no people; and he hadn't been able to figure out why. Years of horror movies made him guess that something traumatic happened, and that's why he couldn't remember anything after stepping off the curb with his girl's hand in his. Something had taken everyone away, and left him here alone. He didn't know why, but he wanted to.

After the sun dropped below the horizon, the sky remained light for a long time. The heavy cloud-cover from his dream had not appeared. Nate went out to the lawn, sitting cross-legged next to a double-amputee zombie that he'd positioned crawling across the dying grass. He leaned back on his hands and gazed at the clear sky, watching for the first pin-prick apparitions of stars. The breeze sighed around him, the continuing breath of the wind he'd become accustomed to over the last few weeks. Bells on a hanging witch's shoes tinkled.

At 11:45, the wind-up alarm clock that he'd set rang. He got to his feet, feeling a bit stiff and cold. Had he fallen asleep? He stumbled going up the porch steps, but didn't fall. It took only a moment to light the kerosene lantern he'd found in the garage with the camping supplies, and he set it on the railing to light the porch. Feeling like an idiot, and glad there was no one around to witness, he lit the candles in the prescribed order. There was a whole big speech in the book, but he knew he'd just feel silly reading it all. The author in many places had impressed that the most important things were intent and emotion. He just needed to be very clear about what he wanted. In this case not what, but who.

Following the directions in the book, Nate lit the incense, wet his fingers in the bowl of water, and tossed a pinch of sea salt over his shoulder. At each step, he checked the page, worried lest he miss an important step. Just before midnight, he lit the votives placed before the photographs, focusing on each person as he did so. Dad with his thinning salt and pepper hair and constant good-natured smile. Mom, who never seemed to find the time to sit down and relax because there was always something that needed to be done. Sharon, the straight A student working toward a scholarship so she could go to college somewhere miles from this little town. Then Calleigh, the perfect girl for him. He'd never told her that he loved her, afraid that it would change things between them. Now he didn't care. If nothing else, before Samhain was over, he wanted to let her know how much she meant to him.

The alarm clock rang again, and he quickly silenced it. Midnight on Halloween, the magic moment promised by the Book of Shadows. Yearning with everything he had, he willed his family to appear to him. The book said it could happen. He would just believe it hard enough that it would be true.

The breeze picked up, becoming stronger. Nate swore as it blew out the candles. His kerosene lamp still cast bright white light over everything, but all other lights had been extinguished. Even the incense fell over and stopped smoking.

"I just want to know!" Nate yelled, not worried about appearing stupid anymore. "Where did you go? Where did everyone go?"

The wind roared, gusts destroying his decorations as they had in his dream, and the kerosene lantern sailed off the railing to land on the front walk. The glass shattered, and flames caught the foam headstones and plastic zombies, burning and melting them into dark globs.

"Why didn't you take me, too?"

***

Barbara stood on one side of the hospital bed, Calleigh on the other. Randall sat on a hard unpadded chair with his daughter beside him. His contagious smile was missing tonight.

Barbara looked down at her son, her eyes wet although she didn't let the tears fall. When she looked across the bed at the young woman who might have one day been her daughter-in-law, she ignored the fading bruises and the sling that held one arm. Calleigh was very lucky to have survived with injuries so light. She was lucky that Nate had seen the car coming and pushed her— mostly—out of the way. Barbara knew that Calleigh blamed herself for Nate's condition. He'd saved her life, but had been unable to get out of the path of the oncoming vehicle himself. In the following weeks, Calleigh had rarely left his bedside.

"It's time, dear," Barbara said softly, her voice rough as she fought to control herself. She would not break down. Not now. She could do that later, at home.

Calleigh nodded, clutching Nate's unresponsive hand. The doctor said nothing, just flipped the switch that turned off the life support systems. For the first time since Nate had been admitted to the hospital, the wheezing rushing sound of the ventilator fell silent.

When the world finally ended, the wind didn't blow anymore.

The Notebook
By
Randy Attwood

(Jeremy)

I had two phone calls from Don before he killed himself. Each call should have tipped me off. Maybe not the first one, but certainly the second. I couldn't have gone to him anyway; he lived in another state far away. Still, I could have done something. Called somebody. I wonder if Don knew at the time of the first call–the first contact I had had with him in three years–he was going to commit suicide. When do suicides know for sure? Just before they pull the trigger?

He had called that first time to say hello, but instead of wanting to hear an update on my life, he had launched into a rambling account of his own. Then he told me, "You know, the other day I suddenly remembered I left a notebook in the attic of that house where I had my college apartment."

"What's in it?" I asked. The mention of his college apartment had brought back memories of heaps of books, his cluttered desk, stacks of papers. A mess, but organized, it seemed, to make an impression of disorderliness.

"I can't remember. Poems, story ideas, philosophical arguments. Maybe nothing," he replied. "I can't imagine why I hid it. I was in one of my states, I suppose."

Then two months later he put a bullet in his brain.

But not before he had called one more time. He had to confess, he said. Confess to something horrible. I didn't believe him. I simply couldn't believe what he was telling me. It was too outlandish. What he told me occupied my thoughts when I should

72

have been wondering about his mental state. The incredible confession had been the sign of a tormented and deranged mind crying out for help. A cry I hadn't heeded.

I should have gone to him, but I hadn't.

Now he was gone from me, gone from the world.

That was five years ago. I really hadn't thought about him until I happened to return to our old university when I was asked to deliver a paper on the patrons of Victorian art. Driving up and down the old streets, I passed by the house where Don had had his second-floor apartment. Seeing the home made me remember the notebook and wonder if it were still where he said he had hidden it in the attic.

The brick streets, the towering elms, the early fall. It all brought back nostalgia from my college life, and it made me remember how envious of Don I had been. He was what I wanted to be: a Balzac sort of character, up at all hours, writing stories, dashing them off through the night in his cluttered cave of an apartment, and then stumbling out in the morning light, his hair as frazzled-looking as his brain must have been, and feeling he had accomplished something. I feared all I'd ever accomplish was a neat desk.

He'd miss classes, but I kept notes for him. He'd entertain me with the wide range of his thoughts, his ideas, and his passions. I was the neat, orderly, scholarly sort. Now expert on all arcane Victorian matters. Don was consumed with the idea of creating things fresh and new. All I could do was study what had been created in the past and make puny comments upon it that really amounted to nothing more than neat categorizations.

The house was in better repair than I remembered it when Don lived there. I opened the screen door of the small, clean-swept porch and rang the doorbell. Just how was I going to frame this odd request?

(Sarah)

I sat with my cheeks in my palms when the doorbell rang, and wondered why it always rang at the wrong time. Then I laughed and said aloud, "When would the right time be?"

The doorbell rang a second time. I rubbed the heel of my palms into both eyes and across my cheeks to wipe away the wetness and stood up.

He didn't look like a salesman.

"I'm sorry to bother you," he was saying.

"Yes?" I blinked my eyes but knew he could tell I had been crying.

"I know this is an odd request..."

I tried to connect my life with what he told me. He was handsome, but in an unsure sort of way. About my own age, he wore dark-green, corduroy slacks and a matching coat with a soft-colored, plaid shirt and a knit tie. His thick black hair with streaks of gray was parted on one side and cut neat–the way his mother had no doubt had it cut when she first took him to the barber chair– gave him a boyish look about him and seemed vaguely familiar. His eyes were a startling deep blue. It made me look at them a second time, and then a third.

"Do you own the house now?" he asked.

"Yes," I said, and thought the way he said "the house" sounded odd.

"In your attic..."

The attic? Why am I having more and more trouble connecting my life to what people tell me? Why would he want to see the attic? For a notebook. Why would a notebook still be in my attic?

"I really doubt it would still be there," I told him. I don't like the attic. Too many memories. Why don't I just close the door on him if he can't take no for an answer? Why is he still standing there, still talking?

Important? How could a ten-year-old notebook left up in an attic be important?

(Jeremy)

Women consume me. I think that's why I've never married. I always feel faint in their presence. They are such an affirmation of life for me. I can't imagine tying myself to just one. Their variety, and my reaction to that variety, continues to astound me.

That's why I enjoy teaching at a large university. There is always a changing, fresh supply of the creatures. I stand in awe of them. I've yet to meet one who fails to bewitch me. When I see one who's been crying, I want to put my arm around her, draw her near, tell her to shush, and collapse her into me.

The woman before me was handsome rather than pretty. Built solid. Strong-looking arms. Her brown hair should have been cut into a shorter style years ago, but obviously she was stubborn and wore it braided and piled around her head; wisps stuck out here and there.

"I know it's a bother. I really apologize. But, well, you see, my friend killed himself a couple of years ago and I have no idea what's in the notebook, but I thought I'd look. Something of his that I could have."

Smile now, Jeremy. Smile that deep, gentle, kind smile you use when the young undergraduate lasses come to your office with questions, tears in their eyes over the C-minuses on their papers.

(Sarah)

I liked his smile. It seemed to speak from his heart.

"You'll have to go up there alone. I don't like to go up there. It's where my husband hanged himself. Five years ago."

Just saying it made me bitter again. I always said "hanged himself" instead of "killed himself". Killing himself would have been one thing. A dozen decent ways to do that. He could have run his damn truck at 80 miles an hour into a bridge piling and they would have called it an accident. Or he could have gone out into the woods and blown his brains out with one of his damn guns. Instead, I found Roger in the attic, where he had turned himself into a human plumb bob whose point pierced through to the bottom of my gut.

"Come on in."

(Jeremy)

The carpets had been removed. The wood floors stripped and polished, and woven rugs covered everywhere I looked: on the floors, hanging on the walls, lying over the backs of sofas and armchairs. The house should have been a riot of colored yarn, but everything was dusty. Drapes were drawn, and little sunlight made its way into the rooms where the life of color awaited beams of light. Looms were set up in the living room, in the dining room, and even–as I looked down the hallway through to the kitchen–in the eating area, but they looked long unused. Projects started, never completed.

"A brilliant deduction on my part tells me you weave," I said and added, "My mother used to weave." Finally, a smile came to her lips. It was like a smile that had been a stranger to the lips that formed it.

"I owned a yarn store downtown. But I'm no businesswoman. I need to sell these looms off, but I hate to part with them."

"It's such a contrast to when my friend lived here," I said, and reached down to finger a shawl thrown over the back of a nearby rocker. "This is lovely work." I caressed the ugly mixture of dull colors. I hated weaving and knitting. It was why I moved south where I'd never have to wear another damn sweater.

"Thank you. Did the Franklins own the house then?"

"Yes. A nice elderly couple. I wonder what happened to them. They rented out the summer porch upstairs."

"It's my favorite place to weave. I have the 72-inch loom up there. Mr. Franklin died and his wife sold the home and moved to a nursing home. I used to visit her. What was your friend's name?"

"Don."

"His last name? Maybe I knew him. I was in school here then, too."

"Bowerman. Don Bowerman. We were both English majors. I'm sorry. I never introduced myself. I'm Jeremy Broad," I said, remembering to smile, and extended a hand. She took it. Her grip was firm, her fingers dry–somewhat rough–and I imagined the thousands of yards of yarn that had passed through them. My mother's hands had had that same dry, rough feel to them, as if the fibers of the yarn had sucked all the moisture out of her hands.

"Sarah Winston," She said and the smile came again. "Would you like a cup of tea?"

Oh Jeremy, Jeremy. Go very slow, now.

"I'd like that very much."

(Sarah)

As his hands touched the shawl I wove ten years ago, I felt drawn to the stranger, although he didn't really seem like a stranger. His face was familiar. His name, Jeremy Broad, rang a bell, but I couldn't place him. I realized I hadn't felt this drawn towards a man in many years, since before Roger hanged himself.

Weaving had been my salvation. I used Roger's money to buy a yarn store, something I'd always dreamed of doing. It kept me busy, running the store, setting up classes, and then the creation of goods from the skeins and balls of yarn. I wove a protective wrapping around my heart. But the whole thing failed, leaving me with nothing but the one wrapped heart. How had he found a loose end, and why was he starting to unravel it? I repeated his name, Jeremy Broad, as if it had a magic I could use to make full my empty life.

"Why did your husband kill himself?" he asked from the kitchen table.

I felt slapped. I looked at him from the counter where I was laying out the things for tea. People asked that question shortly after Roger hanged himself, but soon the question disappeared. When new acquaintances learned Roger committed suicide they never asked the impolite "why?"

"Why did Don Bowerman kill himself?" I returned the slap, but he didn't flinch. His chin still rested in his hand, an elbow on the table and those blue eyes still staring at me, absorbing, unraveling. There was no hesitation in his answer...

"Don was too intense, too honest, too creative, too brilliant for the world. Such people suffer in ways we never know. They have this brilliance and the world ignores it. I don't think Don could tolerate his brilliance anymore, or tolerate its being ignored."

I tried again to place his face, but couldn't. He spoke with such little emotion, like a lecturer bored with having to deliver the same words. His lack of emotion about his friend's suicide created a vacuum into which I found myself pouring my emotions about Roger.

"My husband was a self-pitying bum. He blamed Vietnam for everything that went sour in his life, including me. Vietnam syndrome or some such crap, they called it." The depth of my own anger after all these years surprised me. I had never expressed it.

I stepped to the table with the teapot and cups.

"You know what he used to do? He had his Vietnam stuff in a couple of footlockers in the basement. He'd stay down there until late at night fiddling with the stuff, drinking beer. Then he started buying all those guns. I hate guns. How did your friend kill himself?"

(Jeremy)

I looked at the wrinkles around her eyes, the furrows in the brow, the cheeks just going pudgy. A face preparing for middle age.

"A pistol," I told her, and put my index finger in my mouth and cracked my thumb. I knew it was a crude gesture. She didn't flinch. Instead, she spoke.

"My best friend was raped and killed when that madman was on the loose ten years ago. She was a beautiful girl. I couldn't understand it when she died. She was so much fuller of life than I was. But when my husband hanged himself I didn't feel so bad. He was empty of life. Life had left him, gotten tired of him, and departed from him. So, really, all Roger hanged was the shell that had been his life."

"Did they ever find that rapist? I remember the panic in the town. The townies were sure it was a college student and the gownies were sure it was a townie. How many girls did he kill? Four?"

"No, five. And no they never found him. Once in a while the paper does a story reminding us all about it."

"Which one was your friend?"

"Lily Straus. The last one. He must have abducted her when she got off work at the restaurant. They found her body two days later in a field. Just like the others. Roger was her boyfriend. It was the week before he returned from Vietnam. We comforted each other. We got married and he hanged himself."

I finished my tea and watched her staring off. I knew the space into which she gazed. That middle ground of emptiness where people search for answers when they don't even know how to frame the questions.

She seemed to snap to.

"The notebook. Shall we see if the notebook is still there?" she asked.

(Sarah)

Every step upon the stair made my feet heavier with the leaden weight of the memory of Lily Straus. *Lily Straus*. I whispered the name from my lips like a death gasp. Did the rapist enjoy Lily as much as I had? The flashing, blue eyes, the black, glistening hair she wore cut short. She would twist away and yet implore you for more. Had she implored the rapist, too? Had there been pleasure in the fear? Surely not.

I could imagine Lily's small hands, beating on his back as they once had pummeled my own back. I could still feel their tiny batterings. The demanding for more pleasure and the hating of it at the same time. The recriminations after. The pledges to not do it again, of staying friends, and then–in the warm, mellow evenings of that summer–the gentle touch that became a frantic fumbling.

Lily's boyfriend was in Vietnam and she waited for him. She didn't date other men; she stayed loyal to Roger, except for me. When Roger returned, he found Lily not alive to greet him, but dead–raped and murdered–and buried. And that domestic violence ravaged the precious few portions of his soul that hadn't already been ravaged by the foreign violence he had just departed. I comforted Roger, and he comforted me. He was a link to Lily. As if, when Roger possessed me, I possessed Lily.

"There's the rope; it pulls down the stairs to the attic."

"Do you want to leave?" he asked. "I can go up there alone."

"No, I want to go up. I want to face it.

(Jeremy)

I watched her reach a hand up to grab the rope and pull down the stairway. As she stretched, her body attracted me. Her hips were full and broadening with the coming of middle age.

"I want to face it," she had said, and I ran the quote over in my head. It looked to me as if she were anxious to face–running to face–gasping at the opportunity to face whatever "it" was.

The stairs were hinged; she pulled them down for the bottom rung to rest upon the floor. The light in the attic had that hazy look, as though filtered through a yellow paper. Dust motes hung in the air from the earthquake caused by lowering the steps. To me, it looked like she missed the third step on purpose. She slipped, fell backwards, and I was there to grab her shoulders and steady her. She twisted her head to look at me. Tears were in her eyes.

I think a man who fails to kiss a woman when a woman wants to be kissed–needs to be kissed–is condemned to hell. A man who cannot recognize when a woman wants to be kissed lives in hell. It is the not the kiss that is delicate, it is the words. You have to say words after you kiss. That is the challenge. But I knew what to say. I had seen through the hallway into the summer porch where Don had his apartment. I saw the bed there, next to the large loom.

She continued to stare at me, tears flowing out of those brown eyes, eyes that looked into mine with a haunting desperation. The life seemed gone from her shoulders, as though only my grip upon her was keeping her from wilting into a pile of will-less flesh. The kiss came easily. Her eyes closed. The pressure of my lips upon her own gave her back her will. First I felt her lips gain life under my own, and then her shoulders tensed in my arms. And the words, too, came easily:

"Come," I said, and led her by her hand. "I want to make love to you in Don's room."

There was no reluctance in her step.

There are times that I am able to separate myself from my own passion, float above and stare down to observe the flow of passion of the woman I am with. Her passion fascinated me. The longing and the need were so intense and so deep my body could only ride with it. It was as if I were in a lifeboat on a stormy sea. You had no choice but to go where the storm took you. To think you could control the boat was silly. All you could do was hang on as the roiling in the depths of the sea caused the surface of the water to whip itself into an explosion of expression.

But then my moment came. The totality of my existence focused itself into that desperate, physical desire to sum up that existence with one massive thrust. And as I did so, I opened my eyes, and even as my loins emptied their fire, they turned to ice. Her face was not her face; her face was Don's, his eyes wide open and staring into mine.

"Don," I cried, and heard her own astounding answer.

(Sarah)

"Come," he said. "I want to make love to you in Don's room."

I followed willingly as he led me by the hand back to the bed beside the loom. I slept there in the summer, with the windows open on three sides to catch the night breezes. I felt drained. It amazed me that I could walk. I thought he might have to carry me. The spark of life he had given me in that kiss was but a tiny battery charge for my heart. Without a further charge, my heart would flutter into nothingness.

He sat me on the edge of the bed and kissed me again. More life came into my body. His lips moved to my neck, and the pulse in my neck leaped to meet his lips. He began to undress me, his hand going to my nipple, and my heart jumped to meet his touch. My hands finally found the strength to pull his head to my breast.

Even as I lost control, I reflected on the fact. But any mental powers I had were lost in the demanding cauldron of need. I haven't had a lover for years; I excused myself, and let loose from deep within me the power to devour him. But he seemed un-devourable. He stayed afloat even as I raged below him until each emotion fused with every other emotion in my body to speed along the wires of my nerves and overload my brain with insane need.

"Lily!" I heard myself cry, and opened my eyes. Lily's face was above me, her blue eyes flashing. "Lily!" I cried again, even as I heard him call me Don.

(Jeremy)

I am rarely satiated. Tired, yes, but almost never satiated. Men get bored with women, but that isn't satiation. I wanted her again.

"Was Don your lover?" she asked, her breathing slowed. The deep gulps of air she took were quieting her.

"We were close, intimate, but never lovers. Neither of us was homosexual. I loved him, but I didn't desire him." My own breathing, too, was calmer, although my stomach muscles still fluttered, sudden spasms of muscle memory triggered by the physical exertion. "And Lily, tell me about Lily," I demanded, and listened to the evening sounds of birds bring night upon the world and dread upon my soul.

(Sarah)

I didn't want to tell him about Lily. How to tell him about Lily, I wondered, even as I realized my mouth was opening and the words were tumbling out, tired of being imprisoned.

"We were lovers. Neither of us had had a lesbian experience before. It surprised us both. Scared us both, especially her. Her boyfriend was Roger. He was away at war in Vietnam that summer when we had our affair. Then she was murdered the week before he was to return home."

"And you married Roger," he said.

"And I married Roger," I repeated. "I married Roger because he was my link to Lily and I was his link to her. But it didn't work out, and neither of us could admit it. Divorcing each other would have been like divorcing Lily for both of us. Roger came back from the war shattered. I don't know if even Lily could have glued the pieces back together. I hardly tried. I think Roger liked being broken, so he could pick each piece up and cry over it."

"Did Roger ever know?" he asked.

"Oh, yes, he knew. I told him. You don't know what it's like to be with a man who thinks he's so macho then dissolves into beery tears. He disgusted me. I guess I was still jealous that Lily could have loved him. I was angry at Lily for loving him. I was angry that he couldn't honor Lily's memory by being stronger. So, yes, I told him.

"I went down in the basement one night to find him wearing his silly, floppy, khaki hat with the medals pinned on it, drinking beer, his belly bulging, and there was the picture Lily had sent him when he was in Vietnam. The picture I had taken. She looked so fresh and alive, and I knew the reason. We had just made love and she *was* fresh and alive. He blubbered over the picture. So I told him.

"I told him I had been the better lover. I knew. I could judge. I had loved her, and him, and I had been better for her. I told him it was a shame he hadn't been killed in Vietnam. He didn't even have the strength to hit me.

"And after I said that, I watched him fade the way colors in a cheap yarn will fade until what link to Lily he provided for me turned to smoke that was puffed away when he hanged himself."

"You found him?"

"God, yes, I found him. His last bit of cowardice and I haven't been up there since. But I want to face it. We can go up there now. There's a light bulb, if it still works."

(Jeremy)

"Not at night," I told her. "That notebook's been up there for ten years. One more night won't matter." I turned on my side and laid a hand on her stomach. The raging seas within her had quieted. I could launch my boat again and this time navigate it, steer it, guide it through the swells and waves and pretend I was in control.

Later in the night I awoke. Her breathing was deep and restful. Crickets lulled the night. The smell of her was strong, but through its pungency I smelled the dust of the attic, and I wondered what ghosts had been disturbed. And I wondered–if the notebook were found–if I would find the courage to open it.

The memory of seeing her face turn into Don's worried me. That same intense face. Self-assured of its own brilliance. Certain of victory. How it used to laugh at me when I would argue with it.

That next morning we had a quiet breakfast. The sky was clean, with that special fall clearness that seems to sweep away depression like dust before a wind.

"Sarah?" I looked up from my breakfast and was stopped by the look of her face. It had changed. Maybe the confession had been good for her, maybe the lovemaking.

"Yes?" she asked, and there was an interest in her voice and her eyes that had not been there the day before.

"A week before Don shot himself, he called to confess something to me. I didn't believe him at the time. He was always making up outlandish stories. He said he had killed those girls ten years ago."

"He killed Lily?"

"Well, he rattled off some names. I can't remember them. Four of them, he said. I was paying attention more to the tone of his words than the words themselves, but I remember he said four of them and then gave four names. Lily was not one of the names. I just thought it was so outlandish that I didn't pay attention to him. I should have. I should have gone to him. I'm sure he wanted me to."

"But now you think he may have been telling the truth?"

"Maybe. He was afraid of women. It was the one weakness in his cocky brilliance. He never dated, despite his good looks. He wanted dates, he wanted to know women, he desired them, but he feared them at the same time. He used to tell me how he would follow a girl on campus and then to her apartment and stake the place out. He said he'd keep logs of her comings and goings. He'd describe her to me in infinite detail. He said he wanted secretly to know all about her before approaching her. But he never approached any of them. Or else he approached them only to kill them."

I had watched the desperation building in her eyes as I talked, and finally it exploded in a pitiful cry. "I loved Lily so much," she burst out and started sobbing, then stopped abruptly, wiped her eyes, and continued.

"She was such a tiny thing. We were so happy together. She chatted all the time about everything. She said we had to stop when Roger came back. What did she see in him? I never understood it. To think I've been living in the house where her killer lived. Let's go see that notebook."

We climbed the steps again to the second floor; the ladder to the attic still rested on the hallway floor. I followed her up.

The dry, dusty smell of the attic became stronger with each step. Her body was halfway through the opening when she turned her head, muttered, "Good God," and sat on the edge of the attic opening and put a hand on the floor.

"What is it?" I asked, then walked past her and turned my own head to see what she had seen. "Good God." I repeated her own exclamation when I saw the rope. No one had taken the rope down. Its cut end still hung there. They had cut him down and left the rope in place. It was thrown over a rafter and tied around a two-by-four attic stud. The chair upon which he had stood lay underneath it.

"Stay here. I'll search for the notebook," I told her, but I don't think she heard me. She was in her own quiet world of memory.

(Sarah)

I could only stare at the cut end of the rope. It seemed to represent the end point of my life. Before that point was the thread of my life. Then it had been sheared off. Now there was nothingness. Never had the nothingness of the past few years been so visible to me. It was not Roger's body that I saw beneath the cut point of the rope, dangling as it had that day I found it. It was a conclusion: my life was as empty as the dry and dusty air that floated beneath the rope and came to rest upon the fallen chair.

"It's here." I heard the voice from far away. There were footsteps beside me and then he sat next to me, blowing dust off the cover of a spiral notebook with a shiny, red cover. I watched as he opened the cover and read with him the words: "The Diary of Murder."

On the next page was pasted a newspaper clipping about the first murder-rape. A picture of the pretty victim–a blonde college girl–was contained in the article. On the next page I looked over his shoulder as he read the close, handwritten notes. He flipped the page, and the notes continued. I tried to focus on some of the words, but my gaze flashed to the bottom of the page, where a lock of blonde hair had been taped.

He had flipped the page, and the story and picture about the second victim was taped to the page. This time I concentrated on the tiny, small, handwriting and then wished I hadn't. I was beginning to feel overwhelmed.

"...their fear almost takes my breath away. It makes me feel faint. The way she tried to wriggle away from me. It gives me a massive erection and tremendous ejaculation...," I read, before he flipped the page and there was another lock of hair, this one strawberry blonde, taped to the page.

Lily, I began to think; my breath coming in short, tight gasps. *I felt faint.*

(Jeremy)

I really wasn't all that shocked. Maybe Don's confession had prepared me–even though I had discounted it–and here, now, was the evidence in my hands that Don had killed all those girls. What surprised me was he had kept such an incriminating record. But then, he would have wanted such a record. Probably planned on using it some time for a writing project. Stashed it away. And it had been sitting up here all these years waiting to convict him. But they could exact no punishment upon him. He had already killed himself. He was beyond their reach.

I turned the page to look at the clipping about the third victim, the headlines growing larger as fear and outrage grew with each dead girl that turned up. His slanted, squat handwriting was easy for me to read: I knew it so well.

"...They are all alike in their begging. They all beg. They all promise not to tell. They all want life. I want life, too. I breathe deeper when they gasp for life. My heart is fuller. Blood races in my head. My muscles are stronger when I hold them. Her scream was a symphony in my ears..."

I flipped the pages and found the fourth victim's story and, at the end, his notes about her. Then just above the lock of black hair these notes:

"...this must be the last. I think Jeremy suspects. If he finds out, he'll tell the police. I've gained so much strength, I think some-times I could kill even him..."

"But what about Lily?" An arm shot across the notebook and her hand turned the page. But it was blank.

I looked at her, staring in panic at the blank page.

"Nothing about Lily here. Why is that?" I asked. "Why isn't Lily's murder here, Sarah?"

She shook her head back and forth.

"Maybe it isn't here because Don didn't kill her. But if Don didn't kill her, who did, Sarah?"

Her mouth was open and her eyes continued to stare at the notebook.

"Was it you, Sarah? Is that it? Was it more than you could stand, having Roger coming back from the war and knowing you'd lose Lily? Did you kill Lily so no one else could have her? You could have strangled her like the other girls had been killed, and even if there was no evidence of the rape, the police would blame the rapist. And then you buried your own memory of killing her, buried it deep within you where even you had no access to it. That's why Roger's suicide really bothered you so much, not that he was dead, but that it made you remember you killed Lily and were responsible for her death and his, too, really. That's why you didn't want to come up here, isn't it, Sarah? But now you remember, don't you?"

I looked at her ashen face. She stared at the cut end of the rope. I watched her mouth open, then close, then open again, the lips parting in the whispered, "Yes."

(Sarah)

"Yes," I whispered, and my mind was flooded with the memories.

Lily's body under my heavier body, pressing against Lily's light frame. Knowing that Roger was returning in a week. The despair. Knowing I would lose Lily as a lover. The despair turned to a desperation that had filled me with an unspeakable dread.

"I can't share you, Lily. I can't lose you," I said, as I put my strong, weaver's hands around Lily's thin throat and started pressing, squeezing, and felt Lily's sweet, little body thrash beneath me, tiny fists beating upon my back, the nails dug deeply into my skin until all was still. I had the scars for weeks. And as those scars had healed, as the newspapers told me the rapist killed Lily, I had believed it, and the scars were gone.

Roger returned and we consoled one another. And now the scars were back, huge, gaping things on my heart. I could feel the blood gushing from my soul.

"I know a lot about repressing memories," the man beside me said. There was something different in his voice. Something that drew even my shattered attention back to the world around me. "Jeremy's been repressing me for years. Thought he'd killed me off."

His eyes were different, the set of his face, and suddenly I recognized him. His was the face in one of the pictures in Mrs. Franklin's nursing-home room. I used to go visit the house's former owner, and each time there was the ritual of looking at all her pictures. In one of them, she and her husband stood by one of the students who had rented from them. They had particularly liked him, thought him brilliant. Yes, that's why the name was familiar, too. Jeremy Broad. It was Jeremy Broad, not Don Bowerman, who had lived here, had kept this diary.

"You? You're Don Bowerman? You killed those girls?"

"I killed all these girls," he said, and reached down to finger the lock of hair on the last one. "I'm so glad to have the notebook back. I hid it up here to keep it from Jeremy. His force was becoming stronger. He didn't like me killing girls. He'd taken some psychology courses, and had it all explained.

He said I was just trying to get back at my mother for her incest with me. Jeremy with his reasons and his logic and his smoothness. He pushed me back. I've been gone for a long time. Jeremy even thought I killed myself. It was a trick of mine. If I was dead, he wouldn't think he'd have to worry about me. But I am alive and here sitting next to Sarah Winston. Sarah Winston who killed Lily Straus."

He rested a hand on my thigh. I froze, but not in fear. I froze in wonder. I marveled at the words my brain told my mouth to form. I had no interest in his story, because the solution to the emptiness of my life was clear. The solution was so justified, so deserved. Join the emptiness. The emptiness where Lily Straus and Roger had gone. The emptiness that had beckoned me ever since that day when I felt the life of Lily expire under my hands. The prospect brought joy to my heart. All the dread and guilt I had felt was gone. I felt wonderful. I smiled, put my hand over his on my thigh and let my mouth form the whispered words: "Kill me."

I continued staring down at my hand over his and said, "You have to kill me. I might go to the police and tell them about you."

"I know," he said, and the change in his voice made me look at him. Don was gone and Jeremy was back. The transformation of his face was astounding. It was Jeremy. His face bathed in sweat.

(Jeremy)

"I know," I said, and smothered Don within me. I couldn't let him kill a woman I loved. She was mine. There was no reluctance in her step either. She followed me to where the rope hung. I untied it from the two-by-four as she watched the rope in the kind of fascination with which a small animal will watch the snake coming to kill it. I retied the rope to another stud, and the cut end of the rope slipped closer to the floor. I asked her to take off her clothes, and she shed them as though happy to be rid of those last bits of earthly impediments.

"I had to work it all out for myself. I couldn't go to a psychologist. I took psychology classes, read, and reached my own understanding of my own split personality. The reason was simple: one of the most common. Incest with my mother. She seduced me and I enjoyed it. I hated her and she had to pay, and that became Don. But I enjoyed the sex and wanted to seduce women to get even, and that became Jeremy. Only Don turned violent so I had to pick between the two and I picked Jeremy."

I don't think she was listening. Her eyes were glazed, and I reached my head forward to kiss a nipple and watched it spring erect. I tied her hands behind her back using her pantyhose. I righted the chair and stepped up on it with her. As I tied the rope around her neck, I felt her body press against my own and her lips opened. "Lily," she whispered, and then said it one more time as I stepped off the chair and kicked it free.

The body struggled. "The body always struggles. It gives up life only with a fight, no matter how strongly the mind has called it quits," I heard the voice say within me. Don's voice. The dreaded voice, the voice I had to still once and for all. I untied her hands and they dangled beside the hips. I ran my hand lightly over the downy hairs on the stomach, then leaned to kiss a spot below her belly button, at just that spot where Mother would direct my head. I don't know if they were my lips or Don's upon her skin.

I picked up the notebook, walked down the attic steps, closed them, made the bed beside the loom, picked up all my things, and walked around the house one more time with the notebook tucked under my arm. I set the front door to lock when I closed it, and walked across the street where my car was one of many parked in a row. Sometime in the future, who knew how long, they would find Sarah and conclude a suicide. The files would reveal her husband had hanged himself in that very spot, and that would hasten their conclusion.

I drove a small ways out of town and turned on a dirt road. I stopped and took the matches out of the glove box and walked to a clearing beside some trees. "Jeremy, don't do this," Don spoke to me. "You know your life is fuller with me." I was tempted to read the words Don had written as I tore each page out of the notebook, but I knew the attraction they would have for me: the awful, powerful attraction. I made a pile of the crumpled paper and struck a match, but could not bring it to the pile. It burnt to my fingers and the shock of that pain gave me strength. I struck another match and threw it on the pile. It caught fire quickly and I added the bright-red cover. I watched Don Bowerman turn to ashes. Only the wire spiral binding remained and I ground that spine into the charred ash and dust under my heel.

E N D

Impure Breed
By
Ken MacGregor

Niles stood in the open back door of his house. He leaned against the frame and watched the alley. Clive had been gone for twenty minutes, which was ten minutes longer than usual. The dog's name was supposed to be a joke: Clive Barker. But it turned out to be a girl dog, so people always asked why she had a boy's name. No one got the joke.

Putting his hands in his pockets and fiddling with the contents, Niles found a crumpled bill and pulled it out. George Washington looked at him sideways. The large A matched the smaller A at the beginning of the serial number. Niles had never noticed that before. Folding it in half, Niles slid it back into his pocket and looked again at the alley mouth. Clive was nowhere to be seen.

A scraping sound snapped Niles's head around. There was Clive, limping toward home. Niles ran to her and felt all over, his panting matching Clive's as his fingers felt for wounds. He couldn't find any, but Clive smelled like rotten eggs and was favoring both her back legs. After a bath, Clive smelled like herself again but still seemed out of sorts.

The next day, his dog was still moving stiffly, so Niles called the vet. The woman on the phone said it didn't sound like an emergency, but that she'd be happy to look at Clive if Niles brought her in. The vet had an opening the day after tomorrow. Niles had seen her at the office a few times; her name was Rebecca. Her long, burgundy-dyed hair framed her high cheekbones well. She had a slightly upturned nose and her eyes were the green of a tropical lagoon. For a doctor, Rebecca dressed casually but well: designer jeans or pencil skirts and a button-down blouse. Every time Niles saw her, he caught himself smiling a lot.

The examination room, one door away from the lobby, was decorated with animal cartoons and pictures of kittens and puppies. Clive lay on a small, waist-high table in the center, listlessly wagging her tail. Rebecca talked to the dog while looking her over, explaining what she was doing in a calm, quiet voice. Niles found this comforting, too. After 15 minutes or so, Rebecca scratched Clive behind the ears, gave Niles a smile that made his heartbeat stutter, and gave Clive a clean bill of health.

Within a week, the dog seemed back to her normal, healthy self. Clive lost the limp and was soon playing tug-of-war with the foot-long rope that was her favorite toy. She did seem to be eating a lot and putting on weight, but otherwise seemed fine. Until she started throwing up all over the house.

Niles took her back to the vet. Signing in at the front desk, Niles joked that he wished he could buy health insurance for his dog.

"Very original, sir," he deadpanned, giving him a tight smile and flat eyes.

Niles frowned at him but kept his own mouth shut. In a lobby chair, stroking his dog's fur, Niles waited until the other guy wasn't looking and flipped him off.

The door opened to reveal the veterinarian, wearing a skirt today, he noted. She led Niles and Clive into the other examination room. Rebecca inspected Clive for a long time, frowning and performing the same steps over again before turning to Niles with her eyebrows arched up.

"She's pregnant," said Rebecca.

Niles stared at her. Behind her designer glasses, she blinked those green eyes at him.

"She was spayed in this office," Niles said. "If I recall correctly, you were the one who did it."

"I was. And I know. Technically, this isn't possible. A dog that has been spayed should never get pregnant. I've never seen or heard of it happening. This is basically a miracle."

Niles had no memory of the drive home from the vet's office that day. Going through the motions, he ushered Clive into the house and out the back door so she could relieve herself in the alley. The air was crisp, and the wind carried hints of autumn through the leaves. Niles rubbed his upper arms with his hands and jumped a couple times. He let Clive in and closed the door.

"Have to turn on the heat pretty soon, bub," he said. Clive wagged her tail. Niles fed her and thumped her ribs with his palm.

Cracking open a beer, Niles slumped in his chair by the front window. Reaching for his book, a true-crime novel he was struggling to finish, Niles glanced out the window. A movement caught his eye, a flash of pink in the fading light of dusk. Niles watched for a while but saw nothing else.

The next month was uneventful. As Clive got heavier, she seemed to slow down. She spent most of her time lying near the heat vent, only moving to eat or go outside. In the alley, Clive would only walk six feet from the back door to relieve herself. Toward the end of October, Niles was helping his dog across the room; she was only four but was moving like an 18-year-old dog.

On November first, as Niles was taking down Halloween decorations, Clive started whining loudly. Niles set down the cardboard skeleton and knelt next to his dog.

"What's going on, girl? Is it time? Are puppies coming?" Niles stroked her sides with one hand and scratched her ears with the other. Clive gave a yelp and jerked under his hands. Air escaped her back end and Niles looked. Blood spattered on the carpet behind her. Niles hugged his dog, stroking her fur and talking to her in a soothing voice. With another pained *yip,* Clive convulsed and gave birth.

Niles leaned over his dog to see the miracle puppies. There were three of them: tiny, fuzzy, pink things. They looked like long, skinny Hostess Sno-Balls with legs. Fuzzy, pink, stretched-out tennis-ball wiener dogs.

The creatures made tiny, pathetic mewling noises. Niles had never seen a dog give birth before, but even his amateur eye could tell these were not normal puppies.

Clive stretched her head around to look at her young. After niffing them, she sneezed. She shook it off, growled, and grabbed one in her jaws. Whipping her head back and forth, Clive bit down hard, and the tiny creature was in pieces.

"Clive, no!" Niles yelled. He scooped up the two still-living animals and held them to his chest. Clive gave him a reproachful dog face and spat onto the floor the part of her offspring still in her mouth. She nudged it with her nose, but it was still.

Clive's chest hitched, and she gagged. Her claws dug furrows in the hardwood. The dog coughed and sneezed several times but seemed unable to draw a breath.

"Clive?" Niles asked, still holding the pink fuzzies to his chest. "You okay, bub?"

Clive was not okay. She convulsed again, and blood flowed from below her tail. She wasn't getting any air. Clive lunged forward, jaws snapping; it looked to Clive like his dog was trying to bite a lungful of air. She shook her head back and forth, chest heaving. Niles set the babies down and held their mother. He cried as his dog struggled for air but couldn't help her. In minutes, she was dead.

Niles was on the floor, weeping softly into his dog's fur, when he felt something. The little pink guys climbed onto his leg and nuzzled him. Holding the two helpless creatures to his stomach, Niles cried until he had nothing left.

Once he could control himself again, Niles called the vet's office. After a moment, he got Rebecca on the phone. He told her what had happened. Niles couldn't keep the tears out of his voice.

"Are the other puppies okay?" Rebecca asked.

"I'm not sure," Niles said. "I guess so, but I don't think they're normal."

"Niles, I'm about to go to lunch. Why don't I stop by to look at the litter? I can also pick up Clive and the other puppy for you so you don't have to, you know."

Niles thanked her and hung up. He put a throw pillow in a cardboard box and set the squirming, pink, furry animals on it. Without looking at his dead dog or the dead baby thing next to her, Niles picked up the clutter in the living room. There wasn't much; Niles lived alone and kept his place neat.

Twenty minutes later, Rebecca arrived with a dog carrier and a quart-sized Chinese-food carton. She said hello, set down the food, and with great care loaded Clive and the dead pink newborn into the carrier. She closed it up and turned to Niles. He showed her the two living offspring.

"I don't think these are dogs," Rebecca said. "Whatever mated with Clive must have been really interesting." She spent several minutes checking out the creatures and stood up, stretching her back. Niles watched her breasts push against her shirt, pulling the fabric tight.

"What should I do?" Niles asked.

"Take care of them," Rebecca said. "Whatever they are, they're babies. Here. Call me if there's trouble." She handed him a business card with a handwritten phone number on the back. "That's my cell."

Rebecca lifted the dog carrier; Niles held the door for her and watched her leave. She turned back once, and Niles waved. Rebecca smiled at him and got in her car after sliding the carrier into the back seat.

When he was alone, Niles cleaned up his dead dog's blood. Then he tried to figure out what to feed his pink pets. They wouldn't drink milk or eat dog food; they didn't touch yogurt or raw hamburger. He noticed the carton on the table and opened it; inside was chicken fried rice. As the smell filled the room, the little pink guys mewled and swayed their heads toward Niles.

"You want this?" Niles asked. He squatted and held the food in front of them.

A slit appeared in the animals' tiny heads as they bent over the Chinese food. They slurped it up like fuzzy pink four-inch Dustbusters; there was about a pint in there, and it was gone in about two minutes. They loved it. Niles grinned at them and made a sandwich for himself.

The animals grew fast. They were definitely not dogs, or at least not completely. Aside from the tiny mouth, they had no features on their heads. After two weeks, vestigial ear nubs popped out of the top of their heads. A week later, little bumps pushed through the space above the snouts; they might have been eyes. They craved contact with Niles, and he often held them, humming lullabies.

Months went by. Niles spent a great deal of money on chicken fried rice. His pets always seemed to be hungry. Niles watched his fuzzy pink pets get bigger and better defined week by week. They were bigger than dachshunds after five weeks. At three months, the animals had grown to the size of pit bulls. Their eyes, which came in around that time, were wide, shiny, and dark brown. Their mouths filled with teeth- grinding molars in the back, needle-sharp canines up front. He got so many nips that Niles wished he owned stock in Band-Aid.

The animals' tails had grown, too: they were long sinuous things with minds of their own, wrapping around table legs and making the animals stop short. The big pink quadrupeds constantly had to untangle themselves.

One of those tails caught Niles around the ankle as he crossed the room holding a glass of water. A little sloshed out of his glass and fell on the one he called Sno. Part of the creature dissolved. There was a long, pale scar where the pink fur had vanished. The other animal, Pinky, sniffed the scar, but Sno seemed okay. The scar never healed. Still, Niles was glad he hadn't brought them out in the rain.

"I haven't brought you out at all," Niles said aloud. These animals ate but didn't create waste. "Maybe that's why you grow so fast." Sno unwrapped his tail from Niles's leg and made a *chuff* noise.

Most days, when Niles came home from work, the big pink animals rubbed against him the moment he walked in. Since each of them outweighed Niles, this move pinned him to the wall. Their hot breath on his face smelled like soy sauce. It made Niles's stomach rumble.

"Good news, boys," he said one day, grinning and shaking the rain off his umbrella. He called them boys, but there was no way to determine their gender. "I have a date. With Rebecca! *She* asked *me*, can you believe it?" Niles did a little victory dance around the apartment; the lion-sized creatures picked up on his excitement and dogged his heels.

Niles brought Rebecca home for the first time two weeks later. With her coat still hanging off her shoulders, she stopped and her jaw fell.

"They got *huge*." Rebecca said. She finished taking off her jacket and handed it to Niles. He accepted it with a gentleman's grace.

"This one is Sno," Niles told her. "And this is Pinky. You know? It just occurred to me: you and I are the only people who have ever seen them." Rebecca put out her hands and let the animals sniff first. She tentatively touched one. Sno pushed against her hand and made a low rumbling noise deep inside. Pinky nudged her other hand, not wanting to be left out.

"They're so soft," Rebecca whispered. "Where'd you get their names?"

Niles shrugged. He smiled, a bit sheepish. "Hostess Sno-Balls," he said. "When they were born, that's what they looked like, remember? They're great, aren't they?"

"They're so cool," Rebecca said, turning to address the creatures. "Yes, you are. You're the coolest." Rebecca petted one with each hand. "Hey, Niles, I'm starving. I haven't had anything since lunch. Can I raid your fridge?"

Niles nodded and pointed to the kitchen. He hung her jacket on the hook by the door. He idly scratched Sno and Pinky at the base of their heads, just where they liked it.

"Oh, good. I love this stuff," came Rebecca's voice, muffled by the kitchen door. A chill crept up Niles's spine.

Rebecca came back in carrying a cardboard takeout container and eating out of it with a fork. It was the fork with the bent tine that Niles never used because it always poked the roof of his mouth. The beasts went rigid under his hands. Rebecca's cheeks were puffed out, and she was chewing.

"Oh no," Niles said. His voice cracked. "Not that, please. That's not for you." It was the chicken fried rice. Rebecca lowered the container to her waist, one forkful still halfway to her mouth.

Niles gripped handfuls of fur in his fists. He shushed his pets. Watching the three of them, Rebecca slowly raised the fork.

"Don't," Niles pleaded with her. "Don't let them see you eat any." Rebecca finished chewing and swallowed hard.

"What?" Rebecca asked. She raised her eyebrows, bemused, and put the fork in her mouth.

Niles had no idea his creatures could move that fast. He was jerked off his feet and landed hard on his chin. In his hand, Niles held clumps of pink fur.

Niles looked on helplessly, his scraped chin burning, as his animals pounced on his would-be girlfriend. Sno knocked her down and Pinky wrenched the carton from her hand. They both sucked up the food that fell out, leaving no trace of it. While they ate, each kept a paw on Rebecca; she couldn't move.

When the chicken fried rice was gone and the carton licked clean, both beasts turned their heads to Rebecca. The fork was still sticking out of her mouth. She turned her head to the right, keeping her eyes on the animals, and let the fork clatter to the floor. Niles couldn't move; sweat trickled down his ribs.

"What's happening, Niles?" Rebecca asked. "What are they doing?" Niles shook his head.

Pinky lowered its muzzle and sniffed at Rebecca's mouth. It looked at Sno, then sniffed its way down the woman's throat, chest, stomach.

Pinky made a *chuff* noise. Sno bared its mouthful of canine teeth in Rebecca's face, and the crotch of her jeans went dark with urine.

"Oh God," Rebecca said. "Sorry. That's a fear reaction. How embarrassing."

Sno *chuffed*, and both animals tore into Rebecca, using their needle teeth to rip her open. She screamed. Blood flew outward from their muzzles. The beasts used their paws to pull apart Rebecca's flesh, to get to the chunks of rice, chicken, broccoli, and watercress.

Niles stared, unable to move; he was barely able to control his own fear reaction. It was a pink, fuzzy train wreck in his living room. The animals licked her clean, clearing away every trace of their favorite food.

When they finished, they turned their bloody muzzles to Niles. Their tails writhed like serpents behind them. They looked nothing like the cute, fuzzy, pink pets they had been moments before. Niles wiped his hands on his pants, took a deep breath, and walked into the kitchen. He had to step over Rebecca's eviscerated corpse to get there. Niles tried not to get any blood on his shoes.

Niles's pets followed him. They sat side by side on the tile floor, both heads cocked to the left. It would have been comical without Rebecca's blood on their faces. Niles turned on the hot and cold taps full blast on the kitchen sink. He stood there watching the water for a moment. He cupped his hands in the water and splashed his face, once, twice. Niles yanked on the spray trigger and pulled its hose as far as it could go. He turned around, water dripping from his jaw to his shirt, and he pointed the trigger at his pets.

Sno *chuffed.* Pinky *chuffed.*

"I'm sorry guys." Niles squeezed the trigger and sprayed them both. They stood there and let him.

Gooey pink sludge ran off the animals and into the floor drain. Both beasts whined in pain and confusion. They dwindled fast, and in less than a minute, nothing was left except their eyes and teeth.

Niles scooped up the four brown eyes with a spatula and dumped them in the drain. He turned on the water again and ran the disposal. Niles listened to the wet grinding for a few seconds before turning both off. Silent tears fell over a jaw clenched tight as he worked.

Niles gathered up the teeth with his fingers, careful to hold the jaw by the back and not to touch the canines. He put them in the sink, too, and washed his hands with dish soap.

Niles toweled off and called the police.

"I've killed my girlfriend and would like to turn myself in," he said. He gave them his address and said he'd be home.

Niles returned to the living room and sat a few feet from Rebecca's body. He didn't look at the torn remains as he waited to be arrested. Tears ran nonstop down his face.

When the cops knocked, he got up and let them in. Upon seeing the body, Officer James drew his pistol and pointed it at Niles. Officer Hardy put Niles in handcuffs. Niles didn't resist at all.

"I'm sorry," Niles said. "I didn't mean for that to happen. I really liked her." He didn't say anything about Sno and Pinky, his impossible pets.

Sitting in the back of the cruiser, Niles looked up at the dark thunderheads. He could feel the sudden pressure drop that preceded a storm.

Movement caught his eye from across the street. Something was crawling out from under Bill Madison's porch. As Niles watched, something large and pink slid out under the latticework, scraping its back and leaving a clump of fur behind. It was shaped like a dog, only bigger; its tail snaked out behind, lashing whip-like. *He knows I killed his kids,* Niles thought.

The animal kept its gaze on Niles in the car, padding toward him on large silent paws. Niles looked toward his house. No sign of the cops. He looked back and the animal was running. Above the car, lightning zigzagged across the clouds. The monster sped up.

"Shit!" Niles yelled. He slid across the seat to the driver's side and pounded on the bulletproof glass. The creature slammed into the cruiser; the door buckled inward but held. Its jaw slammed against the glass, yellow spit smeared by razor teeth, lips flattening out to show black gums.

His back against the door, Niles pedaled his feet on the seat, trying to get even further away. He heard muffled voices behind him and turned his head. The two cops were outside now, each staring at the pink monster and going for his sidearm.

The beast was clawing at the car now, leaving furrows in the steel. Niles could see the cops split up, Officer Hardy going around the front of the cruiser, Officer James around back. They both shot the creature, but it didn't seem to care. It just kept trying to get to Niles. The passenger side of the car was caving in, and the bulletproof glass was a wild network of cracks. The cops put a few more bullets in the pink monster. The roof of the cruiser began to give, the reinforced frame bending under the onslaught.

Thunder boomed, loud enough to shake the ground, and everyone stopped. The cops, the monster, and Niles all looked up. The rain poured from the sky like someone had upended a bucket. The cops were drenched in seconds, and the pink creature bellowed and shrank. As it died, it still tried to get to Niles, digging its teeth into the door handle. In about twenty seconds, a pair of brown eyes fell to the asphalt. The razor-sharp canines dangled from the handle, attached to nothing.

The rain slowed, becoming heavy and steady. Officer Hardy nudged the lone set of jaws with the end of his automatic. He looked in at Niles; a dark stain was spreading across the man's crotch.

"I hate this neighborhood," said Officer James. His partner nodded.

The Fun House
By
Jo-Anne Russell

"Don't be a pussy!" Jessica said then turned and faced Hope with a smirk.

I'm not a pussy, and I'm sick of you calling me that!"

"Then go in."

Hope pushed past her friend and stopped at the foot of the steps. The odd-shaped door of the fun house reminded her of the horror novel's cover she was reading. She placed her foot on the first step then paused.

"Get out of my way, Pussy," Jessica said as she pushed her way passed, and raced up the steps. "You're always going to be Scared Little Hope. You're no fun at all. I don't even know why I hang out with you anymore!" She disappeared inside.

Hope honestly didn't know why either. At eighteen, she was what would be considered a lady; she didn't smoke, drink, do drugs, or even really date. Her focus was on her future; a future that she was working very hard to accomplish. Camera equipment wasn't cheap, and wasting money on partying and boys wasn't going to help.

She placed a protective hand over the camera dangling from the strap around her neck and followed Jessica inside. The tiny misshapen hallway rocked from side to side as a strobe light blinded her. Feeling her way along the wall, she entered a room.

"Jess?" Hope rubbed her eyes between blinks, and looked around the dark room, with only a single, small wattage bulb hanging from the ceiling. Much good it did her. She could barely see anything in the dim lighting. Hope rubbed her eyes again and waited for them to come into focus.

The walls were coated with old, chipping black paint. Spider web cracks filled the spaces between the old-fashioned picture frames, housing frightening images of creatures, and bodies covered in blood. One such picture depicted a clown with blood dripping from his eyeless sockets, and a smile of jagged teeth that glistened, accented by the lighting.

Hope raised her camera and adjusted the settings. The view on the screen was too dark, so she placed it up to her eye, and looked through the viewfinder. In the seconds it took her to click the shutter, a pair of yellow eyes appeared in the image. A rush of panic spread through her. Her legs gave way and she stumbled to regain her balance.

Two hands with long nails met her back and shoved her forward. She let out a scream, and scrambled to the center of the room. Her breath coming in quick gasps as her ears filled with the sound of cruel laughter.

Hope spotted Jessica standing against the far wall with her hands covering her mouth. Her light complexion glowed with the redness of her outburst.

"Oh my God, you should so see your face right now! You look like a toddler about to cry, ha-ha-ha!"

"That's not funny, Jess. I saw something weird when I took a picture. There were eyes looking at me."

"Sure there were. We're in a fun house for crying out loud. You're supposed to see weird stuff. Let's go look some more."

Hope looked at the picture. "I'm not kidding. That clown was eyeless, and as soon as I hit the shutter button, they appeared."

"They probably have some creep hiding in the wall, flashing fake, lit eyes, when scared little girls like you come along. I bet he's busting a gut right now."

Jessica flipped her hair out of her eyes—an annoying habit to Hope—and smirked as she walked into the next room. She made moaning sounds, imitating the undead. Hope rolled her eyes as she continued to follow her friend.

The moment she entered the room she smelled it. The putrid, sour odour pierced her nostrils and made her eyes water. Hope looked around for the source, but found nothing more than a circular room full of bizarre shaped mirrors.

The sharp sound of a slammed door cut through the pungent atmosphere. She turned in the direction of the sound only to see the glow of the bulb was gone.

Jessica squealed with delight. "Finally, some action!"

The frames of the mirrors glowed toxic green, lighting their images. Hope watched as Jessica ran from mirror to mirror, laughing at her misshapen reflection. The oval one she stood before now made her body too thin on the top, while her bottom half ballooned out like an old weeble toy.

Hope laughed and raised her camera to her eye.

"Don't you even think of—"

Before her friend could finish, Hope snapped the shutter. She giggled as she backed away from Jessica, knowing her friend was not going to let her get away with any shot that would ruin her "oh so perfect," image.

"Give me that camera," Jessica shrieked, as she lunged toward Hope.

Hope jumped backward, curling her limbs around her camera as she fell. Jess's foot dug into her ribs, as she watched the top of Jess' body pass over top of her. The ear-piercing scream that followed, rendered Hope unconscious.

She woke with one arm still curled around her camera. Her head pounded with a whisper of a scream echoing still. Panic raged through her.

"Jess? Jess?"

Her eyes searched the empty room. Hope stood then walked to the mirror beside her. Jess had to have hit it, but there was no crack. She raised a hand as a misty resemblance of Jessica's face appeared. Frozen on her cloudy image, was a look of pure terror.

Hope gently touched the mirror. It disappeared under her warm touch, as a ripple passed over the glass. She tried to pull back, jerking her hand away, but it remained. The liquefied mirror spread up her arm, slowly reaching her shoulder. She screamed, and tried pulling off her denim coat.

The liquid spread faster, covering her screaming face. Pain, like nothing she had ever felt before, spread through her as the mirror slithered over every inch of her. It seeped into her pores, and her ears, and mouth, drowning out her screams. Just as she was sure she was going to die, coolness spread through her toes, and fingertips. It soothed the tortuous pain she suffered. Jessica's face flashed in her mind, and for a moment, she wondered if Jess had felt the same thing.

She wiggled her fingers and tried to stay calm, as control came back to the rest of her body. She watched the remaining mirror slink off her skin then stood. The liquid reformed within the frame, creating a window-view of the room she had just left.

Where she stood was neither room nor a space of any she had ever seen before. Even the air brought with it a tingling within her lungs during each breath. Hope placed a hand to her throat, and ran it down the strap to the dangling camera. She raised it, and examined the device for obvious damage. Satisfied it was cosmetically unharmed, she turned in a full circle.

The space had neither walls, nor ceiling, yet beneath her feet laid a brown, rubbery surface. She randomly picked a direction and started walking. Strange whistles and other sounds echoed in the distance, but gave no distinct clues as to where they came from.

"Jess? Jessica?"

Her own voice trailed off, and blended with the other sounds. After walking and calling Jessica's name for what seemed like hours, Hope sat cross-legged on the strange brown rubbery surface and inspected her camera further. She pushed the power button and watched the view screen light up.

Hope scrolled through the pictures until she came to the painting with the eyes. They stared at her, making her shiver, and feel as exposed as a nude in a coliseum. Her finger tapped the right arrow button. A surprise spread across the screen Jessica, in mid-flight, had a pair of liquid hands wrapped around her throat. The rest was a pink blur of Hope's flesh. The surface quaked beneath her, but before she could get to her feet, it split. Multi-sized shards of glass shot out of the crack and landed in a pile. They quickly assembled themselves into a jagged square, and clouded.

Hope, frozen by both fear and curiosity, tentatively swiped her hand across it. The cloud cleared, leaving her hand cold and aching. She watched Jessica's image appear, frantically calling out for help, as she pounded on the walls of her confine.

"Jess!"

Jessica spun around and faced her, but her voice disappeared. She pounded furiously on the other side in futility.

Hope sat as if glued. A haunting voice spoke to her, but Hope couldn't find the will to look up.

"Pity not this creature, for she is not worthy."

A gentle hand, patter her on the head.

"What?" Hope stood then, and faced him. The tension rose within her as she faced the yellow-eyed image, from the painting in the hall of mirrors.

A smile spread across his cracked skin, exposing his yellowed, jagged teeth. His eyes glowed with soft light.

"Don't fear me girl, fear what you have become. Fear what lies ahead, for you have laid a path of pain and agony for yourself. Your life will end by your own hand, and for good reason."

"W-what do you mean? Who are you?"

"I am he who is neither here nor there, the darkness and the light, the guide for those who face their true likeness. I am simply a reflection of all who were, and all who are—even you."

"I don't understand. I want my friend back. Please, let us go."

She looked back to the mirror, and upon her friend, who now sat cradling her drawn legs, peering at them with a tearstained face.

"The key to your freedom lies not with me. It lies before you— within the one upon which you gaze."

"What do you want from me? I don't understand your riddles—I don't even care. I just want to go home." She wiped away the tears that trailed from her eyes, hoping he wouldn't realize how terrified she really felt.

She furrowed her brows as she attempted to interpret his facial expression. He was either mocking her, or looked compassionate—

but with such a gruesome face, the answer was beyond her. She changed her tactic.

"Explain what you mean, and cut out the riddles."

"Look," he said, as he touched the glass.

The image swirled, and she saw herself at school from the week before. She was in the darkroom of her photography class. Even with digital technology, the students were schooled in photo development. Old school. She gazed at a drying line of photos when the darkroom door flew open. A burst of light flooded the tiny room, and before she could protest, Jess came into view. Her face red with angry lines tracing their ways to the corners of her eyes and mouth.

"That stupid bitch—what does she know anyway? Its muffins, not rocket science!" She folded her arms across her chest and took a seat on the stool.

"What's wrong with you?" Hope looked back to her pictures and prayed they were not ruined.

"Mrs. Braxton, that's what! She's always on my ass. According to her, I am a danger to myself and anyone else in the same vicinity of where I'm cooking. She told me I should focus on something less dangerous—like horticulture. Can you believe that?"

Hope tried to stifle the giggle that erupted.

"Really? You're going to laugh at me? At least I try to do social things like cooking. I'm thinking about my future, and my future friends. You're going to end up alone, and friendless. You're boring. You barely do anything that involves anyone beside yourself. Why am I even wasting my time talking to you? I'm out of here!" With that, she hopped off the stool, and stormed to the door.

"Jess, wait!"

"Don't bother. I have a lot more friends that actually care if I'm upset, and they won't laugh at me. Know why? Because unlike you, they are not social Neanderthals!"

This wasn't the first time Jess had really hurt her feelings, she did that on a regular basis. Her tone held so much malice. Hope overlooked so many things about Jess, and still made an effort to be her friend. Even when other students tried to deter the friendship. Hope had ignored the warnings and rumors, always trying to make Jess feel good about herself, and for what? Jess' words stabbed at her soul. She used Hope's secrets and fears against her, and that hurt more than anything.

The clown touched the glass again.

Jess walked to the back corner of the school, where students smoked. She stood with a group of girls who spread gossip faster than poison ivy. Jess leaned in and took a smoke from one of the "lower rank girls."

She smiled as she exhaled. "You'll never guess what I just walked in on."

She puffed a bit as the other girls looked at each other. They gave her looks of anticipation.

"What? Tell us!"

The "leader" took the smoke and finished it. "Yeah,? What did you see? Sounds juicy." She dropped the smoke, and stomped it into the dirt.

A smile spread across Jessica's face, her hands made jesters at ninety miles-a-minute.

"I went to see Hope—she was in the darkroom—and you'll never guess what I caught her doing in there!"

"What?"

"Yeah, what was she doing? Tell us!" someone else chimed in.

Like a pack of starving hyenas after a carcass, the crowd surrounded her.

"I surprised her. I guess she wasn't expecting anyone to come in. After all, who really cares about photo shop? Anyway, there she was leaning on the stool." Jess took a breath, absorbing all the attention from the eyes upon her.

"So," said the lead. "What's so big about that?"

"She was masturbating!"

"Oh my god! Are you serious?"

"As if—"

"I know, right? Who would have thought she even had feeling down there!"

All of them laughed. But it was the laugh that came from Jess, that stood out. It wasn't her regular, warm, giddy laugh that Hope had heard so many times over the last few years, but a laugh that seemed deeper, and colder.

Hope let the tears flow freely.

The clown touched the glass again.

Hope saw herself lying on her bed reading the new horror novel her mom gave her. She had been away from school for the last two days, and the weekend had finally arrived. She hoped the rumor someone started would die down before Monday or she might have to change schools.

She heard the knock, but the door opened before she could say a word.

"Hey. You're mom said you were up here. Can I come in?"

"I guess." Hope put the novel face down on the mattress, careful not to lose her page.

"Well, I got two tickets to the carnie for tomorrow. I thought you might want to go."

It was supposed to be an apology. Jess never really said the words. She did things instead.

"I don't know Jess. I have a photo project I'm behind in. I really need a good grade in this class—"

"Perfect! I'll be here tomorrow at ten. You can bring your camera, and take all the shots you want while we're there. It's going to be so cool. I heard they have a few new games. Bring some cash. The prizes are always so cute, but you have to trade up for the really good stuff." She started backing out the door.

"Wait, there's going to be kids from school there too. I really don't want to deal with that right now. Things need to cool down, you know?"

"Suck it up, Hope. You have to grow up, and stop being such a baby. So what if some kids are there? What can they possibly do to you? Really, get a freaking backbone!"

Hope inhaled, readying herself to protest, but Jess was too quick, slamming the door behind her. In other words: it was final.

The next morning brought her baggy eyes and a headache from lack of sleep. She shook as she poured a glass of juice, skipping anything that might come back up in lumps if she upchucked. A knock sounded from the other room, and the mirror clouded back over.

"I still don`t understand," she said, as she stared up at him. All her sadness gone, replace by anger and frustration. "How does *that* help me?"

"You must decide. Your choice is the future, and your freedom. I must show you one last thing." He waved his entire hand before the mirror.

Hope stood at the steps of the fun house. Jess rushed past her and inside, but that's where things changed. The view moved to the back of the fun house where a group of girls stood around, smoking and talking to each other. The same lower rank girl looked really nervous.

"What if we get caught? My dad will kill me then ground me until I'm, like, twenty-five!"

"Quit your bitching." The leader stubbed out her smoke, and then lit another. "Did you tell someone?"

The lower looked like a startled rabbit. "No!" She said it too loud. "I mean, of course not, I wouldn't—"

"Better not have, or you know what'll happen to you."

Lower sparked a smoke, and quietly puffed away.

"Okay, so when Jess comes out, we go in. Remember, there is barely any light in there, so make sure it's her you're stripping, and not one of us. I want lots of pics too, just in case some of them don't turn out. Between the six of us, and Jess, we should have this all over school and the net before lunchtime on Monday. Now, get ready!"

A painful thud entered Hope's chest. Her stomach churned, but instead of upchucking, an inferno of anger and hatred exploded from within her. All the bullying, sadness, and years of aching for someone to be a true friend, had finally taken their toll. Hope decided then, that people were ugly no matter how pretty they thought they were.

An emotional wave hit her, knocking the breath from her, and the desperation from millions of people just like her. People who were worthy, but misunderstood, different, and alone. Their pain pulsed in her veins like hoards of tiny pins. She tingled everywhere, but the sensation was welcoming.

The mirror clouded over.

"Now you see," he said. She looked at him, and finally saw him for the first time. The illusion faded away, and before her stood a young man, beautiful, with soft glowing eyes. His warm and honest smile.

She nodded, and placed her hands in position on her camera. This time when the liquid engulfed her, there was no pain, nor fear. She found herself standing as it departed and solidified, leaving her in the hall of mirrors.

Hope stepped closer and adjusted the lens. Jess was red-eyed, and angry. She screamed obscenities at the mirror, and at Hope's image on the other side. She was as ugly as her personality. Small reflective material closed off Hope's ears as she snapped the shutter.

"Smile!"

Jess' skin burst into pulsing lesions, and then flames. Her flesh melted away slowly as she ran about screaming, smearing the mirror in blood and puss. She never lost consciousness until the very end.

The caps receded inside her ear canals, and a friendly voice whispered to her.

"You did well. Even she couldn't argue the fact that you have a backbone."

Hope smiled. She knew what she had to do. Her soft yellow eyes glowed, as she made her way to the door; the girls were waiting.

Neighbor in Apartment B
By
Matt Scarlett & Jesse Duckworth

When I left the airport in Philadelphia, it was obvious I wasn't in Kansas anymore. Cabs blew past me and when I finally got one to stop, a middle-aged man in business attire jumped inside ahead of me and took off. Several attempts later, another cab stopped. I told him my address, and even though he spoke little English, within thirty minutes I was at my apartment, standing on a rollercoaster of a sidewalk.

In the first moments, I just soaked up the sight. The wood porch had seen better days. Paint chips reminded me of flower petals that bloomed off the railing. When I put my hand on the railing, they crushed like dry leaves. On my right, brushed stainless steel mailboxes were inset into the wall.

I slid a key in the old, rustic lock and turned the knob. The door was stuck. Using my shoulder, I nudged it open, revealing faded wood floorboards that testified of the building's age. Upon walking through a hallway to the stairs, I noticed there was only one apartment on the first floor: Apartment A. Its door was old and worn; the bronze knocker hung loosely on a screw. A stack of old newspapers sat in front of the door. *Vacant.*

A flight of stairs went up and a flight of stairs went down. I decide to take a peek at my new apartment on the second floor. I've always hated basements anyway. Walking up the narrow steps, the aging wood creaked with each step, announcing my presence. As I approached the top of the stairs, a thick musty smell filled my nostrils.

God, I hope this odor goes away.

My apartment was on the right, Apartment C. Upon opening the door, much of my excitement of having my own first place dissipated. The apartment was small and dingy. The walls were beige, accepting a grey contrasting wall, and the outlets were still taped off as if the last tenant had left in a hurry with no time to finish painting the living room. I set my things just inside the door and decided to take a walk outside to get acquainted with the area.

I had never seen anything like it. So much history, unlike McLouth, the small town in Kansas of which I was born and raised. Passing by a group of tourists, I heard them describe the architecture as "gothic." Sure, I'd heard that term before. Although, I never had a clue what it meant until now. If this was "gothic," I liked it. The building faces were imposing and ornate in design. But, all the buildings were crammed together, much like the line I had waited in to get on the plane. When I viewed the houses from a certain angle, they appeared as one continuous house and the gaps between them a mere seam. It made me long for the Kansas countryside.

I stopped at a diner at the end of the street, ordered a coffee and picked up a newspaper that happened to be sitting on my table. It was rare for me to look at a newspaper, but I needed something to pass the time before my coffee arrived. The front page of *The Philadelphia Inquirer* read, "Missing Person." My eyes were drawn to the picture of the girl.

My age…same long, blond hair….pretty.

It made me think about my sister, Ally. I was going to miss her. We'd never been apart like this before. Twins aren't supposed to be separated.

"Ma'am?"

I jumped. The waitress had arrived with my coffee. "Thank you."

She smiled, nodded and went back to work.

I dumped three sugar packets in and took a drink.

Perfect.

Setting my cup of coffee down on the newspaper, I noticed it spilled.

Shit!

I picked up the cup to clean it with a napkin. When I looked back at the paper, a perfect coffee ring circled the words "Missing Person," captivating me to read on.

"Ashley Davis, 22, last seen on—"

That's my street!

Upon reading the rest of the article, I discovered that three other females disappeared near my apartment in the last few months. Anxiety inched its way up my spine. I went to take a sip of coffee and I noticed my hand shaking. My breathing quickened. I inhaled and exhaled slowly to calm myself. Then my phone rang, causing me to spill coffee down the front of my shirt.

"Dammit!" I patted my shirt and wiped off my hand with the coffee stained napkin. Then I looked at my phone. "Landlord" was displayed on the screen.

I answered and said, "Hello?"

"Hello Jen. This is John, your landlord. I just wanted to see if everything's going alright. How was the flight?"

"A little bumpy, but, thankfully I got here in one piece. Everything's fine. Getting a cup of coffee right now."

"At The Corner Diner?" he asked.

My eyes darted to the soiled napkin on the table. "The Corner Diner" was printed in the center with a black circle around it. My heart raced as I inspected each person in the diner.

"How'd you know?"

He laughed. "It's the closest place for a cup of coffee. How was the apartment?"

Jen, quit being such a baby. "It's great." I lied.

"Perfect. Do you have any other questions?"

"Umm…" I started. I wanted to ask who the last tenant was, why they had to move out or if he knew any of the girls who went missing. "Nope. I think that's everything."

"Okay. Don't hesitate to call if you need anything. Have a good night!"

"You too. Goodbye." I hung up the phone and reread the article about Ashley Davis.

***

It was dusk by the time I returned to my apartment. I was unlocking my door when I saw a flash from behind me. I spun around. A faulty light brought my attention to the apartment across from mine, Apartment B. The light dimmed and brightened as if it had a mind of its own. It highlighted duct tape that sealed off the entire doorframe almost like a crime scene.

What the hell...

"Excuse me. Can I help you?" a gentleman asked.

I nearly jumped out of my skin. My eyes met his. A tall, dark-haired man stood on the landing between our apartments. His wavy hair, gorgeous green eyes, muscular frame, reminded me of Viggo Mortensen in the Lord of the Rings. Surprisingly enough, he looked like a guy I could take home to my parents, provided he hadn't already fallen for an elf and the blonde wins him this time.

He cleared his throat. "Hello, can I help you?"

I forgot to introduce myself, or speak for that matter. My body temperature rose and I could feel my face turning red. "I'm sorry, my name's Jen. Just moved into Apartment C." I tried to laugh but it came out as an awkward giggle. "And you are?" I asked, holding out my hand.

"I see," the man said, turning toward the door of Apartment B. He methodically pulled the duct tape off the frame without harming the paint underneath. After unlocking his door, he turned and stared at me. "Welcome!" he announced before disappearing into his apartment, leaving me still standing there with my hand outstretched.

Nice to meet you too!

I ran a hand through my hair. It felt oily and gross. I remembered the stain on my shirt. *I wouldn't have been interested either. I'm a mess!* I took one last look at his door, then went into my apartment and unpacked.

***

No matter how much better I looked, this happened every time I saw him for the next few weeks. He never muttered more than two words, "hi" and "goodbye". He never led with a question.

A month went by and I still didn't know his name. Then I stopped seeing him altogether. He would leave before I woke up in the morning and wouldn't come back until I was asleep. But I knew he was still around.

His peculiar behavior and the duct tape around the door fueled my curiosity. Watching him became my addiction.

By Saturday, I devised a plan. I set the alarm for five o'clock in the morning. When I awoke, I made a cup of coffee and watched his door through my peephole. My breathing became louder and louder the longer I waited. Every possibility streamed through my mind about what kind of person he was.

Hermit? Murderer? Vampire?

I had never seen him during the day before. I shook my head and laughed at myself. *A vampire…now that would be fun.*

The creaking of stairs pulled me out of my daydream. He appeared in the vision of my peephole. After removing the duct tape, he stopped and looked back at my door. I ducked as if he could actually see me. I heard a door shut.

When I looked back through the peephole, his door was taped off again but he was nowhere to be seen. The light started to flicker again, but this time, it went out completely. I moved my eye from the hole and rubbed it. Looking back out, the same darkness still loomed. Then light flooded my eye, instantly blinding me. When I could focus, I saw the man's face hovering in front of my peephole.

I yelped and fell backwards. Covering my mouth, I tried to prevent any further noises. Then I heard it. A few small taps sounded as if someone was moving their fingers in a walking motion toward my doorknob. The handle started to turn.

I scurried away, falling onto the stairs behind me. The next moments played in slow motion as fear rendered me paralyzed. Absentminded, I stared at the knob. It stopped turning but it was minutes before I could move. Like a mouse stuck to a glue trap, I was incapable of peeling myself from the stairs. I would've chewed off my own leg if it would've helped me to reach the door.

I slithered to the door, using the handle like a crutch to get to my feet. Against the voice in my head, I looked out of the peephole.

He was gone.

What the fuck?

For a moment, I just waited. Still, no one appeared in the hall. My heart continued to race, as I couldn't see the stairwell in its entirety. I hoped the man wasn't waiting for me out there.

I held the doorknob and turned it.

My knuckles whitened because of how hard I gripped the knob. I eased the door open. A soft creak echoed past me and into the apartment. I put my left foot onto the landing, leaned out of the door, and looked down the stairs.

Nothing.

Instantly relieved, I turned my gaze to the door of Apartment B. Curiosity won out against the voice in my head that was urging me to go back inside my apartment. I crept to his door.

I have to know, I just have to.

Stepping back from his door, I found a bent corner of duct tape. I took it and pulled downwards. The light rippling sound filled the silent stairwell. With all the duct tape removed, I tested the knob. To my surprise, it was unlocked. I pushed the door open and stared into an abyss.

***

I flipped a switch and no lights came on to comfort me. Adrenalin charged through my veins as I went over my options. I could go back to my apartment and live in fear or I could push forward and prove there was nothing to fear. I moved into the darkness, each step slower than the one before it. My right foot bumped into something. My hands felt a wooden railing that led up a set of stairs, guiding me as I ascended. At the top, a doorway faintly appeared, silhouetted in light. I opened the door and light washed over me, like an entrance to a cave.

The smell of feces and urine was undeniable. It poured into the hallway, embracing me. I walked in, shielding my eyes from the bright light that assaulted them. Once my eyes adjusted, I felt my stomach drop and I screamed.

I stepped back in terror as a cacophony of voices overpowered my own.

"Help me!" shrieked a naked, skinny girl, reaching her boney arm through the bars of her cage. "Please hurry, before they get back!"

Every cage had at least one person inside it, except one. The prisoners were naked and shaved clean from head to toe. A glimmer of hope appeared in each of their eyes when they saw me.

"You must hurry! He won't be gone long, never is," said a bone thin man as he glared at me. I took a step back, then froze, not knowing what to do next.

"Please, don't leave us! You have to help!" another said.

"I'll help!" I heard myself burst out. "Are there any other people here?" I ran to the cage nearest me. A naked woman lay against the back of the cage with her eyes closed.

"She's dead! You must be faster!"

"Where're the keys?" I yelled. Each cage had massive, unbreakable locks. I shot glances around the room to find them. There were no keys in the room.

I'll need to look elsewhere.

They pleaded with me not to leave but I had no choice. I backed into the hallway and frantically searched the rest of the apartment. It was eerily silent outside of that room, but I could still hear their cries in my head.

The apartment was so barren. Tables, counters, everything was clean like no one lived there at all. In one room, I saw a cord dangling down from an outlet. Upon closer inspection, I discovered that it was a phone charger.

My phone! I searched my pockets. Empty. I had left it charging in my apartment. *Why didn't I bring my phone? God dammit!*

Many of the other rooms had no light either. It helped that the apartment seemed to have the same floor plan as my own. Consequently, I found the kitchen. I slid my hands across the granite countertop, feeling a heavy liquid cling to my fingers. In my mind, I knew what it was but I smelled my hand anyway.

Blood!

My legs felt weak and shock hit me like a bolt of lightning. It took all I had to stay on my feet.

A floorboard creaked behind me, and when I turned, I felt something hard strike my face. Instantly, light blinded me as pain seared through my limbs. Another strike put me on my back. My vision doubled and two silhouetted figures stood over me. They each raised an arm and brought them crashing down upon me.

***

"Wake up my sweets. It's time for a little haircut."

I heard a buzzing sound. My head pounded, and even more so after I opened my right eye. My left eye wouldn't open, neither would my arms and legs move.

I'm tied up!

"What do you want from me, you crazy bastard?" I screamed at the man. "Who the hell do you think you are?"

"My dear Jen, I've had my eye on you for weeks. Ever since you started snooping around at my door, I knew it was only a matter of time before you came to meddle in my apartment affairs. Just like all the others."

"Fuck you!" I tried to kick him, which only made the chair totter.

He seized my hair and ran the clippers down the middle of my scalp. I threw my head to the side with all my might and tipped the chair. The clippers dug into my head as the chair fell on its side. I felt the hot liquid trickle down the side of my face.

"You stupid bitch," he said.

He returned the chair back upright. Before I could speak, he struck me across the face. I felt more blood pour from my nose. I didn't protest while he shaved the rest of my head. After he finished, he untied my feet and then positioned himself behind me. He grabbed the knot that held my hands together and kicked the bottom legs of the chair out from under me, sending me toppling to the floor.

He dragged me down a hallway. I did everything I could to stop him, to no avail. Nothing fazed him. We finally reached a door and he tossed me into the room.

"This oughta suit ya," he said in a thick east coast accent. Having never heard him speak more than a couple words, I hadn't noticed it before.

On my hands and knees, staring up at him, I said, "Please let me go, I haven't done anything wrong!"

"Oh, but you will make me so much money, my sweets!"

The tall, handsome man I had once crushed on walked towards me. He had a mallet in his hand, probably the same one that he originally hit me with in the kitchen. I fell back onto my feet with my hands poised in the air, protecting me.

"Please you don't need to do this!"

***

"I told you to hurry! Now you're going to rot, just like the rest of us," a male's voice spoke into the darkness.

"Maybe he'll kill her first, ship her overseas or let that evil ass landlord have his way with her," someone whispered.

They spoke of me as if I wasn't there or I wasn't human. Like I was just another animal waiting for slaughter. Anxiety crippled me. I had to focus to breathe. But I choked on my breath when I heard the familiar sound of duct tape being pulled off a door. The door downstairs opened.

The faint sound of a woman's voice echoed up the staircase.

"Hello. It's me, Gale, again. Have you contacted the landlord about that musty smell?"

The malevolent first encounter I had with him screamed in my mind. I heard him speak and chills ran through my body.

"I did. No answer yet. Would you like a drink?" he asked. I heard the door close.

***

Mud clang to my boots like tar, anchoring me down into the watery abyss at my feet. Thick jungle foliage stifled my sight. Occasional bombs flashed in the distance like lightning and roared through the dark canopy of the jungle. My breaths were steady as I ran with my team to our newest checkpoint.

"Private Cason," screamed our first officer, leading the pack. I was in the middle of the squad, enjoying our journey through the jungle. "Move your ass, soldier. Two minutes until we reach our destination."

"Aye sir," I yelled out, straining harder as I ran against the sucking mud.

Near the front of the pack, a small light pierced through the overbearing forest. It lit up the eager faces of my four brothers. We were specialists, sent from hell itself: mercenaries. Loyalties were near zero, money was our common language, a better team at extracting vital information there was not.

Best and brightest! I laughed to myself. *These despicable excuses for humans deserved the fate that was bound to them.* Every mission brought forth the true reality of how much I hated our own kind. "Purely insane" is how most would describe our roles in society, but I see it as a cleansing. A natural order that must take place. The survival of the fittest.

Arriving at a small hut concealed amongst the jungle, a dark figure stood silhouetted in the doorway.

I smirked at him. "What's up doc?" I said.

"Mr. Cason, excited to get this underway?" He said, an evil grin spreading across his lips.

The hair on my neck stood on end. I nodded.

He ushered us into the hut. The stench of blood flooded my nostrils. Intensity overtook me as I gazed at the already bloodied man tied to a chair in the middle of the room. Reaching for a knife harnessed on my hip, I felt the unsteady state of my nerves.

The man's eyes grew wide upon noticing the long blade. I gingerly tapped the top of my knife with my thumb, as if contemplating the next move. Licking my lips, I unsnapped the two buttons holding my instrument of death in place.

The doctor moved past me to confront this poor, helpless bastard in the chair. He choked the bloke until drool oozed out the sides of his mouth. We all laughed as the man's face reddened and he struggled to breath under the doctor's powerful hands.

Releasing him, the doctor gave him a violent punch to the face. Turning, he looked at me. His eyes filled with hatred.

"Cleanse him of his sins," the doctor said. A warped smile spread across his sunken face. He motioned for me to come over.

A razor sharp knife with jagged edges glistened in my hand. The man's eyes were locked on the knife before they darted up to meet mine. Staring at the dying man, I grew anxious.

Practice makes perfect.

This was just another war-criminal. I must not fail. Execution was always the hardest task for me. Torture and capturing were easy in comparison, but taking a life still had a lasting effect that weighed heavily on me.

The menacing knife became sweaty in my hand. The doctor said something, but it took a few seconds for me to unscramble his words.

"Who's the next victim?" He asked.

"Her name's Jen. From Apartment C," I replied. Looking down, I noticed my hand violently shaking.

"You okay son? Having another flashback?"

Sanity came back to me as the doctor tapped me on the shoulder. I was back in my living room, realizing it was just a flashback.

"Don't worry. Take these. It'll calm you down," the doctor said in a soothing voice. He held two blue pills in his outstretched hand. I snatched the pills and swallowed them. The effect was instantaneous. My hands stopped shaking.

We walked back to the blood-drenched table to grab our instruments. I picked up my gore-covered knife, wiped it on my leg, and put it back in its sheath.

"Are the flashbacks getting worse, Cason?"

"No," I lied. "I've just never beheaded someone before."

"Sometimes a gruesome death is the only way," he said, placing his instruments gently back in his case. He never showed remorse or the slightest care. "Dispose of the body quickly. The duct tape will only work for so long. Then get some rest. This flashback was the worst one yet."

He placed a hand on my shoulder and we stood in silence, gazing at the headless body that still twitched in the chair next to us.

The doctor was the closest thing I had to a father. I owed him more than my gratitude. I followed him to the door not saying another word.

***

The next few days were uneventful. Routines were my life and I never strayed from them. Today was different. Coming back from my morning errands, a person was waiting on the doorstep. She looked almost identical to Jen.

"Excuse me, can I help you?" I said, slowly walking up the stairs towards my apartment. She was staring at the duct tape lining my doorjamb. It took a few moments for her to notice my presence.

"Hi. My name's Ally. My sister moved in next door a month ago. She looks identical to me," she said, then gave a half smile. "Jen was supposed to be here, and her car's outside, but, she won't answer the door."

"You sure you're in the right building? How'd you get in here without a key?"

"Yeah, this was the address she gave me and the door was slightly open. I let myself in." She answered as she pulled a small piece of paper from her pocket.

"No one's lived there for weeks. You should check another building." I turned and removed the duct tape from my door.

"Please! This has to be correct. I'm worried about her. She's my twin sister!"

I opened the door and walked into my apartment. "Sorry I couldn't help," I said before closing the door. Standing silently in the darkness, I watched her sister through the peephole. She was still at my door.

Persistent bitch!

A vibration in my pocket stole my attention away from Ally, the bitch on my doorstep. I answered the phone and a voice boomed on the other end.

"Have you made contact with the girl in Apartment C?"

"I have the girl. She being prepped. Did the doctor tell you we lost another the other night?" I said.

"Dammit! He's getting too careless!"

"We had no choice! The guy was losing too much blood. Wouldn't have made it through the night."

"Bullshit Cason, this wasn't part of the deal. Just make sure you keep the girl alive for a bit longer than the last one."

"Yes sir. But we have a problem. Her sister's here looking for her."

"Don't let her leave! We can use both of them. I'll call the doc. We'll have to move faster than planned. Try not to make too much of a mess. Remember, the next subject has already moved in."

"Copy," I said, hanging up the phone. I peered through the peephole. The girl sat curled up against the door to Apartment C. A rush of adrenaline coursed through my veins as I reached for my knife.

***

My chest heaved hard against the steel-cage. So cold…weak. And this man never shut off the damn florescent lights, making it hard to sleep. Rationed food portions were just enough to keep us alive. It was their method of slowly killing us.

I couldn't stop shaking. My teeth chattered from fear and the fact I was naked with no hair left on my body, not that the hair would have done much good. Uncomfortable with my naked self, I sat in a crouched position, shielding myself from the others.

God, please get me out of here!, I don't deserve this fate…

Never knowing when our tormentor would return kept me on edge. Fear of what he has done to the others plagued my mind. Soft cries began to escape my mouth.

A Hispanic man in the cage next to mine laughed. His broken, yellowed-teeth and sunken face showed no mercy towards me. "Ha, you're next! Wonder what he's going to do with that pretty face and sexy ass." He taunted.

"Screw you!" erupted from my mouth. More laughing was his only reply. Glancing at the other cages, I looked for a friendly face.

"Don't worry about him. He's been here the longest. Constant tortures have rotted his mind." Came a voice from a cage adjacent to mine.

I turned to look at the person speaking to me. Her appearance made my stomach churn.

What in the hell happened to her?

Each hand had been lopped off at the wrist. The wounds were soldered shut. Grotesque scars accented the burnt flesh. Her stomach, leading to her breasts, had too many stiches to count. She might have been beautiful once. But that was a different life.

This is a nightmare! What terror awaits me here?

I started to cry and buried my head into my hands.

"Quiet, you stupid bitch or he'll come gut you!" The Hispanic man said, laughing again. My predicament appeared to please him.

Before I could reply, footsteps sounded from somewhere in the apartment outside our room. I heard a faint knock and then the echo of heavy boots on the staircase. A creaking door brought forth hushed groans from the others in the room. My own heart fluttered, scared of what was to come. The door closed and I could faintly make out soft voices.

"Welcome, Doctor!" one voice said.

"How's our newest girl doing? I trust you didn't harm her too much?" another voice answered.

"She's in the front room, just waiting on the anesthesia to kick in."

"Good! I need to see the others. The General wants a progress report on the experiments."

I heard a few more murmurs and then nothing. Scanning the room, I saw fear etched on everyone's faces. *Is this it? The butchering of my body? I won't die in here!*

Squeaking and thuds from footsteps sounded outside of the door in the hallway. It reminded me of the sound a gurney makes when pushed. My hands gripped the bars of my cage tighter as the sounds stopped outside of our door. The duct tape was ripped off. Our door creaked open. Blackness draped my two tormentors. A man in a white coat appeared first. The coat dragged against the smooth, white-tiled floor. He wore a dark blue suit underneath of his cloak. Small bifocals set snuggly on his skeletal face. Smiling, he looked at each of us. He sinisterly gazed at me, draining the marrow from my bones.

He wheeled a chair above a rusted drain, in the center of the room. The crimson chair resembled one you would find in a dentist office; only this one had multiple straps. It was meant for torture and the fear of its use made my body turn brittle.

The doctor pointed at a cage containing the Hispanic man. My abductor quickly retrieved the man and strapped him to the chair.

"Get away from me, you sick fuck!" The man cried out.

The doctor grabbed his bald head and forced his mouth open. "I see the cyanide has done its job well," he said, sneering. Opening a black suitcase, he rummaged through it. I moved into the back corner of my cage.

I don't need to bring attention to myself. Whatever happens, don't scream!

"Ah ha, here it is," the doctor said, holding a small bottle containing a yellow liquid in one hand and a large syringe in the other. He shook the vial and used the syringe to draw out its tortuous fluid.

"Sulfur Dichloride with Ethylene, also known as mustard gas. Symptoms are only known from direct contact on the outside of the skin. What we want to know … how will your body react to an injection? Where should we start first?"

The doctor moved the needle over the man's body. The man cried and squirmed, straining against his restraints that held him to the chair. He finally showed his fear. Not that show he put on for me earlier.

My captor, who I once thought handsome, walked up and hit him in the back of the head. "Stop moving you prick, so we can prick you." He said as he laughed, then stepped back, allowing more room for the doctor.

The Doctor plunged the needle into the man's bony arm. The yellow liquid disappeared slowly from the syringe. After a few minutes, blisters rapidly formed locally on his skin and his arm began to turn a charcoal black. The man shook as if he were having a seizure. He screamed and tears streamed from his eyes.

Red-orange blisters bubbled, highlighted against his blackening arm. His cries started to wane as his consciousness faded. Minutes passed and his entire arm was a puss-filled blister.

"Put him back in his cage. We'll examine the aftermath later. I want to inspect that girl. Bring her to me." The doctor said. He had a greedy look on his face as he pointed at me.

The man that once reminded me of Viggo Mortenson was no future king. He was just a pawn of this doctor. And he did what he was told like a trained pet. He walked towards my metal tomb. I closed my eyes as the lock clicked open, allowing the man to enter my cage.

"Be strong!" whispered the woman who had spoken to me before.

Callused hands grabbed my arm, scratching against my skin. I let all of my weight drop to the floor.

He'll have to drag me, if he wants his prize!

***

As the lock clicked, any sorrow my cold heart could muster did feel for this poor girl. What the doctor had in mind, even my deranged world couldn't imagine. He enjoyed punishing the victims, but he loved killing them. And as of late, he had killed many.

When I grabbed her arm, her fragile state was evident. She fell limp, letting her dead weight try to inhibit any progress. Easily enough, I scooped her into my arms and carried her towards the chair.

Strapping her in, I felt the cold, dark glare of the doctor, like a wolf waiting to devour his meal. That evil grin kept spreading across his lips. It even gave me chills.

After securing Jen, I turned to the Doctor and waited to receive further orders. He advanced toward the chair. Jen kept her eyes closed as the doctor calculatingly ran his hands down her body. I watched her breasts spill out on either side of the strap that ran over them.

"Cason," the doctor muttered

"Yes."

"Please go get our next test subject," he said, licking his lips.

I stayed for a moment too long, staring at Jen.

"Cason!"

"Yes sir!" I bellowed as I left the room. Making my way through the dark apartment, I headed back towards the living room. I hadn't felt this conflicted since my first mission as a soldier, before all of this shit. I felt my mind again begin to wander...

"Cason! Get your ass down!" Screamed my lieutenant as a bullet whistled off the wall above my head.

I immediately hit the ground. More bullets clattered against the tiled wall, showering me with white dust. I took in the scene around me.

The lieutenant was motioning and screaming but the loud crackle of gunfire drowned out any audible words. Soon after the firing started to wane, I finally relieved myself from the rubble-covered ground.

"Sir, what the hell is going on?" I asked, although I couldn't hear my own voice over the constant ringing in my ears.

"The reinforcements for the rebel soldiers have advanced on our location. Right now, only a few men are holding the American Ambassador captive. We are to infiltrate this location and get her out of this county," Ordered the lieutenant in a commanding voice.

There were only five men in our crew. We were the Special Forces unit for NATO: a secretive black operative group, reporting only to the leaders of the United Nations. This was my first time really "in the shit," as the other men would say.

"Cason, follow Browler down the hall to the main living quarters, and secure that area. The Ambassador will most likely be held there. We will flank them and advance from the back side." Lieutenant Marks had barely finished his statement as he disappeared around the corner of the building.

"Let's do this boy," Browler said.

"Roger."

We climbed the fire escape on the outside of the building and entered the third level through an open window. The captors were sure to have positioned themselves on the main floor, which was on the second level. Having the high ground was the only possible way this mission would have any success.

The third floor of the embassy was strewn with broken glass from office doors and littered with clusters of paper. The dark hall between the glass window offices flickered on and off from broken lights.

File cabinets were piled against the main doors to keep the intruders out. It was a sad attempt, the four bodies lumped in a small pile proving evident.

We kept our pace steady and quiet, pushing into the lobby of the third floor. The Embassy was a circular building with an open center on each level. Moving on our hands and knees, we crawled to the railing as the soft murmurs of the rebels sounded below.

"This isn't goin' to be pretty, if you know what I mean." Browler said then laughed.

It wasn't a nervous laugh either. He truly enjoyed every moment of this. I racked my weapon and waited for the lieutenant to get into position. Peeking over the rail, I saw the Ambassador tied to a chair. She was a striking blonde. Even from here, I could tell she was the type of women to turn heads in a room.

"In position," the doctor said.

Before I could respond, a loud shot echoed throughout the lobby. I instantly sprang to my feet, only to see the body of the ambassador lumped over in the chair. Her blood pooled at her feet as it dripped from the open gorge in the top of her skull.

"Cason, snap out of it!" The doctor yelled, shaking me.

It took me a minute to realize that I was back in the room. My hands had a death grip on the metal bars of the gurney. Jen was screaming a beautiful scream. I looked down to see the meager half-sedated face of her twin sister. My eyes returned to Jen. Her bloodshot eyes bulged. Again, I felt sorrow. This girl looked strikingly similar to the Ambassador that I couldn't save.

"Cason, grab my bag and retrieve the three black boxes." The doctor demanded, pointing toward the closet.

I did as I was told and retrieved the boxes. I laid the three medium sized black, leather boxes on the instrument tray.

"Here. Take this. It'll calm you down." The doctor said, holding two blue pills in his hand.

"Don't do it!" Jen screamed as I reached for the pills. "Do you even know what those pills are? Maybe the doctor has plans for you too!"

I stopped for a moment and hesitated. The doctor looked on intensely.

"Now Cason, we want to get rid of those horrible flashbacks don't we?" he asked in a sympathetic tone.

"Yes sir, but what are these?" I asked meekly.

"Don't you mind, your brain wouldn't be able to understand it anyways. They make you feel better right?" the doctor asked, but this time in a more serious tone.

"Yes." I replied.

"Then take the pills and let's move on with our newest subject."

I tossed the pills into my mouth and swallowed hard. Just like last time, the effect was instant. I looked to the doctor as my hands once again steadied.

***

The strap pulled tight around my throat. I could feel my blood pulsing its way around it like sand through an hourglass. Somehow, I still managed to scream at the doctor. "Let her go, you son of a bitch!"

He didn't reply.

The sight of my twin sister, Ally, lying motionless on the gurney, left an empty hole in my stomach.

"Please, let her go!" My voice was cracking from fatigue and stress. I sobbed.

"Oh my, now isn't that original? Just let her go, she says. Well, since you're willing to negotiate … how about we play a little game?" he asked, picking up one of the black boxes from his tray.

"Fuck You! I won't be a part of your sick games. I'd rather die first!" I spit at him with all the venom I could manage.

Looking at my sister's naked body, I already knew what was coming, even before the doctor spoke.

"Now that's not how you play with others. I'm sure your parents taught you better manners than that," he said playfully. "Cason, please grab the smelling salt from my bag. It's time we reunite these two."

Cason passed by me and picked through the bag that lay next to my chair.

"You don't have to do this," I whispered. "He's just using you, Cason. Please … that's my sister over there. Her blood will be on your hands."

Cason didn't respond. He walked over to Ally. Holding the salt, he waived it in front of her face. Ally's brow furrowed and she coughed as she came back to her senses.

She blinked and then seemed to notice her straps for the first time. They groaned against the gurney as she tried to move her arms. It took her a good minute to realize that she was stuck.

"Ally, don't scream." I begged, trying to think of anything that may deter any onslaught of punishment.

My attention went back to Cason who was handing the doctor something. A large pair of black and chrome bolt cutters. Once Cason gave the doctor the bolt cutters, he turned and glanced back at me. For a moment, I thought I saw some sort of pity or sorrow in his eyes.

"Now let's try this again, shall we?" the doctor asked eagerly. He seemed to be chomping at the bit to start the torture. "Jen, will you play our little game and spare your sister or not?"

"Go to hell!" It was as loud as I could scream. Afterwards, I felt sapped of whatever energy and strength I'd had.

My sister was finally awake and trying to comprehend the situation. She cried out and sobbed. Tears streamed from her eyes.

"It's going to be okay, Ally. I promise … everything's going be okay." I tried to reassure her. The guilt of her predicament started to fill my mind, but it was too late.

I heard a loud snap, crack and shriek as my sister writhed in pain against her restraints. The doctor had snipped her ring finger off at the knuckle with the bolt cutters. The blood from her gushing wound misted her naked body and sprayed onto the floor.

I couldn't hear anything over her screams. Blood-curdling screams echoed throughout the apartment. It didn't stop until the doctor smacked me across the face. I hadn't noticed that the screams were my own.

"Cason! Go get the iron. We wouldn't want our subject to bleed out just yet. I mean, Jen still has nine more chances left to play the game." He chuckled.

Cason exited the room and returned promptly, plugging the iron into the wall. The doctor licked his lips as he looked down upon my sister who was dry heaving. When the iron was reddening, the doctor made me watch as he pressed its searing surface against the open wound. My sister cried out again in pain. Her shriek pierced my ears and skewered my heart. The smell of burnt flesh invaded my nostrils and I couldn't bear much more.

"Stop! Stop, I'll do it. I'll play your fucking game!"

"Good." The doctor said, making it obvious he was satisfied with his plan. "Now, will you please unstrap and escort our dearest Ally over to the accommodations we've made for her?"

Cason released my sister from her restraints and carried her limp body to the cell I previously inhabited. He shut her in and walked back to the doctor's side.

"Now Jen, you will choose one of the three boxes? Each box will contain a form of punishment. The box will also contain a number. This number will represent one of our fine candidates from around the room." He carried the tray the three boxes set on over to my chair and set the tray next to me. His boney face wrinkled as he smiled wide.

"Choose a box."

"The middle one," I answered, timidly.

The doctor pulled out a neatly folded piece a paper with pristine cursive handwriting from the center box. "The number is cage seven and the punishment … death by the ratchet strap. Perfect!" He moved excitedly toward his bag and pulled out five yellow straps. "Cason, please retrieve our nice and calm Hispanic friend again."

I looked in the direction of the man's cage and saw fear once again spreading across his face. Even with his hateful words and spite, I still didn't wish this fate upon him.

Cason moved fast and had the man strapped to a gurney as the doctor barked out instructions. A strap hung loosely from each limb of his body. The fifth strap dangled from his neck.

"Jen, you're going to need a hand to roll dice!" He said, motioning for Cason to free one of my hands. The doctor held two die. He offered them to me.

"What if I decide not to play your stupid game?" I mocked.

He looked down at me from over the frame of his glasses and smiled. "Simple. We'll strap your sister back to the gurney. Mr. Cason and I will play the game ourselves and then have our way with her rotting corpse." His sadistic tone left no room for reasoning or question.

I grabbed the dice from his outstretched hand and looked over to the Hispanic man, strapped to the table.

"I'm sorry," I said. Tears breached the dams of my eyelids. He understood and nodded his head as tears streamed down the sides of his face as well. I tossed the dice into a small box the doctor held.

They tumbled and rolled, moving from number to number. The dice stopped.

"Lucky number seven," the doctor called out. "Cason, that will be seven ratchets. Please make sure you start in a counter-clock-wise direction."

Cason moved methodically, pulling each strap tighter until it clicked once. The doctor again held the dice in his hand. I hesitantly grabbed them, glancing at the poor man. The blisters on his arm had spread to his upper chest.

After the first tug on the strap, I could see the blister popped and oozed out onto the remains of his charcoal colored skin.

"Roll the dice," the doctor hissed.

I closed my eyes and prayed for a small number, but when I heard a loud laugh from the doctor, I knew the worst was about to happen.

"Twelve! Great roll my dear. Yes, very excellent indeed!" The doctor was jubilant with the outcome.

Cason proceeded in tightening the straps, which were snug after the first round. The man wailed. I gathered the courage to look at him. The skin on his blistered arm peeled off from the tension.

Making his way to the final strap, which was situated around his neck, Cason tightened it down. The man's cries were cut off as the strap constricted his breathing.

"Now finish him off, Cason! Use that knife of yours and put him out of his misery."

Cason unsheathed his knife and held it in both hands, directly above the man's head.

"Cason, you don't have to do this," I screamed out. "The doctor is using you. Haven't you ever wondered why he gives you those blue pills?"

"Shut up, you bitch!" the doctor boomed and smacked me across the face. "You're next."

He approached Cason, who stood frozen over the choking man.

"See Cason, he doesn't want you to know the truth," I cried, grasping at something…anything…and then it came to me. "You're the real test subject!"

Cason gazed at me. His eyes bore through me as he looked to be searching for an answer.

"It was always you! We never mattered. The doctor's job was to control you. Make you the ultimate soldier of terror and fear. One who would act on emotion. That's what those blue pills are for, to turn you into a zombified killing machine." I had to say whatever I could while I had his attention.

Cason's eyes narrowed and his glanced at the doctor. "Is this true?" he asked. "Am I the real test subject?"

The doctor leaned close to Cason and put a hand on his shoulder. At the same time, I used my free hand to loosen the straps, securing me to the chair.

"Listen, you will be the greatest solider to walk the earth when this is all over. Think about how many lives you will save, Cason." The doctor said in an almost fatherly sort of way.

"I … don't understand. Why not tell me?"

"Soldiers obey and Generals give orders. Is that clear?" The doctor's tone changed to a commanding one. "That's right soldier, I'm the general. I'm the one protecting the innocent, you and this goddamn operation. Now do as you're told and kill the subject!"

Cason turned to face the doctor. He lowered his knife, and started toward the door. The doctor grabbed Cason from behind and spun him around.

"Listen you son of a bitch, we have a mission to complete. A job that needs done ... and I will be damned if I let some stupid whore ruin our operation." He smacked Cason in the face and turned him back toward me.

Having already unstrapped my legs and arm, I fell on my hands and knees. The General pushed the chair out of the way and stomped on the middle of my back, sending me crashing against the floor. He savagely wrapped his hands around my neck and lifted my head off the ground.

"I'm going to enjoy this," he said.

"Go to hell," I mouthed.

His grip tightened around my neck and he violently jerked, sending my face crashing onto the floor. Another second passed and again my face met the tile. This time I felt my nose give way against the hard surface. Blood spattered onto the floor and down my face.

I waited. The end of my life should've come, flashing before my eyes. Pictures of Ally, bonfires, and all the family campouts we had once a month filled my thoughts.

What I wouldn't do for a pair of ruby red slippers...

Time stopped. I sucked in a long, cool breath of air. Closing my eyes, I squeezed them tight. It had to be soon. I heard a distinct sound of cracking bone and a gasp of air. I fell to the floor. Turning around, I saw the end of a chrome knife sticking out of his chest.

Cason was sitting on the floor next to us, watching as the doctor reached for the knife in his back in disbelief. I was able to push him off me.

I backed toward the cage containing Ally. Cason got to his feet. He started to advance in my direction. I looked around for something to defend myself with. He stopped in front of me and reached into his pocket. I turned my head and waited for it all to be over. But then I heard the sound of keys jingling and bouncing off the floor in front of me.

"Go," Cason said in a voice laced with exhaustion. "Please go, you must hurry."

Cason turned and marched to the doctor who lie twitching on the floor.

I sprang to my feet, moving quickly to unlock all the cages in the room. Ally was first. When she got out, we had the longest embrace of our lives. Never had I felt so lucky to have my sister and best friend.

She pulled away and said, "Come on! Let's get everyone else out!"

I quickly opened each cage then Ally helped me usher everyone toward the door. The once beautiful woman was the last to be released. She hugged me, wrapping what was left of her arms around my shoulders.

"Thank you!" she said. She ran out of the apartment.

When Ally and I reached the threshold of the door, I stopped and turned back.

"Jen, we have to go now!" Ally said.

But I didn't budge. I watched Cason as he hovered over the doctor's body. His red, tear-filled eyes met mine. He stood and walked toward me. Light shimmered off the crimson covered knife he held. Ally screamed at me to run but I couldn't. I was mesmerized.

Cason stopped within striking distance. He stared at us for what felt like minutes. He then grabbed the door and said only one word.

"Goodbye." Cason slammed the door shut in my face.

Ally shook me and the spell seemed to wear off. There was something about him. Something that made me want to go back in.

She pulled me down the stairs and nearly out of the apartment complex before I heard the gunshot in Apartment B...

The Shoggoth
and The End Of The World
By
Roy C. Booth & R. Thomas Riley

"Gibson, it's time to get up!"

The boy moaned and pushed deeper beneath the pleasantly warm cocoon of blankets.

"Gibson! Rise and shine!" called his grandfather once more.

Gibson pried open his eyes and glanced at the clock beside his bed. The glowing green numbers were bleary, but he knew it was god awful early because it was still dark outside his window.

A pang of sadness washed over him as he thought of his parents. He missed them. He missed them so much. He stirred at his grandfather's heavy tread on the stairs.

The door creaked open and Gibson squeezed his eyes shut as his grandfather flicked on the bedroom lights. The harsh glare filled the room.

"Eggs aren't gonna get themselves," said his grandfather with practiced manufactured cheer. "Pancakes and bacon soon as you're finished with the chores."

The bed shifted as his grandfather sat on its edge. Gibson breathed deep and opened his eyes. The light pained his eyes and fresh tears sprang into them.

His grandfather frowned and patted his leg. The gesture was meant to be comforting, but came off rough. Gibson groaned as his tired muscles flared.

"Hey," said his grandfather. "Big boys don't cry. Especially not Blount boys."

The unspoken thought of his parents hung heavy between them.

Gibson moaned. "What time is it?"

"Up and at 'em time," said his grandfather, laughing.

"I'm up," said Gibson said, throwing back the covers. The coldness of the early morning startled him.

His grandfather rose from his perch and walked over to the door, pausing on the threshold. He didn't turn around, but said, "I know these aren't the ideal circumstances. You're still smartin' about your parents. I miss your father, too, but this is the hand life's dealt us both. I've let you slack the past few weeks, but you can't mope forever, Gibson. You just can't." His grandfather sighed. "Your parents didn't die in an accident. It's time you know why they died protecting you, Gibson. Your parents died protecting you from *them*. They want to turn you to their side," continued his grandfather. "Every time you start anew, they come for you."

Gibson blinked. *Anew?* He thought some more. Finally a single word came out: "They?"

It's my job now to make sure you choose and get on the right path, boy."

With that, his grandfather closed the door.

***

Gibson grabbed the basket just outside the henhouse and breathed deeply of the morning air. It smelled of manure and fresh cut hay. He'd come to live with his grandfather just a month before. Adjusting was slow. At first, he'd missed the sounds of a busy city and he'd had trouble sleeping without the sounds of blaring car alarms and sirens. He'd only met his grandfather on two occasions before his parents died, something happened between Gibson's father and his father a long time ago, but Gibson never knew what it might have been. He was old enough to realize that sometimes parents and children simply didn't like each other or get along, for whatever reason.

He was fortunate his grandfather had taken him in. If he hadn't, Gibson would've been lost in labyrinth known as Child Protective Services.

He shoved those thoughts away, because they would inevitably lead to thoughts of his parents and the night of the accident, as he unlatched the door to the henhouse.

Sure, his grandfather woke him well before dawn and the chores were many and varied, but at least he didn't have to defend himself against some weirdo family he might've been placed with by CPS.

His father had always told him 'Blounts come from a long line of strong stock and you should be proud to be a Blount.' Gibson clung to those words in this new existence like he clung onto his blankie when he was younger. He had to.

The hens stirred as he entered the building. Their stench made his eyes water. At least he told himself it was their stench and not fresh tears. He swiped the tears from his eyes and began gathering eggs.

As he made his way down the rows, his mind drifted to the night of the accident. They'd been coming back from a night of family fun in the city. It'd been late and the roads nearly deserted. His mother and father chatted animatedly about the film they'd just seen and Gibson dozed in the backseat, half following the conversation.

The seat belt cut into his chest and neck as his father slammed on the breaks. Gibson's eyes sprang open and he saw the truck in front of them. The black vehicle blocked the intersection. His mother turned in her seat. He'd never seen her so frightened.

"Gibson, honey," she said urgently. "Stay down, baby, stay down!"

His father shifted the car into reverse and the car rocketed backwards. "It's them," he said.

The windshield filled with light as the truck gave pursuit. The next thing Gibson remembered was a feeling of weightlessness as the car smashed through the bridge's guardrail and the shock of icy water flowing over him.

Flashes of his mother red hair undulating in the murkiness like fire-colored seaweed. Flashes of his father struggling to shatter the window as the water rose about his chest. Flashes of the pain sluicing through his lungs when he couldn't hold his breath any longer. Flashes of some stranger pulling him from the water. Flashes of him screaming for his parents and the stranger shaking his head sadly as police lights bathed them in reds and blues.

At first, he'd blanked the truck from his mind and when he did remember, Gibson never told the investigators about the strange truck or the reason his family's car had ended up in the river. On some level, he'd known not to.

He reached beneath another hen and it pecked at his hand, drawing blood. He hissed and pulled his hand back. His hand glowed.

"What the . . . ?" he whispered as he turned his hand over and opened his palm.

The egg gleamed beneath the harsh lights of the henhouse. Translucent hues of gold, green, and silver radiated from its center. The hen clucked loudly and Gibson tore his eyes from the egg. Three more glimmering orbs, they couldn't be eggs, were in the nest. Suddenly the story of the golden goose popped into his mind and he shook his head. He sucked in a breath as he eyed the orbs. The hen's beady eyes flashed and it stuck out its neck to peck at him once more. For just the briefest of moments, Gibson saw a slimy mass in the nest. Black, oozing eyes covered the mass and agitated purple tentacles writhed.

He stumbled back and his feet tangled beneath him. He landed hard and his teeth clacked together soundly. Stars danced before his vision and his jaw ached. He closed his eyes to stop the room from spinning. The egg in his hand grew hot as his fist clinched.

***

Gibson heard his grandfather's voice, but it sounded so far away. The voice grew louder and Gibson opened his eyes to find his grandfather kneeling over him. "Are you all right, Gibson? What happened?" asked his grandfather, concern evident in his tone.

Gibson's head felt like it was stuffed with cotton, but when he moved his head, cotton turned to razors. He groaned and cringed as pain blossomed behind his eyes.

His hand felt sticky and he turned his head just enough to see why. "There's something wrong with the eggs," he croaked.

"What?"

"The eggs are weird."

His grandfather glanced down at his hand and sucked in a breath. "Where did you get that?" He reached for the orb in Gibson's hand, but Gibson closed his fist and pulled himself into a sitting position. He suddenly didn't want his grandfather to take the strange sphere from him. The orb was pliable to the touch and it kind of tickled his palm as it gave beneath his fingers.

His grandfather stepped back and eyed him with a strange look. "You need to give me that," he said, his voice tense.

"No," said Gibson. He brought the orb to his chest and held it protectively.

"What you have there in your hand? It's dangerous. There are things that are reaching out to you. Because of what you are."

The orb felt like it was melting into his flesh and the sensation scared Gibson, but he found he couldn't open his hand to drop the strange thing. He saw the greedy look in his grandfather's eyes. He just wanted the egg for himself.

"The walls are thin, son," said his grandfather, holding out his hand for the egg. "Whatever that thing in your hand is? You need to give it to me . . . now."

Gibson gained his feet and backed away. "It doesn't want me. It wants you." Gibson paused and frowned. How did he know this?

His grandfather snatched his hand back and frowned. "Listen to that voice in your head, Gibson. That's a good boy."

His grandfather turned and stumbled from the henhouse. Gibson put the orb back in the nest while the hen eyed him with suspicion. That is, it would've, if it could actually do an expression.

I. Am. Clay.
By
Donna Marie West

Flashes of light. Smoke. Children screaming in the distance. I'm alone. Choking in the acrid air. Running . . .

I'm awake! I want to pinch myself to make sure, but can't. I can't move at all.

As I transition from groggy to fully conscious, the first physical sensation I have is of lying flat on my back on a cool, flat surface.

Definitely not my bed.

The second thing I notice is the smell: a faint antiseptic scent, nothing organic about it at all.

I open my eyes and squint in the harsh, white light.

Definitely not my home.

Struggling to suppress a rush of panic, I try to rise only to find my hands, feet, and shoulders strapped down tight. I can only move my head.

As my eyes gradually adjust to the painful light, I dare to look around. The ceiling and what I can see of the walls are shiny, metallic silver. Sterile.

Perhaps a hospital.

I twist and pull against my restraints in vain. "Hello? Is anyone there? I'm awake over here! Someone tell me what's going on!" My voice is no more than a rasp, despite my trying to yell.

My mouth is dry. Desert in the summer dry. I feel as though I've been asleep for months. It occurs to me, in a feverish sort of way, that I might have been in a coma or something similar. But why? I don't feel sick or injured.

A red light flashes somewhere on the edge of my vision. A siren shrills right beside my head, so loud and piercing that I fear my eardrums will rupture. Mercifully, it doesn't last more than a few seconds.

Through the residual ringing in my ears I hear a low whoosh, perhaps the opening of a door, followed by soft, hurried footsteps. Seconds later, three creatures tower over me, leaning in on me, their hot, foul breath almost suffocating me.

They walk upright, and they're huge, three times my height and weight. They're dressed in close-fitting white suits, only their undersized brown eyes and red slashes of a mouth showing through transparent face masks. In their hands---disfigured hands with one too many long, narrow fingers---are metallic trays laden with unidentifiable and terrifying instruments I know are meant for me.

My mind shuts down for a moment at the sight of those trays, but I come right back to the here-and-now when one of the creatures emits a series of deep, guttural sounds. The second creature replies in an equally repulsive voice. Their voices are muffled by the masks. I wish the experience had been indefinitely postponed.

The first creature grasps my arm and holds it tight while the second sticks one of the instruments into a vein in my wrist.

I scream as fire races up my arm and down my neck, and to my heart, responding immediately with a heavy thud and slowing down.

The third creature, smaller than the others---if any of them can be considered small---pokes and pinches the inside of my nose with an instrument that looks like pliers from hell. The second creature, with the needles, sticks a second one in my arm. I feel sick to my stomach. My bladder empties, urine runs hot down my leg. My vision blurs, and the white light swirls through yellow to green to black.

More nightmares.

I wake up for the second time, heaving, the bitter taste of bile didn't quite come up all the way, sticking to the back of my throat. I remember chaos. Explosions. Panic and loss.

I know I've been moved long before I open my eyes. The air is cooler here, almost crisp, and the smell is different, bitter and definitely organic–urine and feces and sweat, born of fear. I'm no longer lying flat on that table or bed, but curled up in a fetal position in a cage. Wires of some unfamiliar, dull metal bites into my back and shoulder where I've been leaning against the side.

I'm humiliated to find I'm utterly naked, though no longer bound or restrained. I crawl forward to the front of the cage.

The light isn't as harsh here. More yellow than white, and I can look around without needing to blink or my eyes tearing.

The room is long and narrow. Across from me stands a row of cages in varying sizes. I recognize the animals in some of the cages; familiar species from home. They're yowling and pacing listlessly in circles. I wonder if they're as confused and scared as I am.

Above the cages, and at the one end of the room are metallic cupboards covered with a series of straight and curved black lines. I assume they're the aliens' form of writing–identifications or instructions–and sudden clarity sends a chill racing down my spine.

This isn't a hospital, but a laboratory. And I'm a damned guinea pig, just like those poor animals over there.

"Hello? Is anyone else here?" I ask in a tight whisper, not daring to shout for fear of setting off more sirens and flashing lights. There are solid partitions between the cages, but I hear sounds of movement and a subdued reply somewhere down my row of cages to the right.

I'm not alone!

"My name's Clay," I hiss. With a jolt, I realize this is the first time I've recalled my own identity, as if until this moment I was nobody. "Who are you?" I can barely hear my voice over the blood pulsing in my temples.

"I'm Sandy." The voice is male. It speaks my language, but it sounds old and worn out. An old man's voice.

I think for a moment. Ask the right question, in case there's only time for one. "How many of us are here?"

Silence.

Finally, a hesitant answer. "At first there were many; a dozen or more. They . . . Somehow they put us to sleep, and they've been waking us up one or two at a time. When one of us expires, they bring in the next."

"How do you know that?" I ask, although I've already guessed the answer.

"The one before us told me."

"What? Why are they killing us?"

"I don't think they mean to. I think it's the food. It---it's not right for us. But they do experiments. Horrible experiments . . . Oh God. They make me think dying might not be such a bad thing."

Before I can say anything more, three of the creatures come in to the room. I think they're the same ones as before–two tall, thick ones and the shorter, thinner one---each wearing a long, narrow tank on its back. The taller ones stop at the end of my row. I hear their voices, deep and flat and threatening, though I don't have a clue what they're saying.

Perhaps, it's better this way.

Sandy pleads to leave him alone. There are sounds of a scuffle, and a muffled grunt of pain from Sandy. The creatures wheel a gurney carrying my comrade by my cage. He looks at me with wide, terrified eyes and struggles against his restraints. I learn he's no more than a dozen years older than me, and nothing but bones, beard, and pallid skin. I shudder for him and whatever he's about to endure, and I wonder when my turn will come.

The smaller creature brings a round, flat bowl to the front of my cage. It pushes the bowl

between the wires and places it on the floor. The lumpy brown contents look like farmyard slop and smell even worse, but I'm starving as well as thirsty. Despite what Sandy said about the food, I can't help myself. I fall into the bowl, shoving handfuls of the nauseating gruel into my mouth, licking and slurping like an animal, and forcing myself not to gag.

The creature stands on the other side of the cage, watching me. When I'm done, it reaches cautiously into my cage and snatches the bowl away.

I wipe my hands on my thighs and relieve myself in the corner of my cage, feeling all the more like an animal; dirty, disgusting, and helpless.

I try to remember more than my name: where I come from, and what brought me here, wherever 'here' is. I suppose it's shock or perhaps the drugs, but my mind is blank and my head hurts when I think too hard. I find myself looking forward to my dreams. They only give me scattered bits and pieces---and I wake in a cold sweat---but they help. After several more dreams, things begin snapping into place.

And then, all at once, I remember everything. I almost wish I didn't.

We'd been hearing about unidentified flying objects and alien abductions for years, but no one in their right mind thought they were real. I sure didn't. Not until the night the ships burst through heavy clouds, and my people had an answer to the question we'd been asking since the dawn of history: we're not alone in the universe!

There was a brief, fierce conflict in which we were completely overpowered. My village was ravaged. The women and children who survived the initial onslaught fled with the old men to safety in the underground shelters, but the young, able-bodied men, such as myself, stayed to defend what was left. I watched friends and strangers fight and die. The last thing I recall is one of the aliens, only steps away, pointing its awful weapon at my chest.

I'm on one of the aliens' ship. God help me . . .

In a flood of emotion that makes me faint, I remember my parents, sisters and brothers, my wife Emma and baby daughter Lily. All of them hopefully alive and safe, and grieving for me. I have to accept I'll never see them again except in my dreams, but the thought of them gives me strength.

The experiments continue. Sometimes, the aliens put me to sleep for whatever procedure they're doing. Other times they don't, and I experience horrific, excruciatingly painful explorations of my anatomy: from my eyeballs to my navel to my genitals. They stick long, thin needles into every orifice. Occasionally, they take things from me: hair, blood, semen, a fingernail, even an upper back molar. I'm sick for hours afterward with pain and the feeling of having been violated.

Sandy says they're studying us, taking resources and specimens from our world to theirs. It's only a guess, he says, and it's obvious he's past caring. Responses from him have become shorter, weaker, and more sporadic. Until the time comes when the creatures wheel the gurney past me; instead of Sandy, I see a still, narrow form covered by a white sheet.

I wait for the aliens to bring in someone else---Sandy's re-placement---but there's no one.

I know of all my people who were on this vessel, I'm the last. I huddle in the back of my cage, and for the first time since awakening in this God-forsaken place, I weep. I weep until my burning eyes have no tears left.

The smaller alien watches my breakdown like I'm entertainment, and when I can turn my mind to something other than my fear and heartache, it occurs to me that the creature is surprised by me.

Does it think I feel no pain? That I have no thoughts? No emotions? Or does it simply not care?

This same alien comes often. Sometimes with a bowl of gruel or water that tastes slightly like iron. Sometimes to replace the tray that slides out from the bottom of the cage after I've soiled it. I notice its eyes aren't brown, but blue. Its voice is higher pitched than the others', and its movements are slower and gentler.

I come to believe it's female, although there's no way to know for sure. I ask her for clothing and a blanket, but of course, she doesn't understand me. I suppose I sound like nothing more than a chattering animal to her, but I'm determined to communicate.

My life depends on it. Sandy was right. The food's no good for me. While the animals in the cages across the room seem healthy enough, I grow thinner and weaker, my head and stomach ache more and more, and my stool comes as putrid brown goo. I'm stinking filthy, my teeth chatter until they chip, and I can't get warm no matter how hard I try. Back on my world, I was a simple farmer. Here, I'm something even less . . . less, still, every day.

I think about it hard and long, yet as tempting as the thought of release might be, I can't allow myself to die this way, fading to nothing the way Sandy did.

I don't know why or what my future will be---or even if I have one---but I choose to survive.

I start paying attention to the combination of clanging, banging, screeching and moaning, which apparently passes for music on the aliens' world. It plays frequently over an invisible sound system. I try to isolate the sounds I hear most often, the ones I presume are made by a living creature. I begin imitating them when the aliens aren't around. At first, it's impossible to force those sounds from my throat and past my lips, but eventually I get the hang of it.

The first time I say a word in their language to the female alien, her eyes open wide enough the whites surround the blue. The corners of her mouth turn up in her people's version of a smile and I notice the small, even white teeth behind her lips. I don't know what I said, but it doesn't matter. I have hope now that she'll see I'm a civilized, sentient being.

From then on, the effort to communicate goes both ways.

Time passes---days or weeks---no way to tell in this place, except by the lengthening of my hair and nails and the way my ribs become more prominent beneath my sagging skin. The horrific experiments in the operating-room-slash-torture-chamber are replaced by language lessons in a cold, white room furnished with two soft chairs and a metallic table; where I'm allowed to move freely. One of the other aliens I think of as male stands like a guard inside the closed door. I'm fairly certain if I make a move to escape or harm the female, he will kill or incapacitate me. I'm not looking to confirm the theory.

The female alien shows me colorful images on a flat screen taking up an entire wall. There are scenes from my world before and after the invasion---nothing much left of my village afterward but smoking rubble and a few ruined stone foundations. There are many more images of what I assume is her world, which has seas and plains and snow covered mountain peaks. Just like my planet, and a myriad of peculiar looking animals---both feathered and furred---that fuel fresh nightmares for a half a dozen sleeps to come.

I work to master some alien words and the female makes attempts at my language. We gesticulate and verbalize, neither one of us able to understand what the other is saying but aware, at least, that we are saying something. We're so frustrated at times that I scream and fly into rage, the female stomps from the room, and the guard throws me into my travelling box to carry me back to my cage.

And then, a breakthrough!

"My name is Clay," I say for the hundredth time in my language, slapping my chest with the palm of my hand. "I. Am. Clay."

The alien studies me in silence for a moment. Then she points to her own chest with one of her long, gloved fingers, and says something which sounds to my ears like, "Ai – mee."

"Clay!" I yelp in return. "That's me!" I start making extravagant motions of covering myself. Now that she knows I'm saying something, perhaps this action will transcend the language barrier. "I'm freezing here! Is that so hard to understand?"

I find myself holding my breath when Aimee leaves the room, but I can't hold it long enough and it eventually slips out of me with a wheeze. She comes back and hands me a length of rough blue cloth wide enough to cover most of my body.

Sobbing with gratitude, I drape it around my bony shoulders and tie the corners in a knot to hold it on. I never imagined I would appreciate such a simple luxury so much.

After that, we make tremendous progress. When Aimee brings me the inevitable bowl of brown slop, I push it away and say firmly in her language, "No." In my people's words, I add, "It's killing me."

After I refuse to eat five consecutive meals, she brings me a bowl of greenish slop. It smells and tastes marginally better than the brown stuff, but I eat it and hope for the best. I tell Aimee thank you in my language, and she replies with a word in hers.

For a dozen meals I eat the green food, and as disgusting as it is, I begin to feel better. No more stomach aches or foul loose stools. I grow stronger and the fog fades from my brain.

Aimee brings me a warm, wet cloth and a second dry one, and I'm able to remove the worst of the grime from my body. We begin to make progress with our language lessons. If I understand the aliens' words correctly, they're planning to send more ships to my planet once this one gets back to theirs.

My determination to survive is renewed.

All I used to want was to raise my family, work my land, and grow my crops. Now I see myself as a sort of ambassador for my world. I want to teach the aliens my language and tell them my people have history and culture and hopes for their children's future. I want them to know what they've destroyed, and I want them to see how what they've done to my people is wrong. If I can prevent one more village or person from going through what my village and I have, it will be worth all my suffering and loss.

Aimee gives me a small white suit similar to hers to put on, and I know we must be close to the aliens' planet. I presume I'll need it in their atmosphere, just as they need one in mine. I'm terrified all over again, but I'm excited, too. I want to see the undeniably beautiful, cloud-shrouded blue sphere the aliens come from---even if it doesn't have much of a name.

They call it Earth.

156

Paul's Rose
By
Joshua Sterling Bragg

I

Paul sat on the front porch, in the freezing February air, drinking a cup of coffee and smoking a cigarette. Six a.m.: daily routine, step one, in progress. He probably thought the cigarettes were his little secret, but I watched him every day as I stared out of our second-story window, hoping to see what he appeared to be waiting for. It never seemed to come.

When he was satisfied, he came back inside, poured himself another cup of black, heavy, dark roast, and stomped up the stairs. He didn't mean to stomp; I doubt he even realized he was stomping. Joint issues and general wear and tear were starting to set in now that he's older. Mentally, he was still twenty-five, but in reality, he was nearly twice that. I had grown accustomed to the sound of his oversized feet thump, thump, thumping up the stairs every morning. So much so that without it, I'm sure I'd wake up at 6:26 every morning wondering what was wrong.

As per his routine, he headed for his office at the top of the stairs, located across the hall, diagonally from our bedroom. He placed his secret death sticks into the closet, where they remained hidden above the door frame, held in place by an old electrical wire. Then he walked quickly to the washroom, where he completed step two of his daily routine: showering off the smell of tobacco while drinking his second cup of coffee, in the shower stall. I have often wondered how he does this without consuming half a cup of shower water, but it's been years since he's invited me in with him. Drinking coffee in the shower was another one of the innocent little secrets he thought he kept from me.

The rest of the routine was not much to speak of. He sat and wrote, then sat and edited video, then sat and watched video, then edited, then e-mailed. He rode his bike every day before lunch, which consisted of two scrambled egg whites wrapped in a burrito shell with a few slices of cheese that he didn't tell anyone about. Then back to sitting and editing and writing and watching. He loved it. I thought it was boring, but it didn't matter. I had my own things to tend to, but this…this was Paul. There were other things he did, but this was who he was, how he preferred to be.

Ours had not always been a quiet marriage. We used to do things and go out to adventure around the neighborhood. We'd make time for each other; we'd have dinner once a week in some mediocre restaurant that somehow always felt like The Plaza Hotel to me. It's the gesture. Any marriage can survive on just a few simple gestures per week. A back rub, some flowers, cleaning something up without being asked to…they don't all have to be intimate things, just something selfless that one does for the other. As soon as that selflessness stops… well, that's when things can fall apart.

Once in a while, I'd poke my head in on Paul, trying to catch a glimpse of his creative process. We lived in a very old house with lots of old energy floating around in it, so it was sometimes difficult to sneak a peek. The doors and floors creaked, but what I came to realize was that there are buildings, and more specifically, pockets of energy around our world, that heighten one's senses. People are born with an innate ability to sense the world around them, and these pockets enhance those abilities. For example, that moment, when you know someone is watching you. That feeling of burning in the back of your head like a hot sack of rice. It's heavy and very present. Then you turn and make eye contact with that other person and think, "How did I know?" That's the pocket: old energy fueling your senses. Our house was one of those places. And on this day, just like on any other, he knew exactly the moment I cracked the door to peek into the room.

"Not now, Rose. I'm on a roll." He spoke, gently, without ever turning around. I paused for a moment, soaking in his creativity.

"Please…I just…I need to finish this," he reiterated. I wasn't hurt. I could understand how my presence was distracting. So I shut the door and left him to his (hopefully uninterrupted) cognition.

I knew he hadn't forgotten me. I still lived there. And although he spoke to me on occasion, I still felt the need to leave him little reminders, nonetheless. Small things that said, "Don't forget your wife!" For instance, I'd move the keys away from where he'd left them. I'd switch off the light right before he did. I'd pull out a picture of us from an album and leave it on the floor by the bookshelf. It was exhausting, but I feared losing him altogether. I wasn't supposed to go this early.

II

"You have cancer. You have cancer and you are going to die." That's not the way he said it, but that's exactly how I heard it. Life had been so perfect until this moment. Until this… interruption…this unwelcome guest who will now be using my body without permission.

"How long does she have?" Paul asked.

"About six months."

"My God. Is there anything we can do?"

"No."

That's all I have from that day. A vague recollection of the bullet points of my inevitable death. But what does it matter? Why should I struggle to retain details about something I no longer care about, if it's all going to go away in six months? My first reaction was to get angry. But then I saw how crushed Paul was, and I knew this wasn't really about me; it *couldn't* be about me. I wouldn't allow it. I needed to make the next six months as wonderful as possible for Paul. I would hide the pain and the fear and focus on the good. Continue to make new memories, ones that would be even better than the ones we already had. This was going to be my final gift to Paul.

In the beginning it was painful for both of us. All he wanted to talk about was what we were going to miss out on. We would never raise kids together, we would never see South Africa, we would never this, we would never that. We began to argue about everything. My attempt at tranquility was just sending him further over the edge, and his stubbornness was keeping him from grabbing my hand and being pulled to safety. I needed to do something drastic. The cancer was after me, but I'd be damned if I let it take my marriage as well.

Lost, I started going to church again. It had been years since we stopped going. Paul and I both went freelance about six years ago; he for writing, I for painting. We found Sundays to be the only time we could truly spend together without work dominating the day. We still went to services on Christmas and Easter and tried to pick a few days in between to keep ourselves on track. It's funny how people can rationalize anything they want to; we felt we were good people and that we were grounded in our faith, so why should we have to attend every week?

What I started to realize, after weeks of meditational Sundays, was how an entire part of me had been closed off. I started to feel like there was a part of this world that had been dark before, and that now it was opening up and soaking me in light. Just as with the pockets of old energy, there are man-made pockets of glory. Wherever a group of people meet in God's name, there is energy flowing that seeps into our spongy brains and works mysteriously inside us. I believe this energy is God itself, and that when I was there, in His presence, He could truly hear me. I prayed for help, for guidance, and for peace for me and Paul. And after some time, I found it, like a tiny ringing bell over the mountains: *I found my peace.*

Paul and I had a few more adventures together. I refused hospitalization and treatment to minimize the cost of my death, and we took the money we'd saved and put it towards traveling. During the day, I would muscle through, keeping a smile on my face, soaking in every glorious moment of life. At night I would hold him as he cried himself to sleep. If ever there was a moment that I doubted Paul's love for me, it was wiped clean in these nights. This man was perfect, and I never wanted to leave him.

It took almost a month to realize I had died. To me, it felt like we were naturally drifting apart, which was okay, considering the effects the cancer was having on me. I became frail. Paul bought me a bed and set me up in my own room for the final weeks. I did not want him to have to deal with my sleepless nights, or to have the emotional burden of waking up next to his dead wife. I found solace in this space, knowing that I was able to minimize the burden on him. My time was getting close, and I saw him less and less. Eventually I was unable to speak and all I could do was look at him and try to tell him with my eyes that I loved him and that everything was going to be okay. Sleep became easier. The pain became muted. And just as I had gradually started feeling worse, I gradually started feeling better. Bit by bit, I was regaining my strength. Paul didn't come in to visit me anymore. *Maybe that's because I can't speak*, I thought. *He may not know I'm awake.*

There is a strangeness about the afterworld, a clarity. The world we know is filled with thoughts and actions and chaos every which way we look. But in the afterworld everything is clear, concise, and singular. My thought was to call for Paul, and because of that single important thought, I neglected to realize the days going by, the lack of food and water, the never needing to use a restroom. There was nothing but working up the strength to call out to Paul to let him know that I was there and I was feeling better! I could hear him throughout the house, walking about, developing his routine. Every day, as he reached the top of the stairs, trailing that tobacco smell behind him, I would try to reach him. I would try to speak, to call him into my loving arms again.

And one day, nearly four weeks later, when my strength was finally charged enough to mutter a single word, I spoke his name. And the door opened. And there was my man, easily 12 pounds thinner, with a beard that I had never seen, standing before me. I tried to tell him I was getting better, that I would be well soon and that we could go on more adventures, but I used up all of my energy. I could not speak or even move as he looked around the room, looking straight through me. And all at once I knew I was no longer alive.

III

Paul sat on the front step smoking, freezing, clinging to his coffee. Snow was blanketed over our modest and secluded New Hampshire home. I wanted to tell him to come inside, but I had saved my energy for something different that day. On that day, I knew exactly what Paul was waiting for: a guest. A guest for me.

It had been two months since I'd called out for him from my deathbed, and I had grown much stronger. It was as if time, for me, were running backwards. Each day, I grew just a little bit further from death, and I wondered how long this would go on for. Would I keep un-growing until I was an infant? A fetus? Would I just evaporate into nothing? Or would my energy be reborn into a new life? I suppose if it all continued like that, it would not matter, because my consciousness would unravel and therefore need to be rebuilt. When would I get to go to heaven? Did I have to find a passageway, or would it come to me like one of my clear, afterworldly thoughts? My thoughts were not feeling very clear yet, but I ascribed that directly to the new and confusing situation I was in. I thought there would be a clearer sign…not that I was ready to go…and maybe that's just it. Maybe the path is only there when you *are* ready. If this was at all true, I had thirty-eight years left to decide. Or did I? If I reverted back to a sixteen year old, would I be sixteen forever in heaven? Would I even remember Paul?

The doorbell rang— a welcome shock back to the now. I had to get myself together if I was going to welcome our guest. I followed Paul to the door to find, standing on the other side, Patti Sentrate, P.P.M.D. (Paranormal Psychologist and Medium to the Dead). Paul wasn't messing around. This lady was the real deal. Even before he got to the door, her thoughts were in my headspace:

Hello Rose, I can sense you. I am not a threat. I am here to help.

I did not respond. I was saving my energy for when I really needed it. But I was impressed. She had not yet entered our house, and she knew exactly how to communicate with me.

Paul opened the door, and there she stood. She was just about five feet tall, with a short, crisp haircut exactly at the shoulders and bangs that ended precisely at the eyebrows. Her hair was red, which she must have dyed herself because it was slightly unnatural-looking. She was in her late fifties, seemed to be in relatively normal health, and dressed in all black. Her coat was like a cube of black floral fabric cut out of an old gothic couch and stuffed with shoulder pads. One good thing about dying early in life was that I would never be burdened with the limited clothing options for senior living. I could just follow Paul around and watch his clothes get closer and closer to being shaped like an old ice box…or a coffin.

Patti came in and sat in the living room with me as Paul brewed tea, shouting apologies from the kitchen like "I wasn't sure what time you were coming over! I would have put the kettle on ten minutes ago." But my new friend and I did not take much notice of his jabber. We were having "mind talk," a concept I was not prepared for. To the living, mediums appear to be sifting through dirt when they communicate with the dead. Most of us, when we hear the term "medium," think of a person holding their fingers to their temples and straining to find a clue amongst a sandstorm of interference. After two seconds with Patti, it was blindingly apparent how wrong we all had been.

The human brain functions at breakneck speed: thousands of thoughts happening at once, and when we talk, we focus in on a handful of them. Then we order them and spit them out one at a time in a neat little row called speech. But when two minds are connected seamlessly, there is no need for order. Patti and I sat across the room from each other, having thousands of conversations at once. No thought was unheard or unanswered. Within the five minutes it took Paul to gather up some hot water, teabags, and cookies, Patti found out all that she needed to know about us. Then, with amazing mental control, she narrowed her connection to me to a single passageway and focused in on Paul.

They talked for two hours, getting nowhere close to sharing the amount of information Patti and I had exchanged. She walked him through the house, and he told her where all the "hot spots" were, places where I had contacted him through a sense or a small action. She already knew all of this, of course, because of our conversation, but this part was for Paul. She was helping him come to terms with the fact that this was real. It was actually happening, and it was a good thing. She encouraged Paul to speak out loud to me whenever he could feel my presence and made us do an exercise. At her command, I reached out to touch him, which made him very cold. Then Patti had him speak out loud to me to acknowledge my presence.

"Hello Rose. I love you more than life itself. I miss you so much."

I couldn't hold myself back. I hugged him, causing him to shiver, and I whispered into his ear: "I love you too."

Before Patti left, she taught Paul some exercises for opening up his paranormal-perception skills. She warned him that communication would take much more energy on my end than on his, and to be patient and not overbearing. He needed to let me rest between sessions. Sometimes for a few days. Paul had so many questions after she left, I could see him getting frustrated with the time it took to connect. And it was aggravating for me as well. I couldn't always answer, but he could always ask. And it was this frustration that drove him to buy the Ouija board.

IV

There has always been something about it that makes me uncomfortable. The Ouija is not a game, it is a device. Everyone knows that. There is an unwritten rule that you do not play with it, and it is a testament to its power that it is still around despite most people's avoidance. But Paul was feeling desperate. His heart was sick, and the only cure was alone time with his ghost wife. So, ignoring all of the signs, he set up the board in our bedroom, lit a circle of candles, and switched off all the lights. As soon as he sat before that board, I felt the old energy of the house swell. All this time, I had looked at the energy as residue from times past, but in this moment there was an awakening. The house was a child rubbing its wool socks on the carpet, and the Ouija was the metal door handle tempting a static shock.

As Paul sat there with hesitation in his heart, I could feel the energy coil on itself, as if the house were being cranked like a music box. The energy was gathering, continuing to grow, to swell and to pulse. There was a noise in the air—not an audible noise but a physical noise, like film grain or television static. It was a presence, and it felt bad. I had to warn Paul to stop, before something awful happened, but I had no energy left from his constant contact this week. I was exhausted, I struggled to speak out, to be heard, but when my energy is gone it's like screaming into a pillow. It's useless! All I could do was watch as he slowly closed his eyes and took a deep breath, sucking air down into his toasted lungs.

The old energy was leeching off of him, tasting his depression like an old man sneaking a piece skin off a perfectly cooked chicken before dinner. I focused on the purity of the afterworld, the divine focus that had been granted to me for communication. I picked one thought, and reduced it down to one word. If I could just force enough energy out of myself to speak one word, ever so gently into his ear, if he could just hear my warning, I might be able to save him from this evil that was getting ready to pounce.

His fingers inched towards the planchette, ready to adventure, as I drifted towards his ear to stop it. The old energy was cresting like a tsunami, ready to wipe me and everything I knew and loved off of this plane of existence. It was ready to unleash a truly powerful force that neither Paul nor I could possibly survive by any stretch of the imagination. I don't know how I knew this with such perfect certainty, but there was not an ounce of doubt in my mind that if Paul touched the planchette, it would all be over.

Finally, I was next to his ear. I was close enough for even the slightest crackle to be heard. My remaining energy flared into action, funneled tightly into one perfect word to end this awful moment. Then, without warning, lightening split open the sky on the other side of the windows, illuminating the entire room like a flash bulb. Every nook popped with brightness, like a curtain being raised, revealing the three of us alone in the room: Paul, myself, and the impossibly dark mass between us. As I spoke, the old energy consumed my word so perfectly that it was as if I had never thought it. And just in case that wasn't enough, just to be sure there was no more hesitation in Paul, as his fingers came to rest on the planchette, there was a clap of thunder loud enough to mute the world. And for a brief moment, it did.

V

The old energy was stretching after a long hibernation. The planchette spasmed, sending pins and needles up Paul's arms and down his neck and back like an aftershock. I had released the last of what I had left, leaving me like a mere glowing ember amidst the growing blackness of our bedroom. What was once our safe space, where Paul used to make me cry with joy while we made love, was now nothing more than a void in existence. We were inside the pocket.

The heavens opened up, and the rain began to fall. Large heavy drops exploded like bombshells on the roof above us, an appropriate noise to mirror the electrostatic encapsulating the room. After shaking off the chills, Paul closed his eyes again and spoke out to the room.

"Rose, it's Paul. Your husband. I'm doing this because I love you. Because I need to know you're okay. This past week since Ms. Sentrate was here has been…difficult. I sensed you were here before, but…I wasn't sure. Now that I know, it's impossible for me to get comfortable with all of this until we can talk. And I think that's what this board is supposed to do. I'm not even sure this will work, but I think I felt you here just now. Like pins and needles all up my arms and my back. So…so I guess I should start this with a question. Are you willing to give this a try?"

As if triggered by the punctuation of his question, thirty-eight beautiful beams of light rose out of the board. They were glowing blue pillars of energy, *real* energy. There was one for every letter of the alphabet, one for each of the single numbers, as well as a pillar for "yes" and a pillar for "no." The final pillar rested at the bottom of the board over the word "goodbye." These pillars of light would be the energy I needed to communicate. It did not matter how expired I was, the board would be my focus, my fuel. What I would later understand was that the Ouija had a great hidden power: the ability to take energy from human beings and pass it through to the afterworld. The problem on my side of the board was that there was no way of controlling who took the power or how it was used.

Before I could make a move, I saw the dark mass grab hold of the "yes" pillar, as the planchette dragged Paul's hands to the answer. That's not fair. Why was it allowed to answer? Paul was talking to *me*! I reached out and grabbed the "no" pillar, watching as Paul's hands were dragged back to the opposite side, and the relief in his face changed to confusion.

"I'm confused. Are you willing to give this a try?" Paul questioned.

Again the void answered "yes" as I answered "no," and now the planchette was racing back and forth between the answers: "yes, no, yes, no, yes, no, yes, no…"

"Rose, are you there?" Paul asked, as his blood pressure was heightened, adding energy to the board.

The old energy and I both grabbed at the "yes" pillar, and the planchette raised Paul's hands into the air, slamming them onto the board over the answer. There was a gust of energy as all the candles extinguished at once. Paul's heart was racing. He was scared, unsure of what to do next. That only forced more power into the board. I could feel myself growing stronger, my presence building, which could mean only one thing: the old energy must have been growing as well, and I would have to fight to protect my husband.

Another surge of power, and the candles were lit again, only this time the flames were a deep crimson. Paul was afraid, and his fear was funneling straight through the board and into the old energy. I could feel it soaking in the power. The noise thickened as Paul sat there afraid of his next question. I tried to take in as much as I could, but the fear didn't energize me like it did the dark mass. I had gained more power from Paul's love, curiosity, and good intentions; the same things that drew me to him and fueled me in life were giving me power in the afterworld. Suddenly, I knew how to win: I had to get Paul to stay positive. But how? My thoughts were being stifled by fear. I couldn't focus, because I was afraid the next question might end the game.

"Rose?" Paul hesitated. "Is that you?"

The planchette raced back and forth, "yes, no, yes, no, yes, no, yes, no…" Then I slipped, and the game was over. I lost my divine focus when I looked into Paul's exhausted and terrified eyes. He was so afraid and filled with regret that I was becoming weakened and afraid myself. The divine focus I had been directing towards him shifted from determination to worry. That was enough for the old energy to stop what it was doing and begin to take from me. This only sparked more fear, which in turn gave it more power. It sucked me dry until I could no longer play the game. I was out; now it was Paul versus evil.

The Planchette moved with speed and accuracy, sending the first clear message from the afterworld. "Say…my…name…" Paul read it out loud in a weak but curious voice. It continued to move and spell: "Set…me…free…"

Paul's eyes sunk with devastation. "I was hoping you would stay here," he spoke aloud, assuming it was me, assuming that I was asking to be led to the light. I could do nothing to stop it as the darkness continued.

"I…will…" it told him. "Say…my…name. Set…me…free…"

Paul hesitated and then spoke: "Rose." A surge of power came to me.

Again: "Rose!"

Like with an injection of adrenaline, my consciousness grew! But the evil in the room saw what was happening and was already spelling out its final message. "A-N-D-R-A-S." Paul read as it was spelled out over and over, faster and faster, "A-N-D-R-A-S—A-N-D-R-A-S—A-N-D-R-A-S."

Paul's love was pouring out of him, but so was his fear. I began to focus my energy to speak again. I had to get a message to Paul to stop all of this…to never say that name for fear of what might happen next. Maybe now the old energy would be too distracted to stop me. I had to try. I had to muster all of my energy, even if it meant that I would stop existing on any plane. I had to get the message to him at all costs. And just as my words were beginning to form, Paul spoke.

"Andras."

The candles burst into pillars of living fire, dancing together like naked hookers as the planchette rose into the air above the board. It hovered there as the dark mass, the old energy, began to take its true form. The static was gathering like atoms, slowly forming a shape from the blackness—what looked to be Paul's shadow. For a second, it was a perfect mirror image. Then it began to evolve. The shape of the head was growing and mutating. Below its shoulders, long, thick bones jutted out like another set of arms. They grew thick and full, coming to rest like a heavy armored cape at the shadow's back. Standing before Paul was a figure of a man's body with the wings of an angel and the head of a great owl, holding the planchette. I watched helplessly as the demon, with its new form, smashed the planchette onto the board with a force that broke it in two. Pain rippled through Paul's entire body. A gust of energy surged through the room, sending Paul flying backwards into the wall, knocking him unconscious. And just as the candles went out, I saw the owlish demon move towards the door, and the planchette fell perfectly into place over "Goodbye."

VI

Paul woke up in bed. The room was empty: no candles, no Ouija… just the faint recollection of a painful dream. I watched him as he struggled to piece it all together. But as light from the sun began to fill the room, the memory gently faded until there was nothing left. From that moment on, things were different. Paul had slept through his routine that day—and the day after, and the day after that. He was in a funk. Something about that dream kept picking at him.

Three days passed after the game, and I also began to wonder if it was a dream. Or maybe it was some sort of shared consciousness that we had tapped into. But I knew better than that; I could feel the charge of the house around me. It was alive, and we were in its belly. The walls were swelling and contracting ever so slowly, as if it were breathing, or worse, trying to digest us.

The old energy, the "Andras," was more present than ever, filling every inch of the house with its noise. It had been here all along, but now it was awake. And it was that very thought that kept Paul and me from communicating during those three days. He knew I was there, he could feel me beside him, but he did not dare say a word until he was sure we were alone.

On the fourth day, things began to happen around the house. In the morning, Paul tried to force himself back into his routine. Heading towards the front porch, he tripped while carrying his coffee. It burned him as it splashed onto his hands, which caused him to drop his favorite mug—the one with the goofy smile that I'd stolen from the Red Arrow Diner in Manchester. We had gone there for breakfast so many times, and he was always joking about the mugs.

"No one could ever have a bad day with a mug like this. Look at it!"

I never wanted Paul to have a bad day, so one December, when he excused himself to the restroom, I slipped one into my purse and wrapped it for him to open on Christmas. He never used another mug again.

But today was not going to be a good day. I watched as his perfect mug shattered on the kitchen floor, as he stepped forward to regain his balance, and as he slipped on the steaming liquid beneath his naked feet. Falling to the tile below, his elbow smacked the floor first, hard, as his foot shot towards the cabinets. Paul's heel slid into the biggest piece of jagged porcelain with the once goofy (now menacing) face printed on its outer curve. Pinned against the wall, the grimacing shard pushed deep into Paul's thick callused heel, releasing boiling blood from his throbbing foot. I watched the whole event unfold, unable to do a thing. There had been nothing there for him to trip on, except the shadow of an angel's wing: *Andras.*

Paul limped up the stairs, using the banister to keep the weight off of his bandaged foot. He had finished his coffee at the kitchen table and skipped the cigarette. I tried to remain positive. Maybe he'd unleashed a special anti-smoking spirit, and this was all an elaborate plan to save his lungs? The idea cheered me up for a moment, but just the same, I reprimanded myself for the thought. I dared not even think his name. *Andras.* Too late. Just then, the banister wobbled as one of the spokes kicked out, striking Paul in the ankle. He lost balance and landed with all of his weight on his injured heel a step below. Luckily, his grip was strong, and Paul narrowly avoided falling backwards down the stairs.

I had to take control of the situation; I had to speak to Paul. So I rushed ahead of him to his office, where I found his computer already on. The past few days of rest had allowed me to save up enough energy to send a nice clear message to Paul. So I worked up my divine focus and tuned it towards the keyboard. When Paul finally reached the office, hobbling on one foot, he made his way to the computer, where he read my message. "Call Patti S."

VII

Patti was devastated by Paul's condition when he opened the door to greet her.

"Good Lord, look what happened," she warbled, her deep Southern accent complimenting the sympathy pouring from her big green eyes. I tried to welcome her inside, but she was not listening. Her guard was up for good reason; there was no getting into her brain. She built up a mental wall, something I imagined to be very difficult to achieve. Paul invited her to sit on the couch, just as before, and facing her from the adjacent leather chair, he tried to explain what had happened. It was difficult to remember at first. But once he got started, the details came back about the game.

"You need a priest," the psychic stated dryly. "What you have is a demon, and I cannot help you."

"You have to do something, please," Paul begged. "I can't handle this on my own!"

"You're not alone," she reminded him. "You have Rose."

"Just talk to it. See if you can get it to go away."

"I can't do that, Paul. It's too dangerous."

"I know it's dangerous," Paul continued, obviously frustrated. "Look at me."

Patti looked to Paul with sympathy but remained firm. She would not be swayed to let her guard down. "I didn't tell you to use the board."

"You told me to communicate," Paul snapped back at her.

"I told you to speak to Rose, not to conjure up dangerous spirits."

"You didn't warn me. It's your responsibility to guide people."

"It's not my responsibility to clean up other people's mistakes that they make when I'm not around."

"This is bullshit," Paul barked, slamming his fist against the arm of the leather chair. The static was growing thick in the room. "You come into my house and stir things up…"

"You invited me here…"

"Tell me to contact the dead…"

"Paul…"

"And then leave me to suffer the consequences? No, I don't think so! You're no psychic, you're a witch! A filthy scam artist! What next? You wait for me to die and then take the house? I'll tell you, it's worthless, honey. No pot of gold at the end of this rainbow, bitch."

Patti said nothing. She just stared past Paul with fear, completely removed from his last statement. I think we saw it at the same time, because Patti and I seemed to mirror a realization in each other. The lamp next to Patti was casting a shadow of Paul on the wall behind him, and as his frustration grew, so did the shadow. With every negative word, the darkness began to change, to grow, until eventually it looked as if Paul were sprouting wings.

Patti, realizing the severity of the situation, attempted to calm Paul down. "Paul, I'm sorry."

"You should be. You destroyed my home! Destroyed my marriage…" Paul began to cry. The shadow-wings stretched as if soaking in the power from his sadness.

Patti leaned into him. "There is still hope. This isn't over."

Paul shook his head, holding his ears, the wings curving as if to embrace them both. "No…no…no…no…"

Yes, Paul. We can fight this…"

"No…no…NO…NO…"

Patti wasn't getting through. Her words were being blocked out, not only by Paul's hands, but by his negativity. Instinctually, she tried to open a mental passageway to Paul's mind, to speak to him, to soothe him. This was exactly what the beast wanted. The shadow behind them stood up, as if this whole time it had been crouching behind the large leather chair. Its owlish head was close to reaching the ten-foot ceiling of our living room, while its wings seemed to curve inward still. And with Patti's guard down, the tips of the wings filtered into a single stream of blackness, and, like trickling sand, that stream filtered into the psychic's ears.

She began to speak out loud, in a voice that was no longer hers. "You worthless pathetic little man. Can't deal with a little death? Can't handle it? Hmm? Don't want to be a part of normal life like everyone else? I bet you're afraid. You're afraid of dying yourself. Well, I can show you something worse than death. I'll make you beg for it. I'll wear your skin as a suit. I'll dance in your body before Satan himself. I'll stretch you like a baseball glove, Paulie."

That struck a bad chord with Paul, because he shrieked at her, yelling in a way I didn't know he could: "Don't call me that! Never call me that!! Devil!"

"I'll make you beg for death, Paulie, and I'll never ever give it to you. Never, Paulie, never!"

"Shut up. Shut UP! SHUT UP! SHUT UP!"

The thing was only beginning to enter her brain, but it was already too painful to bear. I searched the room, not sure of what I was looking for. Something to stop this horrible event. Patti had let her guard down, and if I wasn't able to do something fast, we'd lose her forever, and most likely Paul in the process.

The psychic reached into her purse, searching for something. Paul watched her, upset and completely lost, as she spoke quietly—almost to herself. "You remember your sister Alice. She cut herself until the day she died. Cut, cut, cut. Cut her skinny little wrists. Cut, cut, cut! With a…with a…now where the Hell did I…?" She pulled a sharp metal nail file from her bag. "Ooh. With one of these! Come here, Paulie!"

And with that, Patti lunged forward, stabbing the nail file into the top of Paul's left wrist, squirting blood high into the air like a micro-geyser. She squealed and giggled with excitement, clapping her hands together and bouncing her bottom on the couch like a Saturday-morning cartoon bandit. Furious, I lashed out with a massive burst of energy that knocked over the lamp, sending it smashing to the floor. There was a loud pop and a spark of fire, followed by the tinkling of very thin glass falling to the carpet like icicles. Paul was startled and jumped to his feet, only to im-mediately collapse from the pain into Patti's arms. The shadow disappeared into the darkness, and there were gusts of wind in the room like massive flapping wings. Patti and Paul held each other, the trance broken, bracing themselves for what might happen next. But before anything could, I took what was left of my energy and struck on every light in the house at once.

For a brief moment, the shadow of the demon was there, nearly taking up the entire room, clinging like a cornered spider to the ceiling. And then, as quickly as our eyes saw it, the shadow exploded out in all directions. It was gone, for now. I watched as Patti struggled to get Paul back into the chair, and without even a momentary glance, or even a single word, she showed herself to the door.

VIII

Father Targus tried to keep it together as he spoke to Paul about the house, but I could see straight through him. He was terrified, sitting on the couch, and was using every ounce of his energy to keep the teacup he was holding from exposing his secret. After he was brought up to speed, Father Targus asked Paul how many letters were in the name of the *Thing*. He took out a piece of paper, blessed it with holy water, and scribbled seven sevens with spaces between them. He instructed Paul to write down the letters of the demon's name between the numbers.

"7A7N7D7R7A7S7"

"Oh this is bad. This is very bad." The priest mumbled as the paper began to mist between them, as if being branded by the evil name. "This is not just a demonic spirit we are dealing with," he continued, "but a Great Marquis of Hell. This is a very powerful demon known for sowing discord among those who interact with it. It will do anything and everything to rip you from the ones you love and destroy your life." Paul's eyes searched the room, knowing he could not possibly see me, but he checked anyway before asking "What if my loved one…is dead?"

Father Targus leaned towards Paul. Placing his tea on the table, he whispered with despondency: "It doesn't matter. This is a creature that reaches through all realms. It likely lay dormant here for thousands of years, waiting for an awakening. You're lucky you weren't killed. This demon is known for killing its conjurers."

"I didn't conjure it," Paul insisted. "It tricked me. I thought it was Rose!"

"You conjured it up just the same, with your black-magic board. It waited for you, and you called it out by name. You're lucky it didn't lure you out of the circle of candles. Now it can't kill you."

"What are you saying?" Paul demanded.

The priest's eyes seemed to be glowing strangely. "Had it lured you out of your protective circle, it could have struck you down with ease and dragged your pathetic soul to Hell. You're lucky you survived. The demon broke its own rules by knocking you out of the circle itself. I'd call it 'God's will,' but I have reason to believe it's idiot's luck."

Paul was taken aback by Father Targus's sudden lack of sympathy. He had no words to call upon in response and sat with his jaw open. The priest continued, still leaning forward but speaking more freely than before. He looked at Paul through the tops of his eyes.

"You'd best pray for forgiveness, son, because the world is coming down on you in a hard way, and there's no recovering from making deals with the Devil, you pig fuck." Spit flew in punctuation of the priest's final word, leaving him breathing heavily through his flared nostrils like a bull before the rodeo. And that is when I saw it: the dark cloud above his head.

7A7N7D7R7A7S7 was above him, sowing discord between Paul and the priest. I could not let this go on, for fear of things getting violent. Paul was calm at heart, but like any man he had a limit to his tolerance. I could see this tolerance wearing very thin.

"What do you have to say for yourself, sinner?!" the priest snarled. "Ya give up? Selling your soul to the Devil? For what, Paul? So you can fuck your dead wife one last time?!"

I had to be careful, or I would be pulled in as well. As I focused my energy, Paul rose to his feet, furiously towering over Father Targus, oblivious to the shooting pain in his ripped heel. "Don't you mutter another word about my wife! You call yourself a man of God, but you're a sinner as much as I am."

"Rose the whore, she'll misbehave!
Pleasuring men from beyond the grave!"

The Priest sang in a voice too deep for his own. And that was it. Before I could regain focus, before I could do anything at all, Paul lunged across the coffee table. He smashed the teacup with his knees as he tackled and began to strangle Father Targus. And that was the moment 7A7N7D7R7A7S7 lifted the cloud.

IX

Paul grew dark. In the days following the priest's visit, a heavy cloud came over the whole house. It was a slow, flawless transition, and Paul was oblivious to the change. But I saw everything. He started to drink at night…a few glasses of wine…then a few glasses of scotch. The more time that passed, the harder it was for him to be productive at all. The morning routine drifted from six a.m. to eleven a.m. Coffee and a cigarette on the porch became coffee with a splash of scotch and chain smoking in the house.

At first, I tried to make it apparent that I didn't approve. I would flick the cigarette out of his mouth, or knock over his ashtray. I even tried hiding the cigarettes while he was in the restroom. But these things just made him angry. He would yell out to me, saying hurtful things, blaming me for his condition. "Do you see me, Rose?" He would bellow boozily around the house, still limping on his gimp foot. "Do you see what you've done? I thought you loved me. But you left me…you left me like this!"

Some days he would blame me for giving up. "Oh no, don't give me any medicine, doctor. I'd rather just let the cancer take me away from my awful husband, whose only crime in life was loving me too much. Well, I'm sorry that I smothered you, Rose. I'm sorry I bored you to death with my life's work…with being successful…I'm sorry I didn't play with colors all day like a true artist." He would go on and on, rambling out loud like a maniac. As time passed, his comments only grew more hateful.

One thing he said was true, and I knew it. He did love me, more than anything in the world. My undying love for Paul helped me cope with his dark thoughts. We all have them, whether they be subconscious or eerily present. They sit in the inky corners of our minds like a roach: twitching…growing…and feeding off the darkness. We keep them to ourselves, embarrassed by their existence, hoping they will dissipate. We hide them, knowing that in this life, saying one wrong thing could devastate a person beyond repair. I knew it wasn't Paul that spoke this way but that his filter had been broken. The old energy was darkening his mind and giving the roach open space to wander and play. I could not let myself be manipulated by the demon. I had to keep my distance and devise a way to save my husband. So I stayed away and refrained from interaction. Instead, I focused on gathering my energy for the right time.

X

Paul grew thin. Alcohol and tobacco became his only source of sustenance, aside from an occasional cold cut of processed turkey. The cut on his heel became badly infected, keeping him constrained to the lower half of the house, while upstairs 7A7N7D7-R7A7S7 manifested itself and walked freely. He was killing Paul. Slowly but surely, the beast was taking my husband's life, out of spite, for avoiding his deathly grasp the night of the game. The rules of Hell forbid him to strike Paul down at will. But 7A7N7D7R7A7S7 had full rein of the energy surrounding this house.

To me, it seemed a little too vindictive for an all-powerful being. It seemed almost human. I began to wonder if Paul's life was the key to something…something I was not understanding. A piece was missing, and I lost days wondering what it was. Maybe killing Paul would allow the thing to go back into hibernation. But that doesn't seem like a productive option. Maybe he needed a sacrifice to please the master of Hell. But again, that seemed almost too goofy to be true. We were not living in some sort of film; this was real life. In life, things just happen and sometimes never end up having an explanation. Maybe that was it: The *Thing* wanted Paul dead because it did…period.

I spent weeks storing energy, and I was not sure how much longer I could handle thinking about Paul's death. It made me sick. Even if it would mean us being together as spirits, I would rather have him alive and be able to enjoy the rest of his life than have to endure the purgatory I was suffering.

Purgatory...That's what this was. That word sparked a new thought pattern, not just for me, but for 7A7N7D7R7A7S7. I had to be ready to leave in order to see my path. I had to finish my business on earth just as the demon needed to finish its business before—

I stopped myself. Could it be true? Could Paul be the one thing standing between 7A7N7D7R7A7S7 and the rest of the world? And as if a blue pillar of guidance were rising from the ground, my path was clear. It was my time to pass on.

<u>XI</u>

Paul became still. His malnutrition was worsening his infection, and his body was making to its final efforts. If Paul could not wake up, then Paul could not poison his body, and it could begin to battle the infection. Our bodies are a lot smarter than we give them credit for. As I observed Paul's condition, I thought about my own body. I missed it. I had treated it fairly well; I wasn't too bad to look at for most of my life. I wouldn't say I was stunning, but I knew I was beautiful. Paul told me every day. But I didn't care about that. Mostly I just missed the heaviness of it, the weight that lets you know that you are real.

I stayed there, watching over Paul and conserving energy. I knew that I would need every ounce of it to take down the beast. But I wanted so badly to kiss my husband one last time. In sleep, Paul looked like himself for the first time in a month, and in my mind all was forgiven. I couldn't help myself. When I was alive, there was not a single time we left the house without saying goodbye. How was I supposed to leave forever without even a kiss to send me off? I came in close to him, ready to sacrifice as much energy as I needed to let Paul know that I loved him one last time.

There is so much about the afterworld that I will never understand. No more than an inch separated us when I saw Paul's soul, illuminated as though a fire were raging inside him. *Is this*

180

what I look like? I didn't kiss Paul. I didn't expel any saved energy because Paul saw me too. Being in a coma had awakened his spirit, making him aware of all that was happening around him.

"*I can see you,*" he thought.

"*Yes,*" I thought back. Upstairs the beast stirred, sensing Paul's vulnerability.

"*You're beautiful. Just like always.*" He reached out and connected with me, causing love and power to surge into my consciousness.

"*I love you, Paul. I love you endlessly. But I have to go.*"

"*You just got here.*"

"*No Paul, you're dying. You're dying, and it's my fault. I know how to end this.*"

"*You can't blame yourself for my decisions, Rose. Everything I did was for you.*"

"*I know. You never left. You never left me. Even now. But I have to. I have to be the one to leave, or else the thing upstairs will come for you. And it'll be horrible.*"

7A7N7D7R7A7S7 flexed its power as it came pounding down the stairs. Ancient debris sitting in the deepest cracks of the staircase shook free with each powerful step.

"Please," Paul begged, "I just want to be with you. I'm finally with you, and I just want to stay this way."

"*I'm sorry. I'm doing this because I love you. It is my time. I know it is. There's not a doubt in my mind, Paul. Let me do this for you. Let me go.*"

7A7N7D7R7A7S7 was here, and in full form. Its feathery neck oscillated like a turret as it let out an awful sound from its ugly curved beak. Paul was not distracted: I saw him begin to change, to transform before my eyes, forming a face: his own face. The beast opened its wings wide, filling the room with its dark feathers like a rolling storm cloud. The old energy was thick, filling the room to encapsulate us.

Our love grew thick, like a bamboo forest, slowly forming a barrier between us and the beast. My spirit must have created a face as well, because before I knew what was happening, I was kissing my husband. An energy surged through me like never before, filling me with beautiful energy. In this moment, we shared a consciousness. I was closer to Paul than I ever thought possible. I was a part of him. And he was a part of me.

As 7A7N7D7R7A7S7 devoured the room, Paul took me through time. In that second it took for the house to begin to shake, I lived again completely. While the demon lifted all of the furniture in the room from the ground, I grew up. As it slammed things about, breaking everything we owned, I met Paul and fell in love. A love that could withstand all distractions. Decades passed, and when our lips parted, Paul agreed to what I needed to do.

The building ached with the tremendous power of the demon. More ancient dust shook loose from the throbbing ceiling as my body manifested itself in the room. I looked just as I had before the cancer. I gawked at my hands as the beast swelled with power and let out another screeching call. The static was so thick that it was difficult to move, but it hadn't taken us yet!

"Go, Rose!" Paul shouted. *"Go now!"*

The beast lifted from the ground with a mighty flap of its wings and bolted for Paul's bed. He was vulnerable in his slumber. It would finally be able to finish him off. *"I love you, Paul!"* I called back. *"I always will!"* I cried, as I stepped in front of his bed, wrapped my arms around 7A7N7D7R7A7S7 as tightly as I could, and with a few silent words, sacrificing myself to the Devil, pulled the beast straight to Hell.

This'll Kill You
by
Ken Goldman

"Here's another one you may not like..."
"What did Jeffrey Dahmer say to Lorena Bobbit?
"You going to eat that?"

-Happy Jax, Stand-up Comic

(1) SOURCE MATERIAL

Sylvie didn't know what hit her. Something hard just came from behind, followed by a deep throated grunt—obviously a man's—and then it was lights out.

The Friday ritual began as it always had: a girls' night out with Ginny and Steph, some drinking, a lot of laughing, flirting, and plenty of "touchy-feely" moments with the local horndogs. Sylvie looked her best in her skinny jeans and Toms. On warm summer evenings, she always wore hot pink shorts with the word "Juicy" calling attention to her shapely (and, yes, juicy), ass. But this September night was cool and it was no longer shorts season. The girls' night outs, while always fun, were also the same-old, same-old: a dance club or local watering hole, sometimes a comedy cabaret, featuring some flavor-of-the-week comedian. Friday nights on the town were mostly by the book, and that was just fine since the book was always a laugh. But tonight's last bit wasn't a laugh, of course, due to the smashed skull. No laughs there. But Sylvie had no one to blame but herself for it.

"Stepping out for a smoke," she announced to the group between Acid Reign's head banging sets, and she expected Jeff from the office to jump at the chance of joining her for some alone time. But the young accountant stayed behind his Coors, and Sylvie, having made her announcement, had to follow through with it. She managed a forced moment's eye contact with clueless Jeff, but his cold beer apparently trumped carnal desires, at least for the moment.

"Fuck it," she thought.

The night still was young, and a cigarette didn't seem like such a bad idea anyway. Since the city's lounges had banned smoking, she couldn't legally suck the comforting nicotine deep into her lungs while inside, and there were plenty of times she preferred her mouth around a Marlboro filter rather than slurping goo from some bar hound's manhood. However, tonight was not one of those nights, and had Jeff not been such a blind ass...

That was Sylvie's last thought before Fate stepped in with a set of knuckles that felt like iron and knocked the Marlboro clean out of her mouth. Her next words came several hours later.

(2) OPEN MIC NIGHT

Wh-where...am I...? It was dark. Too dark.

"Hello, Sylvie. Welcome to Comedy Central." A guy's voice echoed. Unless Sylvie's ears were still ringing, that meant this place was big. And he knew her name. That opened up the old worm can big time. *Who?*

"Yeah, I expected you'd be curious. Sorry if I hurt you. I used a bent table spoon in my palm, and *ba-da-boom!* Clever, hey? An old college trick, good for bar room brawls and jerking off ... You're okay, I'm hoping."

Sylvie wanted to rub the bump on her scalp, but couldn't. The guy had tied her arms behind her, and her legs were strapped to a high stool. It was too dark to get a fix on where she was.

"Is this a joke?"

The man laughed. Some focus returned to Sylvie's vision, and even as her abductor stood in the shadows, he appeared vaguely familiar. He wasn't bad looking.

"A joke? Hell, yes! That's exactly what this is! Well put, Sylvie!"

She considered screaming but decided that might not be her best course of action. The room (a large basement?) was much too dark, and this guy couldn't have been stupid enough to bring her where someone might hear her. Then again, he was ballsy enough to pull off the hostage thing.

"You know my name. Do I know you?" Sylvie asked.

"Hell yes! We met a few weeks ago. On stage, actually. You were a big hit with the crowd. Killed them, in fact. A fucking natural."

"I've never been onstage in my entire—" Then she remembered. The Funny Bone Comedy Cabaret, during one of the girls' Friday night adventures. This guy had been the second comedian among three stand-ups; not the headliner, but reasonably entertaining. He referred to his audience as Funny Boners when he called her onstage for one of his acts.

"The ventriloquist act! You needed a dummy and pulled me from the audience! You called yourself Happy "something." I just moved my mouth while you made jokes as if I were saying them. Damn, that was funny—" Sylvie almost laughed, but quickly remembered where she was.

"Happy Jax, joke man extraordinaire, thank you very much. And let me tell you, Miss Sylvie, when you took your seat on my lap that night, I could feel my privates snap to attention, all ready to salute the flag!"

Sylvie refused to smile. "But you don't know me. You don't know anything about me! What am I doing here?"

"You enjoyed your fifteen minutes of fame that night onstage, didn't you? I'll bet you practically creamed your panties up there, eh?" As if the man had read Sylvie's thoughts, he added, "Yeah, I noticed you that night after the show, saw you get into a cab with your girlfriends. So, I jumped into the ol' beat up Chebby and followed you. Remember the late Freddy Prinze? Yeah, he used to call it a 'Chebby.' Anyway, I followed your perky little ass tonight. You're a real party girl, eh? Well, here's your party, girl! You want cake?"

That sealed it. This guy might have been a riot onstage; maybe his act brought the house down every night. But he was probably a bull-goose loony, and she could be in the deepest of shit.

"This is kidnapping, you know. You can go to fucking jail!!"

"'Oh, nooooooo!' That's Mr. Bill, from the old Saturday Night Live, 'member? Him and that other pile of clay, Sluggo, they'd—"

"Skip the punch lines, ass hole. How about you untie me so we can have a good laugh together before I file charges?"

Happy Jax, joke man extraordinaire, pretended to consider this. Then he shook his head like some ornery Gary Coleman wannabe. "Whatchoo talkin' 'bout, Willis?" He pulled a long kitchen knife, seemingly from nowhere, and held it playfully to her throat. "I have to tell you, Sylvie, comedy is a real cutthroat business!"The knife's cold steel made speaking impossible, but Sylvie tried. She knew the word sounded pathetic, but it was all she could think to say. *"P-Please..."*

"Sorry. Didn't mean to scare you. No harm, no foul, okay?" He pulled the knife away. "Better?"

"What do you want from me?"

The comic laughed again as if she had delivered one hell of a straight line. Sylvie figured he would have laughed just as hard had she peed her pants. She worried she just might.

"Well, see..." The guy feigned deep thought and mimicked Rodin's Thinker pose with Hannibal Lecter's voice, one unsettling mash-up. "First, I want to gouge your eyeballs out and stick them in your cunt so you can see me cumming..."

Sylvie needed to breathe, needed even more to scream. She could do neither.

"But mostly, see, I want you to tell me a joke! I want you to tell me the best goddamn joke you ever heard. Some joke no one's ever told before- a joke only you know. I know you can make people laugh. I watched you do it! I want to laugh until I puke."

Holding the knife in his teeth like a pirate, he lowered the mic to her level while Sylvie squirmed against the ropes that held her. "That's…that's crazy! How can I do that? I don't even know any—"

Jax pointed the serrated blade towards her as if he were about to gut a fish. "'You've got to ask yourself one question. Do I feel lucky? Well, do you, punk?' That's Eastwood, hey? Listen, I've seen you under pressure onstage. Having an audience gets you wet, and that gets you going. It's like sex. A little push to the right places, and you're off to the races. So let's get on with the show!"

Jax walked away and flipped a couple of light switches, which gave Sylvie a clearer perspective of where she was. A great gaping black cavern remained in front of her. She was inside some faux cellar created for maximum cabaret effect, a low-lit, curiously cozy place set up with a distinct, underground comedy club type of ambience, complete with the brick wall decor behind her and a pop-up mic in front of her. Celebrity comics' photos lined the walls.

Here was the manic Robin Williams wearing a suit that seemed made from trash bags, and below him smiled a smug Jerry Seinfeld, well coifed and suited up, holding a hand held mic. Nearby in trademark white suit, doing what looked to be his old King Tut bit, was the early Steve Martin before he began taking himself seriously. The gang was all here. Pryor, Klein, Carlin, and Murphy, and the old guard was here too. Bob Hope, Phyllis Diller, and the young Johnny Carson. Personal signatures of each comic appeared on every photo, and Sarah Silverman's added the phrase "Poop is Good!" On closer inspection, Sylvie noticed every signature seemed written in the same handwriting.

This was bad. But what came next proved much worse when the laughing Happy Jax flipped on the house lights.

Cheers and whistles combined with raucous applause from an audience of maybe thirty or forty people seated at tables with drinks at hand. Appearing like some incredible magic trick, they must have been there sitting quietly the entire time watching this scene play out. They were a nicely dressed college-aged crowd hollering and rattling silverware.

This is fucking crazy... she thought.

Sylvie's area onstage was bathed in blinding light, so bright that her audience disappeared behind it. The spotlight belonged to her as she sat tied to the stool. From the corner of her eye she saw someone manipulating a large video camera, the kind you see in a television   studio. Then it hit her, and she understood what was happening. As her audience had done moments earlier, Sylvie broke out in crazed laughter.

"Oh, I get it now! Yes, I get it, you crazy bastards! I'm being punk'd, that's what this is! Like that asinine Ashton Kutcher bull-shit show on TV a few years back. I'm being fucking punk'd! "

Jax stood nearby and had a good laugh.

"That's right, Sylvie. You're being punk'd, you're being punk'd big time. The greatest punk in the history of punks, punk you very much! Now let's see what you've got for us, ah yes!"

He had done a really bad W.C. Fields impersonation, and Sylvie started to understand why Happy Jax had never made it to top billing.

"I'm sorry to disappoint you folks, but what I've got is nothing. If you're expecting a show, you'll have to rip off my top."

That brought the house down. Sylvie couldn't help but feel a little twinge of pride at her quick wit. Jax noticed it too and laughed with the others.

"That's it, Sylvie. See? Improvisation is the soul of genius. A little adrenaline rush and you're at the top of your game! Show us what else you've got."

"That's all I've got. I don't work for free, Mr. Happy Jackass."

That brought snickers from the crowd, but Jax didn't laugh this time. "Then I guess I'll have to take you up on your offer." He stepped up to her and ripped her shirt until the buttons tore apart. "Now that's what I call a show! Bravo! No, cancel that. Make that bra-LESS, ohhh*!* "

The camera guy stepped closer for a full shot. Sylvie felt the hot lights on her skin; a bead of sweat trickled down her exposed breasts. If this were one of those idiot hidden camera reality shows, Mr. Happy Jax was taking his stunt a little too far. Christ, the guy had practically cracked her skull getting her here, and now *this?*

"Listen, I'm spent, all right? I've got nothing to entertain you with. So let's call it a night, okay?"

"Not quite yet, Ma'am. I asked you earlier for a joke, and a joke I shall have!" Jax said, trying a thick Prince Charles English accent.

"I don't know any fucking jokes. I've got no sense of humor. Especially now."

He stayed with the accent. "I realize that with tits like those you really don't need a sense of humor, but we still require some wit with the tit, if you please!" He turned serious, his Jeckyll/Hyde ability to switch gears was disturbing. "You want me to show you how it's done?" Shouting, he added, "Hey Bennie, roll the video, will you?"

A large flat screen emerged from the side of the cabaret, and the monitor snapped to life. The recording showed Jax onstage with some pretty blonde woman seated on his lap. He was performing the same ventriloquist act he had done with Sylvie, although he allowed the young woman in "dummy" mode use her own voice. The girl was really beautiful, but she didn't look like she was having the best time.

"Tell me a joke, will you, Maddy?" Jax asked the girl, a little too politely. But the blonde was drawing a blank. Jax repeated the question. The young woman's face appeared pained as she tried for a suitable reply. She looked about to faint.

"Let me think...Let me think..." Finally, from the comic's lap she offered, "I'm a dummy. Yes, that's right. I'm a dummy, so...I thought *I* was the one with wood. I mean, sitting on your lap, I see *you've* got the wood here..."

Both the audience on the big screen and the one before Sylvie laughed like mad.

"That's good," Jax said to the blonde. "A little rough around the edges, but good. Another dick joke, please!"

The girl mouthed the word "shit". She paused, obviously thinking hard. Then, "I think that little wooden soldier in your pants is disabled!"

"Great! More! *More...!*"

The girl managed a really uncomfortable smile. She added "... he's sitting on two loaded duffle bags, but I don't think he's going anywhere!"

Off screen, there were approving shouts and whistles all a-round. Jax signaled for the monitor to be snapped off.

"You see how it works, Sylvie?"

She sure as hell did. "Those jokes—they were the same ones you used with me onstage when I was just moving my mouth."

"Now you got it! See how creative you can be if you dig deep like ol' Maddy?"

An uncomfortable memory stirred. Maddy ... Was that short for Madeline? Some young local girl named Madeline Kramer had disappeared about a month ago. For days, an all-points alert had gone out, but Madeline remained a no-show.

Better not mention that right now. Better not mention that at all. She thought to herself, but other words found their way out through her lips. "You're insane! This whole thing is insane!"

"I 'yam what I 'yam..." His Popeye impression, right down to the sailor man's distinct snicker. The impression was worse than Fields.

"I want to leave!"

Jax made his overly polite request for a joke again, in the same tone he used with the missing Madeline. He whispered close to Sylvie's ear, "Look, right now we're dying up here, and we have paying customers. Let me pump up that adrenaline some more, spark some of those pretty little brain cells."

Sylvie motioned with her head for the comic to come closer so no one could hear.

"Fuck you," she whispered.

The knife remained in Happy Jax's hand, but the smile didn't leave. Staying in character was obviously his priority, along with his timing. The audience seemed to understand this. The laughs appeared where they were supposed to, and no one dared to heckle. There were rules here, and Sylvie realized she had best not screw with them.

"...or fuck you not," she added, hoping to sound apologetic. She tried to match Jax's pasted on grin but felt her mouth twitch. "Fine. Start me off, okay? But understand, I'm not very good at this, knowing you want to cut my throat."

"I'm not going to cut your throat, Sylvie. Much too messy. But I may have to shoot you."

"At least put the knife away, will you?"

Jax tossed the knife to the ground. For some reason the audience found this hilarious. Some even clapped, and the comic gave a ridiculous exaggerated bow. Maybe everyone in this place was insane. Jax offered her the straightest of straight lines, "So a priest, and a rabbi walk into a bar..."

"What?"

"Come on, dammit! It's the oldest set-up in the book. A priest, a rabbi, a bar, and the bartender says?"

Nothing from Sylvie.

"Sink or swim, Sylvie. *The bartender says?*"

Sylvie was near tears.. "You want a fucking joke from this?"

"Great! There's your punch line!"

Crazy laughter erupted from the crowd. Some guy shouted for more.

Sylvie's head spun. She made a joke, stumbled onto it by accident. But if this was what the comic wanted...

He went for a second try, like a mad man's version of Henry Higgins. "Your mama is so fat..."

Sylvie thought, then shouted, "...the last time she farted they named it Sandy! Yeah, and she's so fat, the bus driver makes her sit in the back of the bus hoping she gets gas!"

The house roared, and Happy Jax looked about to cum through his teeth.

"That was a little more Chris Rock than the Hapster, but you're on a roll. Let's go for the hat trick." And to the tables in the back, "Think she can make it three for three, audience?"

Sylvie could...

"...She's so fat your daddy wears a miner's helmet to fuck her!"

A riot of shouts and hollers burst through the cabaret, and Sylvie's heart raced. She couldn't tell if her reaction came from fear any more. It felt like something else. Crazily, it felt almost good. The challenge to perform gave her a rush almost like sex.

"Hit me again," she said, realizing her panties were feeling moist.

Jax fed her an easy one. "What's black and white and red all over?"

Could there be a straight line more tacky? Her mind responded like a steel trap now. She had no idea where her response came from, but it came fast. "A bi-racial gay couple with the HIV virus!"

Her audience didn't give one shit about political correctness. Many stood, whistling and shouting for more. Deciding to work the crowd a bit, she asked for a cigarette. Several guys rushed the stage to offer her one while silverware tapped in unison against tables, and a rumbling cheer increased in volume. "Syl-vie! Syl-vie! Syl-vie!"

"You'll have to hold my smoke for me, as I'm a little tied up here," she said to the first guy to arrive. He crouched before her, lit the cigarette, and she took a long inhale when the sight gag occurred to her. "You know what this looks like from behind, don't you? Everyone here's going to think I give one smokin' blow job!"

The guy left the stage still smiling, and Jax waited for the laughter to die down. "That's right! Her name is Sylvie, ladies and gentlemen, and you're going to hear a lot about her very soon! Give the young lady a hand! Isn't she great?"

Before the applause died down, Sylvie leaned in close to the mic. "Great enough for you to untie me? What do you think, folks? I can't do stand-up sitting down."

Jax's smile showed teeth. "That privilege you'll have to earn. We all have to pay our dues."

Sylvie's mind raced for the next one liner. "So, this baby seal walks into a club..."

The joke was a sleeper, but then Jax almost pissed his pants. "I knew it! A fucking natural!"

For twenty minutes, Sylvie kept at it, her timing spot-on. She killed, almost forgetting she had remained tied to the stool tits-to-the-wind the entire time. Oddly, her nakedness released the inhibitions, while the crowd's laughter seemed like a drug that pushed her beyond her limits. It even encouraged a few impromptu tit jokes. She had no idea where the jokes came from; it mattered only that they came. It seemed crazy, this rush she experienced. A short while ago, everyone in this place had watched Happy Jax hold a knife to her throat, and now here she was, the fucking star attraction, and the crowd wanted more, more, more.

She gave it to them, at least until she had nothing more to give. Spent, Sylvie sat exhausted on the stool, savoring the applause. As if coming out of a fevered funk she suddenly remembered where she was.

Jax again stood by her side. "You did good, Sylvie. Hell, yes. You did real good." No punch line from the joke man this time. That emboldened her to speak.

"What is this place? Why am I here?"

"You're here to do what you just did. You've come up with some A-list material, kid, as I suspected you would. And this place? Let's just say this place is a very special cabaret, a hideaway for young up-and-comers like myself to hone our craft. Especially when the ol' creative well runs dry. We all need a muse occasionally, and tonight that muse, Sylvie, would be you."

"Your methods of drawing out creativity seem a little unorthodox. You know that keeping me here against my will is wrong, don't you?" She addressed the crowd. "You *all* know that, don't you?"

Dead silence. She felt like someone who had passed wind in church. "Fine. So, now what happens?"

Jax snickered like Popeye again. "Nothing. The show is over." He turned his attention back to his audience, transforming himself into a stuttering Porky Pig. "Th-That's all folks!"

Sylvie stared at the crowd seated before her, still laughing and drinking at their tables as if Jax had uttered some incredible witticism.

"Hey, all of you! The man said it's over! Why are you still here?"

"The show isn't over for *them*, Sylvie. In fact, that portion of our show is just starting." Jax motioned for the guy near the flat screen monitor. "Bennie, roll the rest of Maddie's recording for us, will you?"

Onscreen again appeared Madeline Kramer's improvisational set. Sylvie had almost forgotten about what she had seen earlier. But the young blonde was onstage again and joking like mad, having one hell of a time playing an erection-inspiring wooden dummy on Happy Jax's lap. Her set lasted another five riotous minutes, and while the crowd shouted Maddie's praises, from behind her the onscreen Jax wrapped his hands around the blonde's throat and squeezed hard, strangling her where she sat. Sylvie watched the Kramer girl kick like mad, then slump to the floor. Jax stood to take another exaggerated bow. The recording ended there.

"Shit ... Oh God..."

The audience seated before Sylvie rattled their silverware in approval again. Except, it wasn't really silverware Sylvie saw, at least not salad forks or dessert spoons. They were rattling kitchen knives with long serrated blades, and there were dozens of them.

"And for my closing tonight, a little audience participation, hey?" Jax said. The crowd responded fast and got on its feet. They moved for the stage while the man managing the large camera inched closer for the shot. And then Sylvie understood.

Her time in the spotlight was up— tonight's purpose fulfilled—and Happy Jax had told Sylvie the truth. He wasn't going to cut her throat. But he hadn't said anything about the dozens of young men with their pretty dates— clean cut kids who could have lived next door to Ward and June Cleaver. The men were polite enough to let the women go first

"Syl-vie...Syl-vie...syl-vie!"

The mic onstage picked up and intensified Sylvie's screams, and for one last time she brought down the house.

(3) You're On!

The Funny Bone reached its Friday night capacity again. Its headliner was some hip young upstart who had done Leno and was little more than a no-name himself, but this kid was going places and the buzz on him was pretty good. Happy Jax was envious, but his own time was coming soon, he felt sure of it. The right material would get his foot in the door, and the applause was always loud when he took the stage. Like most comics, Jax had his personal crowd of devoted followers, and tonight they were all present and accounted for.

The opening to a new set of material was always crucial. It set the tone, and it had to be spot on from the start. Jax raised the mic, welcomed the enthusiastic Friday nighters with his traditional "Good evening, Funny Boners," then waited for the applause to fade. His opener had to be fast, a clever zinger meant to get them all in his pocket.

Jax grinned, adjusted the mic, and said, "So a baby seal walks into a club...

Something Is Wrong with Holly
By
Taylor Woods & Brian Woods

His Side:

Walking home from work, I saw this incredibly stunning young woman through the window of a coffee shop that was across the street. I paused to stare at her for a moment. Her slender body fed my starving eyes. She was picture perfect, with her deep green eyes and her long silky brown hair that caressed the small of her back. Gracefully she moved and sat at a table next to the window I was staring through. She was simply magnetic; my attraction to her was intoxicating. I knew I needed to just walk away and return home, but I didn't have the strength to do such a thing.

Without hesitation, I stepped into the coffee shop and made my way to the service counter. I paid the nice man for my coffee, and then I turned around and walked toward the beautiful woman.

"Excuse me. I noticed you were sitting alone, and I hoped I could join you."

She smiled brilliantly at me with a face that should be on television. Now that I could see her facial features more clearly, I discovered how beautiful she was. Her eyes cut me to ribbons. Her cheek structure was lovely, high, and solid. She was perfect; anyone could see this. She held out her left hand to the other side of the table, motioning for me to sit down. As I did, I noticed that she didn't have a ring on that left hand of hers. When she spoke, she did so in a quiet, sweet, and seductive voice.

"Hello, I'm Holly Smith. And you are?"

I sucked in air, trying to remember how to speak. This was ridiculous; I was utterly captivated.

"I'm Brian Harton, and may I say, you are truly a beautiful woman," I managed to get out. She smiled and bit her lip, and my heart began to beat harder and faster as I watched her tongue go over her teeth. It was powerfully alluring.

"Thank you, Brian. You're not so bad-looking yourself." She paused and took a sip of her coffee and then continued to speak. "So tell me, Brian, what do you do for a living?" She crossed her legs and stared directly at me, waiting for a response.

"I'm a photographer. I own a studio on Main Street, right down the road from here." I looked at my phone to see it was only eight, indicating that I had plenty of time. I didn't have to be home until ten, so I could get some work done before I went to bed. I had an hour and a half to spend with Holly. It seemed like such a short amount of time. I glanced back up at her and saw that she seemed fascinated. "Well, Holly," I smiled. "What about you? What do you do for a living?"

"I'm a writer, which is one of the reasons I'm here in Ohio. I am writing about this place near Lake Abram, where a little girl murdered her parents. I became intrigued by it when I saw it online, so I decided to come down here and see for myself. I'm even living in her old house." Her eyes brightened. It was a little creepy to see her get excited over such a thing, but it was interesting, nonetheless.

After a long conversation with Holly, I decided to give her my card. When I went to write my personal phone number on the back, I accidentally knocked my lukewarm coffee all over my lap. Looking down in agitation, I swiftly grabbed the styrofoam cup. As I set it on the table, I felt something press against the top of my thigh. I looked down to see Holly's hand applying a napkin to leg.

"Are you okay?" she asked, pressing another napkin against me.

No, not really, I thought. "Yes, I am. Thank you." I took the napkins from her and tried to dry myself. Now I really had to leave, because my heart wasn't the only thing pounding against its barrier. I handed Holly the card, told her to call me sometime, and left with haste.

Once I arrived at home, I put my phone on the charger, hoping for a call from her. I took a shower to clean the stickiness from my legs. Afterwards, I brushed my teeth and put my robe on. Just as I walked into my bedroom, my phone lit up with a new message. I turned off my light, shut my door, and went to lie down. As soon as I was comfortable, I reached over, got my phone, and read the text. It was from Holly.

It read: "It was nice to meet you, Brian. I hope to see you soon."

Things were looking up. She was beautiful and sweet. She had an exciting life, and she was the first woman I had talked to in about two years I didn't hesitate to text her back.

"Right back at you, beautiful, and I hope you have a good night."

Monday, Tuesday, and Wednesday went by with Holly and me texting each other and occasionally talking on the phone. Quite a few erotic messages were sent between us. When Thursday came around, I didn't get my usual "good morning" text from Holly. I gave it some thought, but after a while, I decided not to be overly concerned. Maybe she was still asleep. I left for the studio to get some work done and to deliver some wedding pictures. They turned out quite nice and they paid me well.

Around five-thirty, which was about closing time, I checked my phone and saw that I hadn't gotten a text from Holly all day. Right before I was about to text her, I heard the bell alerting me that someone had come into the studio.

"We are closed." I didn't look up. I just stared at my phone.

"Even when it comes to me?"

Her voice caught my attention. I snapped my head up to see Holly standing there in a black coat that traveled all the way to her feet, her hair straightened and resting on her back. She smiled, and I did too.

"No, love. It's always open to you." She smiled and walked up to me. She got so close to me I could feel her breath. She looked up and kissed me. It was a sweet kiss that quite took me aback. I placed my hands on her hips and pulled her into me. We kissed until we were both out of breath. I broke the silence, saying, "Baby, it's not that I'm not happy to see you, but what are you doing here?" She didn't seem offended by the question.

Her Side:

"I'm here to get my picture taken." I smiled seductively.

"What kind of pictures do you want?" Brian asked, as if he were excited to take pictures of me. But then again, why wouldn't he be?

"I was thinking...maybe a sheet on the floor, with red and black candles everywhere..."

"With you on the sheet?" he interrupted.

"Yes, that would be the idea."

"I don't have any candles, babe. I usually don't do pictures like that." He was nervous.

I stared at him with mock fury.

"I thought as much. I have a box in the back of my car. There are thirty black candles and thirty red candles. Do you think that would be enough?"

He gave me a "come-get-me" look, and trust me, he was quite tempted to take it.

"Yes, that's plenty. How about you get the candles, while I get the sheets out of the closet in the back?"

When I walked back through the door, I stopped and quietly watched him as he laid the black and white satin sheets over a pillow-top bed on the floor. Once he noticed that I was standing there waiting, he came to retrieve the box from my hands. I remained there, motionless, as I watched him carefully position each candle. It was perfect for what I had in mind. He took his time to make sure that each candle was placed exactly how he wanted it. I could tell by the determination in his movements that he was going to be precise with these pictures. He was excited to do this, and knowing it lit me up.

I had a feeling that no matter what he did, I would get my way. If I wanted them done differently, he would spend hours rearranging them to make me happy. Too bad I couldn't feel grateful, mostly because I really didn't care what he did with those stupid candles. What he would do to me, however, was vital.

When every candle was positions, I pulled him away so we could admire it together.

"Do you like this?" He waited for my approval.

"I love it, Brian. It's absolutely perfect." I smiled falsely. He smiled in relief, knowing he wouldn't have to reposition all those candles. That would be a pain, and more importantly, a waste of my time.

"Okay then. Get yourself positioned while I make ready the camera, and we'll get started."

As he turned around to get his camera, I slowly began to pop the buttons of my dress one by one, letting him hear the snaps. Then I it slide off my body and hit the floor. I saw him freeze. I enjoyed his shock, although I'd prefer he turn to watch me, rather than pretending to play with his camera.

I positioned myself on the satin sheets on my side and waited for him. After he seemed to realize he could no longer stall, he slowly turned around.

His Side:

As I turned around to face her, I noticed everything I thought was wrong, and when I say wrong, I mean dead wrong. She wasn't in her undergarments—she was completely naked. I was glad to have the strap of my camera around my neck because I thought I was going to drop the damn thing.

She was lying on her side, her hand carefully supporting her head. The light from the candles lit her body up perfectly. Her soft, creamy skin was illuminated by a warm glow. I scanned her body, going from her neck to the perfect curve of her hips, to the shape of her legs. I tried to steady my breathing as I struggled to speak. "You're g-going to um…. Have to sign for these later." She laughed. I know my face was as red as those candles.

"Okay Mr. Harton, whatever you say." She teased, moving her legs against the sheets.

I took pictures, one after the other, focusing on the light and the way she was positioned. But truly, what I was doing was trying to keep the thoughts of, *Holy hell, Holly is naked right in front of me*, off of my lips. Her body was just lying there, two feet away from me, surrounded by candles. I was so distracted I almost didn't hear her speak.

"You want to take a break, Brian?" She ran her foot across the satin. "I'm getting a little bored down here."

She stared at me with her eyes that seemed to send flames out at me. I set down my camera and walked over to her. I sat down next to her, not wanting to presume anything. After a moment, when it seemed she was unhappy with my lack of presumption, she pulled at my hand. She pulled my head toward her face and beckoned my lips to hers.

I kissed her back, passionately, as my hands slid down her body and then ran back up her thighs. She welcomed my touch and began to pull my clothes off in a manic frenzy. I couldn't believe this was happening, but I wasn't stopping, and I sure as hell was not complaining. I considered all the candles and pondered why she had brought so many. Holly saw I was staring at the candles. She obviously didn't appreciate the amount of attention they were getting from me, so she blew them out. I smiled and held her wrists as I took control…

One Year Later…

His Side:

When the preacher said, "I now pronounce you Mr. and Mrs. Harton—you may kiss your bride," I kissed Holly, but I also took note that the preacher didn't say husband and wife. But who cared? I took my wife in my arms and had a hard time letting go. When I finally released my grip, we were off to the reception. My sister had done a lovely job of decorating the foyer of my parents' church. Holly said that her parents were not coming down for her wedding because they didn't agree with her getting married. I guess that's why she seemed a little agitated and sad.

The call for the first dance came, and I spun Holly out of the conversation she was having and pulled her into my arms, smiling as we began dancing. Despite her laughter, she still didn't seem happy. I didn't know why, but she seemed cold; there had to be something wrong with her. Something had to be bothering my princess. As we were dancing, I looked at her with compassion and whispered in her ear, "Are you okay, my love? You seem off today."

"I'm fine, honey. It's just that your sister wouldn't talk to me, and she is still not happy for us. I don't know what I did to make her hate me so much."

Leah, my sister, didn't like Holly. Which made no sense, because Holly had been nothing but nice to her. It did aggravate me that she couldn't be nice to Holly for even one day—on her wedding day, no less.

"Leah is just concerned. She will ease up in a week or two. How about this...you and she can hang out when we get back from our honeymoon. Just you and her, so you two can get to know each other." I knew that what I was suggesting could possibly start World War III, but it was worth a try. I so wanted my sister and my wife to be friends.

"Okay, baby. It's worth a try. I would love it if Leah didn't hate me." Holly and I have always thought alike. We fit together better than any two people ever could. She understood me as I understood her.

The dance ended, and I let her go back to her conversation with my mother as I searched for Leah. I found her by the punch bowl and walked up to her.

Her Side:

Talking to Brian's mother was simply boring and dreadful. She wouldn't shut up, and she would talk about everyone in the room and divulge their darkest secrets. I smiled and pretended to be interested. In my head, I was imagining multiple creative ways I could kill this horrid woman. It was a good thing she loved me, 'cause if she didn't, it would give me a reason to do exactly what I wanted to. She continued to talk as my eyes wandered, searching for Brian. I found him. He was talking to Leah by the punch bowl. Leah's facial expression appeared defensive. She resembled her brother some, with her dark brown hair. The difference was that Brian had eyes that were so dark they could be black, unlike Leah, who had eyes that where a pretty, silvery color. I continued to stare as his mother kept rattling on.

"Excuse me, Mrs. Harton…"

"Oh Holly, call me Mom," she interrupted with a gleeful voice.

I smiled. "Mom, I'm going to go get some grapes. Will I see you later?" I had issues with mothers. When I called her Mom, I had a flashback of my own mom, and I must say that I can't stand mothers. Actually, I had trouble with authority figures, period, because I wouldn't like to be overpowered by anything or anyone.

"Of course, dear." She smiled and walked away toward her husband.

I strolled over to the catering trays, which were close enough to the punch bowl that I could partly hear Leah and Brian's conversation. I showed up just in time.

"Why can't you just accept her for who she is, Leah? She has never done anything to you for you to think she is a bad person."

"Brian, I'm telling you, there is something up with her. No one has been through some of the things she has without being messed up!"

This made me very angry toward Leah. She had no right to try to make Brian doubt me. One thing was for sure, I wasn't going to let it continue. I walked toward them, smiling.

His Side:

I was just about to continue arguing with Leah when I saw Holly out of the corner of my eye, walking toward us. Leah didn't smile when Holly arrived, which pissed me off. My sister has never acted so irrationally, not in her twenty-two years of life. Holly smiled as she wrapped her arm around me.

"Hey, Leah, enjoying the party?" Holly asked in a happy voice. It impressed me that she could be so sweet to someone who hated her.

"So far, so good," Leah said.

Holly's smile faded.

"Okay, how about this, Leah. When Holly and I get back from our honeymoon, how about you two hang out? You two should get to know each other better, since you're sisters now." I smiled, encouragingly.

"I would love to spend some time with you, Leah," Holly said. Her voice was as sweet as it could be. We stood there, waiting for Leah's answer.

"Sure, we can do that," Leah submitted.

Holly smiled at the agreement.

"So, does Monday sound good?"

"See you then." Leah's voice was filled with defeat.

Back from the Honeymoon.

Her Side:

I was on my way to see Leah. She wasn't feeling well when Brian talked to her last. I smiled at the fact that this was going to be easier than I thought. I couldn't keep letting her fill Brian's head with doubts about me. Doubt causes suspicion, and suspicion causes people to check up on things. I would not tolerate that.

On the way, I stopped by the grocery store. I went into the aisle, looking for flypaper, and when I found it, I got ten packs. Next, I went and picked up two big cans of chicken soup. I headed to the cash register, paid for my goods, and left. I drove another thirty minutes to Leah's house. She lived in an old apartment down in Loraine County.

Once there, I got my grocery bags out of the back seat and walked up the path to the door. Just before I knocked, Leah answered the door. She looked pale; her hair matted, and her eyes were weak. "Hey, Leah, how're you feeling?" I asked.

She gave me a "like-you-really-care" look.

"I honestly feel like I could die at any moment." Her voice was weak.

She really did look like death was on her doorstep, instead of me. I held up the bag with the soup in it so she could see my intentions were heartfelt.

"I came to make you some soup, if that is okay with you."

Leah seemed to need to think about whether or not to let me in. She finally did. She wasn't walking very well; there was a stumble here and there.

"Hey, why don't you lay on the couch?" I suggested. "I'll make the soup and bring it to you."

Lean was too sick to argue with me today, so she took my advice. I had been in Leah's house with her brother a few times over the past year, so I knew where almost everything was. I got to the kitchen and placed two pots on the stove. I emptied the chicken noodle soup into one pot and the other I filled with two inches of water. I set both to high and waited for the water to start boiling.

When the water was boiling, I put the strips of flypaper. Slowly, the water turned a dark orange color. Then I turned off both burners and poured two bowls of soup, leaving one bowl less full. Next, I turned to the pot with the fly paper in it and pulled the strips out of the water and trashed them. I poured the now orange water into Leah's soup bowl. It was time to end this once and for all. Then Brian and I could go back to being happy, and no one would get in our way.

I entered living room and handed Leah her soup and watched her begin to eat it. I sat down and started enjoying mine, just to remove any cause for suspicion. "So have you seen a doctor?"

"Why do you care? I think you're just over here to kiss up to my brother and to show him how good you are at faking," she barked at me.

I smiled at her directness. It somewhat amused me. She wouldn't be amusing for long. I watched her finish up her soup with a cough. I looked at her forehead and saw that she had begun to sweat.

"I also think you're a horrible cook because that soup made me feel worse." Her voice was even weaker this time, so the effects were starting.

She faded faster than I thought she would. I stood up, watching Leah's breaths become more shallow.

"You know what, Leah? You were right. I don't care for you; in fact, I find you quite repulsive." I wanted to reach out and choke her, but the soup was doing it for me. I smiled, contently.

She began to choke and clutched her stomach in pain. I continued to speak, ignoring her struggles.

"You told everyone that I was a bad person, but the thing is, I'm not a bad person."

She began to throw up. I looked on in disgust.

"Oh, I'm so not cleaning that up." It was nasty, the sight and smell of it. Maybe I should have used less fly paper.

She convulsed a few times and then went completely still. I reached down to check her pulse. There was nothing; she was dead.

I trashed the evidence so it appeared it was only chicken soup that she had eaten. Then I called the police and told them everything. Well, at least everything I wanted to tell them. I also called Brian, and he said he was on his way.

I took a few towels from the closet, a bowl of water and some carpet cleaner, along with a salt shaker. I poured some salt into my eyes so they became irritated and started to water. As false tears ran down my eyes, I began to clean up the vomit, *which I'd said I wouldn't do.*

His Side:

When I got to Leah's home, I dashed through the door to find Holly on her knees. She was crying and cleaning up vomit from the floor. I saw she had already cleaned my sister's lifeless face. Holly glanced up at me with red eyes, then she got up and ran to me, embracing me. I held her while she cried, but even as I held her, I couldn't take my eyes off my sister.

"Holly, what happened?" I couldn't hold back my tears.

"I don't know. I fixed her some chicken noodle soup, and we sat here and were talking about my book as she ate. She was telling me how creepy she thought I was for living in that house before I moved in with you." She paused for a moment to blow her nose.

"I went to the kitchen to wash our bowls and clean up a bit. I must have had the water on pretty high cause when I got back she was..." Holly leaned her head on my shoulder and sniffled. All I could do was stand there and hold her.

Holly and I went into the kitchen so the paramedics could remove the body from the house. I looked around and saw a bag on the table. I picked it up and looked in it to find three packs of flypaper and a receipt. I put the receipt in my pocket and looked at Holly.

"Babe, why did you buy flypaper?"

She looked at me for a moment before she replied. "I needed some for the Abram Lake house. There are so many flies in that house, and it distracts me from writing. I picked them up when I bought the soup for Leah." Her tears stopped for just a moment.

I had forgotten that she had to go back to the house this week to do some more investigating. "Oh. Okay, babe."

The paramedic approached and I had to sign some papers. Then they left with Leah's body.

My mom and dad had been called; they were going to meet the medics at the hospital and decide what they wanted to do as far as the funeral arrangements and autopsy were concerned. I called Mom and told her I was taking Holly home.

I had talked to my sister when Holly and I were on our honeymoon. She had told me she was sick, but she didn't say how badly. She never sounded any worse than she did when she had a normal cold. She told me she would see me today, but now I was too late, and she was gone forever.

Holly fell asleep in the car on the drive home. It was about nine-thirty, and I didn't want to wake her. I carried her into the house and put her in bed. I went to clean out my pockets before changing for bed, and I found the receipt from the bag of flypaper I found earlier at Leah's house. Looking again, it said there were ten packs bought. I only found three, so I wondered, where did the other seven go? I checked in on Holly to make sure she was still asleep, then I grabbed the car keys and headed for the door.

As I drove to the Abram Lake house, I got the feeling something wasn't right. Holly had been acting very strange lately, with no reasonable explanation. She was also very protective of this house. She didn't want me or anyone else for that matter up there at all. I respected her wishes, because I thought maybe it was a need she had to protect her writing space, to make a sanctuary for her working. It never occurred to me, until now, that she could be hiding something from me.

I pulled up at the house and looked past its gates. Trees lined a lake that was blanketed by fog. This place was absolutely creepy, and I didn't like coming here.

The front door creaked open, and I walked through, wiping spider webs out of my way. Just as I suspected, Holly hadn't had time to come up to the lake house before she went to Leah's...

Her Side:

I woke up and checked the alarm clock on my nightstand. It was about ten o'clock. I reached over to grab Brian, only to find an empty space on his side of the bed. I jumped out of bed with an unsteady quickness.

"Brian?" I called out.

There was no response.

I walked into the bathroom, only to see that he wasn't there. I made my way to the staircase quietly and peeked over the banister. I didn't see anything, but I yelled out anyway.

"Brian? Babe, are you here?"

I began to worry as I went back to the bedroom and paced the floor. I looked over to the dresser and saw a piece of crumpled-up white paper. On further inspection, saw it was the receipt from the grocery store. Rage built up in me and I shoved everything off the dresser and onto the floor. I marched over to my phone sitting on the nightstand and called Brian.

No answer.

I ended the call and then hit redial, but again, no answer. I decided to call him a third time, but it went straight to voicemail without ringing.

He must have turned his phone off. Panic started to infiltrate me as a voice in my head began to take over. *He knows, Holly. He knows everything. Take care of him before he takes care of you.* I stood up straight and walked into the hallway and waited.

His Side:

Holly had called me twice before I turned my phone off. This could only mean two things. One, she had woken up, and two, she knew where I was. I had called Greg, my buddy down at the coroner's office, and asked him to do additional tests on Leah's body. I was headed over to the morgue to see what he had come up with. I checked on my phone. It was a quarter after midnight.

Stepping into the coroner's office, I found Greg shuffling through a stack of papers. "Greg, man, did you find anything?"

He looked at me with tired eyes. "Hey, Brian, look, all I could find were signs that she had food poisoning, nothing more."

Somehow I doubt that food poisoning was the cause.

"Yeah, okay." Sure it was.

"Brian, I know this is your sister and all," Greg started, removing his glasses and setting them on the computer in front of him. "But don't read into it something that just isn't there. Leah died of natural causes. Just leave it at that and let it rest." He spoke more like a family member than a friend.

Maybe he was right. Maybe I was trying to blame someone for Leah's death. I should just go home and get some sleep. Get past all the stress and try to figure this out tomorrow.

"You're right, Greg. I'm just going to go home, man; I'm tired. I didn't mean to wake you up."

He smiled sympathetically. "No problem, bro. I'll see you later. Hopefully not in here anytime soon."

I laughed at his attempted humor and walked out of the office to my car. I drove home feeling tired, suspicious, and sad. I felt kind of guilty for trying to pin this on the woman I loved. I drove in silence for the rest of the ride home. No thoughts, no sounds, just sweet blissful silence.

I pulled up at my house, and before I got to the door, I turned my phone back on. Holly hadn't called me after that second time, or at least she hadn't left me a message.

I unlocked the door and walked into the dark house. It was quiet. Holly might have gone back to sleep. I turned around to shut the door, but as I did, I felt something grip my nose and mouth, making me fuzzy headed. *It was chloroform.* I began to fade as I heard Holly say,

"Welcome home baby."

Then I faded off into the darkness, knowing I was going to die.

CHOOSER OF THE UNSLAIN
by
Cynthia Booth and Roy C. Booth

Hans instinctively knew there was something wrong with the soldier – the moment he strode into Decker Hall, the Viennese meeting site – he wore the traditional SS uniform, but it wasn't quite right. Something was off. A little too big, too long in the trousers, too wide in the shoulders. Hans always noticed uniforms. His was a source of great pride. To be a member of the *Leibstandarte SS Adolf Hitler* was a great honor not bestowed upon just any common soldier. Only five were present at the time – the captain, three other guards, and himself. They were the elite.

When the chaos began, *Der Fuhrer* had already been escorted to safety. Three of the guards had already died from the bomber's spraying bullets. Hans tried to shoot the bomber unjamming his machine gun, but his superior, Captain Eckart, stumbled into his line of fire, so he leapt in, attacking with his Waffen-SS dagger, forcing the imposter to drop the time bomb in the shoulder bag. The dagger was soon lost, yet still he fought, even after taking a machine gun stock to the head, wrestling the young man to the ground, savagely pummeling his face with his fists.

He beat him to a pulp.

After Hans was sure the man would give him no more resistance, he stood up, removing his Luger from its holster. Perhaps his captain would want this man for questioning, perhaps not. The *Widerstand* were comprised of many small, unorganized, rag-tag groups. If anything, a public example needed to be made. No one defied Hitler's finest and survived. Leveling his gun at the prone figure, he heard a sound behind him, like wind whistling through a pipe.

Then he felt the pain.

It started at the base of his skull, swarming upwards, a swarm sounding like a million bees nesting in his head. Hans began turning when his sight darkened, feeling the pain again. This time it began at the top of his head, swarming around his eyes. Blood, gore, and bone shards sprayed out of his skull. He gazed down at his uniform, regarding the bloody, stained mess.

A lead pipe clattered behind him.

Struck down from behind.

Hans didn't recall hitting the stone floor, although he surely did. He lifted himself up on all fours, feeling little pain despite mortal injuries.

What the hell is going on here? I should be dead. How...?

A war cry drew his attention upwards. She seemed to melt through the wall like it was a mirage, charging full speed through the air on a massive silver-white winged horse. Naked, save for a sheer clinging tunic and golden belt, she was as tall as any athletic man and just as muscular. She pulled back on the reins, and the winged horse halted directly before him.

"Hans Adalgar," she spoke, her voice thick, yet feminine and assertive. "I have come for you."

She lifted him by his uniform and flung him behind her across the winged horse's back. The winged horse began to gallop, quickly gaining full speed. Air swarmed around them. Hans saw the ground rapidly recede, gripping her long tawny hair to raise himself enough to sit behind her.

So the legends are true.

He had fought heroically and well, and was to die a hero. That was good. Hans looked down at the scene as they rode away, soon squinting and closing his eyes from a bright flash. He felt the shrapnel pierce him, shredding through his arm and leg. He heard his guardian scream out. He opened his eyes and saw her fall, an oath to her high lord upon her lips. The winged horse reared and whinnied in surprise, throwing him off. Hans spiraled down in a rapid free-fall. He searched about for the warrior woman and the winged horse. Neither were in sight.

Hans hit the ground with a hard slam in the same face down position in which he had died. He saw the blood on the floor pooling around his eyes.

What will become of me now? What just happened? He felt very little pain but was drained, fatigued.

Hans passed out.

***

Hans awoke and opened his eyes, not sure how much time had passed. He felt stronger, so he stood up. He had been lined up in a row on the floor along with the dead bodies. A crudely scribbled note pinned to his shirt identified his name and rank.

He ripped it off in disgust. He was not dead. He was a hero and had returned as such, refusing to be a casualty of the so-called pathetic German Resistance, this filthy *Widerstand*. Hans' thoughts swirled around his consciousness, accompanying the swarming bees in his head. He would have his righteous revenge! He could feel them flying into the soft tissue of his brain, buzzing and jumping, urging him forward. Justice and righteous revenge against the guilty. He focused in on the thought. It gave him strength, appeasing the bees.

The first order of business was to search the area. The bees began to circle and buzz agitatedly speaking amongst themselves; flying in a swirling, funneling motion as they communicated, bouncing about the confines of his skull. Schmidt, Behrman, and Fleiss were lined up on the floor. Identical notes identifying them were pinned to their uniforms in his captain's customary black ink scrawl. There was no sign of the assassin, though. Hans searched through the splintered and broken debris of tables and chairs. Shredded maps and papers leftover from the meeting were scattered throughout the room. He fingered through the main part of the rubble from the table. Fragments of glass, ink, bits of cloth. Some of the cloth he found appeared to be a uniform material from one of the shoulder bags. Hans remembered how the man had started removing the time bomb from such a bag. Under a plank of what was a table he found a matching shoulder strap. Moving the plank, his hand brushed against...something. There were some bits of wire charred into the table's underside with the remnants of a tacky substance.

The time bomb had been set to explode there *after* he had been struck from behind.

The bees danced behind his eyes.

This must have been where the time bomb was placed. Was this, then, a second attempt on *Der Fuhrer's* life, hoping he'd be led back to check on the investigation? Continuing his search he found nothing else of the bag. Bits of the wiring and casing from the explosives littered the floor in that area. No other clues were found

Several bees banged against the top of his skull, attempting to find a way out.

There must be more.

The bees banged harder, getting louder. Looking down, Hans noticed for the first time he had lost his left boot. His exposed foot didn't hurt walking along the littered floor, but it was leaving a bloody trail. He inspected his foot, pulling a bit of wire from the underside of his big toe. The sole of his foot was a mangled mess.

Hans soon found a fairly clean bit of cloth and wrapped his injured foot with it. He would have to clean it out later, but metal fragments could be dangerous. He looked down at the rest of his body. Several bits of shrapnel were deeply lodged in his leg, and the right sleeve of his shirt was shredded. The bleeding had slowed to a stop, and he no longer felt the icy cold. Actually, as long as he kept moving and focused he felt quite strong and healthy. It kept the bees at bay. Perhaps that would go away while he healed, a consequence of the concussion.

But how was this possible? By all rights, he should have been dead – from the explosion, the crushing fall, the severe blood loss – from a myriad of possibilities. It was as if his anger and thirst for revenge kept him going. Somehow, he was trapped in a state between life and death, a state of undeath.

He spotted a scrap of paper by his ruined foot. It was partially obscured by the rubble and blotted with blood. It was the same paper as the notes pinned to the bodies. He turned it over in his deeply cut hands. This note, however, was carefully torn and neatly written in his captain's black inked penmanship:

Decker 11:15
4 LSSAH
Wien Westbahnhof 3:20

Beneath this written with a different hand in pencil was a date, last Tuesday, and...he squinted.

500/3000 Deutschmarks

It was circled twice. Every bee began singing in unison now. Had Captain Eckart betrayed his own people? He considered the notion. It was damning evidence. The more he considered it the stronger, more furious he became. Captain Eckart had handpicked him to join his squad. He had believed in this man, followed his orders, drank with him, confided with him. Many evenings Hans had stayed up listening to him speak of his family back home, foreign lands he had seen, foes he had conquered – all for the sake of The Reich. Were they all lies?

Hans searched the floor again, but this time for something different, the instrument of his death, the gore smeared lead pipe. He found it off to the side where he had been laid low. The buzzing was intense. He thought of his captain, and his head nearly exploded. He felt himself burning up inside. The bees sat still, debating. It was all now coming together.

He looked again at the note, then checked his watch. The crystal was shattered, and the hands had stopped. 11:27 it read. He had no idea what time it was now, but the *Wien Westbahnhof* train station was about three miles south of his position. It couldn't be *that* late. He could be there in no time. The bees bounced again, urging him forward. Hans scavenged a Luger from Schmidt, placing it in his own holster. He would need nothing else to track down this villain, this *schweinhund*. He would find Captain Eckart and learn the truth from him. He wanted an explanation for this cowardly betrayal.

He deserved that.

The bees disagreed. No, he couldn't trust *anyone* anymore. For all he knew, their entire relationship was built on lies. Captain Eckart had betrayed everything they stood for, and would pay. A traitor disguised in a uniform, shielded by it, but not anymore. Hans knew the truth even if no one else did. No one else would probably believe him. He would hunt Captain Eckart down like the rabid dog he was. Drown him in his own blood. He deserved nothing better. The thought renewed his strength for the walk to the station. Perhaps he could somehow commandeer a vehicle along the way...

The way to the station was deserted, and he could feel he was making good time. As he reached the road, a young mother carrying a small boy on her hip approached the road walking towards him. As she came into view, she slowed her gait and stop-ped, staring and pointing, horrified. She gripped the boy tighter, stepping back. As he approached, her eyes grew wide and she gasped. She quickly darted to the other side of the road.

I must be a sight, Hans thought. He instinctively reached for his right ear.

It was missing.

He looked down. He had forgotten to grab a pair of boots off one of the bodies before he left. His foot didn't hurt, but it was crooked and wobbled a bit, though. His ankle must have been damaged in the explosion, some tendons torn. He really couldn't tell just by looking at it with all the dried blood around it. He noticed dried blood and clustered chunks that had come down his neck and stained the shoulders of his uniform. It really didn't matter to him now. He wanted to find out what time it was and beat Captain Eckart to the 3:20 train. As he entered the more populated area, people he encountered seemed to have the same reaction as the woman on the road. He was drawing too much attention to himself. There was an old man sitting outside a bar, drinking from a stein. Hans stood directly in front of him and drew his Luger.

"Give me your coat and hat," he ordered.

The old man looked up at him quizzically with bloodshot eyes, blinked and then regarded the hat sadly.

The man relinquished his apparel and Hans put it on. It stunk of sweat and beer. The coat was long, but a little too narrow for his body and the hat fit awkwardly, but it did the trick. He felt alive with vigor now, close to his destination. He continued on. He needed to know what time it was.

As he walked his mind turned inward, trying to come to grips with his condition. It wasn't logical. He should be dead. Hans remembered a lesson from his gymnasium days, a lesson in folk-lore, from the works of William of Newburgh, especially his accounts of revenants. Revenants were animated corpses believed to return to wreak terrible vengeance upon the living, especially those who had wronged them. Was that what had happened with the strange woman and the winged horse? Was he being plucked from life, only to be thrown into some ghastly state in between? Is that what had happened?

Before he knew it, he arrived at his destination.

He entered the station a few moments later. The large clock above the ticket booth proclaimed two minutes until 3:00PM.

He had done it!

The bees that had been waiting and nesting came out now, one by one, each adding their own distinct voice to create one droning hum. Now all that he had to do was find the correct track, watch, and wait.

He checked the departure board. There was a 3:20 train leaving for Zurich. Captain Eckart sought asylum in Switzerland, the most logical place for him to go. Hans walked outside to the tracks and sat on the furthest unoccupied bench. His battered foot and leg were making him weave about, and he was afraid he wouldn't be able to balance on it any longer. It dangled from his leg underneath the bench.

Hans didn't have to wait long. Captain Eckart walked slowly out to the dock, observing each face that was waiting. Hans dropped his head so that his hat obscured the view of his face. He didn't seem to recognize Hans. Hans went to stand and drew his Luger, but his foot gave out on him, and he fell back on the bench. He looked down. His foot remained under the bench, broken off at the ankle, his leg out in front of him. There was very little blood, and it no longer bothered him. The bees roared in his head. It was deafening. They wanted release! He stood up on his one leg. It really didn't matter what happened to him now, vengeance was all that was important. So far no one, including Captain Eckart, noticed him. He slowly hobbled his way forward using the wall as a crutch. The train was in sight just about to enter the station, so Hans stopped right where he stood and fired.

People screamed.

The bees swarmed from their nest, stinging. Captain Eckart, stunned for a moment, drew his pistol and fired off a hasty shot, hitting Hans in the chest.

It didn't stop him.

Hans continued to advance, shambling along. People scattered, running out of the station while the train began to pull up to the dock. Hans dropped his Luger and grabbed his former captain's hand. Captain Eckart managed to squeeze off another shot, hitting Hans in the forehead. Again, Hans should have died.

Now the bees were gone. Vanished. It felt good. Captain Eckart stared in disbelief. Hans ripped the gun out of his hand, taking two fingers with it.

Die!

Hans grabbed Captain Eckart by the throat and threw him at the oncoming train. Captain Eckart collided with the front of the train and bounced down onto the tracks, moments later he was under the train, a bloody smear.

Hans couldn't see the body, but he knew he was dead. He could feel it. A sense of relief and justice. He fell to his knees. His revenge was complete. Now what was happening? The weakness was so overwhelming he couldn't move. He didn't feel sorry for himself, and he didn't care. He fell over headfirst, staring closely at the pavement until his vision faded.

He lay there and waited.

Where was the woman on the flying horse to meet him?

THE END

Mr.Empty
By
Shane Porteous

A chorus of poorly played horns signified that the festival was in full swing. The streets were thronged by a plague of festivalgoers, many drinking, many dancing, many just watching. There was hardly a single person not dressed in a crude costume, making the streets seem possessed by various monstrosities. But amongst this motley crew of revelers, one stood out.

He seemed to fit in with the monsters, but the garments he wore weren't a costume. In a place where so many were hiding their true identities, he wasn't hiding anything. To say he towered over everyone wasn't correct; it was more like he was lurking over everyone, as if he were a specter haunting the street. Even as the drunkards blew pathetically on their horns, the rattle his headpiece made could be heard. Falling like dreadlocks from the top of his head to the small of his back, the bones rattled—finger bones, to be precise. People were too wrapped up in the celebration to pay much attention to the bones, although on close inspection, there was no doubting their authenticity.

They were his trophies, the middle fingers of people he had killed. He didn't take a trophy from all of his kills, just the most interesting ones. He had murdered many before that teenage boy at Rovehit, but that boy was the first victim who didn't die after a single cut. No, that boy took quite a surprising amount of evisceration before he stopped moving. The boy's last movement was raising his middle finger—such a defiant little prick. Still, he couldn't help but admire such gusto, and so he took that finger for his first trophy. The only regret he had had that night was ripping out the boy's tongue. He never did that again. Screams from a tongue-less mouth filled with blood just weren't as pleasant as a normal scream; he enjoyed such a sound.

He wore the garments of a scarecrow: a long tanned coat, tanned gloves, a pair of old slacks that sagged off of his frame, and boots that had been worn to the point of falling apart. But he hadn't come here to scare crows; he had come here looking for a certain someone. Fortunately for the revelers, he didn't believe the one he was searching for was amongst them. Regardless, the idea of turning this festival into a massacre was a delightful prospect. The night was still young: maybe a massacre would be in the cards. But not yet, he thought to himself. He had traveled quite some distance to get here. If he just wanted to slaughter a bunch of drunken idiots, he could've stayed in Idlehelm. Still, it was best to move on; the temptation to silence so many fools was becoming too great.

As he moved on, the crowd became thinner and thinner, and the sea of costumes and alcohol soon ran dry. He enjoyed a good hunt, but this one had taken him further than he had ever been before. In a way, he had been searching for this person his entire life. Since he was born, he had known he was different from other people. Most weren't born dead like he was, and even fewer didn't possess a soul. Unlike most people, he could remember the day of his birth, how Dr. Umer had tried so hard to get his heart beating. On that day, many considered it a miracle what Dr. Umer had accomplished in bringing life to his body. Very few doctors could resuscitate a stillborn, but Dr. Umer had done just that.

Of course, when they found out what he truly was, none of them ever called it a miracle again; after that, the word "abomination" was used far more often to describe him. The few who actually knew what he was, a being without a soul, had given him the name Mr. Empty. It was a name he took in stride, a name that made him feared. When Dr. Umer had brought him to life, he had seen visions of paradise and the underworld. To him, paradise was anything but: no blood, no screams, and no pain—what kind of place was that? But the underworld...now that was somewhere he wanted to call home. Problem was, it was difficult to go to a place where souls were to suffer for all eternity when you didn't have a soul to suffer. Mr. Empty didn't believe he'd suffer if he ever got to the underworld, for he imagined the fingers of demons would make some pretty interesting trophies.

He knew he wasn't invincible, he had almost been destroyed a couple of times. But he was very difficult to kill, considering how many injuries he had sustained over the years. He had never been sick and hadn't eaten anything since he was 15 years old. His body may have been thin, almost skeletal, but the lack of nutrients had never sapped his strength. He had never enjoyed eating: not fruit, not vegetables, not beef or human flesh. Nothing had given him an appetite. He wasn't even sure what would happen if someone or something managed to kill him. Would he cease to exist? This meant he needed another way to enter the underworld and hoped that he had finally found it.

He had been on journeys like this before, searching for those shamans, witch doctors, priests, and exorcists that claimed they could banish demons and the like to the underworld. Mr. Empty didn't have an exact count of how many such seers he had hunted. All he knew was he hadn't taken a trophy from any of them. This was because none of them had proven correct; all of them had been little more than frauds or delusional idiots. He hadn't let any of them live. He had gone out of his way to make their deaths especially violent and bloody. It wasn't only because they angered him or that killing them meant one less charlatan he had to deal with; it sent a message to all the other paranormal frauds not to pretend to be something they weren't.

His plan had worked somewhat. The numbers of people who made such claims had dwindled. Yet no matter how many he killed, there always was someone willing to prey on the ignorant and desperate. It had gotten to the point where he had given up searching and returned to his original plan. He had entered countless temples and other places of worship, killing anyone he could find, hoping to piss off sufficiently any number of gods so that they would appear before him and send him down to the underworld. But 150 such massacres hadn't brought any godly wrath upon him. He never understood why people worshipped gods, considering they did nothing for them. Especially those who were dancing and drinking at the festival, grateful to whatever god had placed them in this shithole of a country.

His search had only resumed when he discovered the supposed accomplishments of one James Groaker. Groaker was an apparent exorcist who had managed to cleanse the 15 most haunted places of his home country. There was even a story, witnessed by over 500 people, that he had sent a live murderer, the supposed Tenzed Slasher, directly to the underworld, saving the villagers of the countryside from further atrocities.

It was a claim hard to believe, but there was something Groaker had done that seemed to corroborate his claims. In interviews with various papers, Groaker had described the underworld in great detail—a place no other exorcist had ever mentioned. The underworld was made up of two layers: a place of eternal fire and darkness, and another layer of cold infinite light. This description was exactly what Mr. Empty had seen when he was brought to life.

He loved those two colors, the sickly yellow of flame and the white of cold luminosity. He loved them so much that he painted the wooden mask he wore with those two colors. No—it wasn't a mask; it was his face. When he was 16, he had decided to remove his own face of flesh, for it was too pretty and innocent-looking, two things Mr. Empty never claimed to be. He was surprised by how much blood there was when one cuts off one's own face. But the blood was the perfect frame for the mask he had nailed into his skull. The blood may have faded long ago but the colours were still bright and realistic.

Groaker had made further claim that the underworld's realm of flames was actually where demons loved to dwell, and that it was the place of cold infinite light where demons were punished. Mr. Empty had long since come to the same conclusion. Demons loved flames and darkness; they would never consider such a place to be a torment. But a chilling arctic waste where there was nowhere to hide from the light? Now that was a place ideal for demonic suffering. If Groaker knew all of this, then there was a good chance that he wasn't lying.

Yet Mr. Empty remained apprehensive about it all. For one thing, he couldn't understand why Groaker had fled to this country. This place was much more rife with mysticism and the old ways than his home country, but the poor exceedingly outnumbered the wealthy here, and Groaker was as much about the money as any of those other exorcists. In any case, even Kikum Somal, the famous skeptic and debunker, hadn't been able to disprove Groaker. Something else was going on here. Now Groaker had simply vanished from mainstream society, seemingly without warning, and Mr. Empty had to find out if he was telling the truth.

He had been searching for a little over two years for Groaker and was now finally standing in front of the building where he supposedly lived. It still didn't make any sense: whatever Groaker's reasons for fleeing his country, he still must be quite wealthy, so why live in this neighborhood? The entire country wasn't much to look at, but this was the worst boil amongst the neighborhoods that plagued the landscape. All of these buildings were ugly and rotten;; whatever purpose they had once served had long ago vanished. Like a once-healthy body now riddled by the disease of poverty, these buildings were the homes of squatters and other desperate individuals.

Just by looking at the entrance, Mr. Empty could see just how radically this building stood out from the others on the block. The door was reinforced steel, much heavier than the decrepit, decomposing wooden doors of the other buildings. If Groaker were trying to hide in this armpit, he should've been doing a better job at it.

Mr. Empty looked around the street. He could see no movement from anywhere. Either they were all at the festival, or everyone was hiding in these tombstone buildings. It didn't matter to him, nor was the reinforced door going to be much of an obstacle. Taking out one of his blades from under his coat, he cut through the locks like baby's flesh, something he easily knew how to cut through. He counted seven locks that his blade severed: somebody was definitely trying to keep something out. Pushing the door open, he was met with putrid darkness. The building reeked of piss and decay. But he was not afraid of blackness or bodily fluid and so stepped into the dark without delay.

In the absence of windows, only moonlight from the opened door battled the blackness inside. It was enough for him to see a set of stairs. Through touch alone, he could tell just how rotted the guardrail was. A child could probably squeeze the wood and turn it to dust. The stairs themselves, however, were a different matter; someone had taken the time to rebuild them using steel.

Listening to the echo of his own footsteps, he soon left the stairs and found another door. Much like the first, it was reinforced steel, and much like the first, it had locks that were easily cut. When he opened the second door, the smell of rot and foulness was completely behind him. He could feel through his boots that he was standing on a carpeted area—not something he was expecting. With his blade put away, he used his long arms to search the walls. He found what he was looking for, turned the switch, and brought to life various lanterns that illuminated the room.

A room like this had no business being in such a run-down building. It wasn't decrepit, it didn't smell, and most of all, everything was new. The carpets weren't messy second-hand lengths of cloth; they were made from fine thread. Mr. Empty could see a desk made from fine oak, with a line of ink blots and quills neatly arranged upon its top. Various sets of drawers occupied the far wall, each made from the same fine oak. A long bookshelf stood beside them. This room definitely didn't belong here. Major renovations had taken place. Obviously the lower level had been left untouched in a bid to deter squatters. Mr. Empty could see several doors. Though sturdy, none of them were reinforced steel. He guessed whoever lived here was satisfied that no one would get through the two reinforced-steel doors and thus felt that further protection wasn't needed. How wrong of an assessment, Mr. Empty thought.

He opened each of the doors and saw that one led to a bathroom, one to a kitchen, another to a laundry, and another to a bedroom. Each room was neat and tidy. He especially noticed just how well-made the bed was. With not a speck of dust anywhere, it was obvious someone had recently cleaned, meaning someone still lived here. Seeing all of this, Mr. Empty seriously doubted that Groaker was at the festival. A rich man, even one in disguise, wouldn't hang around such desperate folks. Mr. Empty wouldn't be surprised if they were willing to eat him alive, considering the lack of viable food in this place. Besides, someone who used reinforced-steel doors wouldn't be an overly social type.

Mr. Empty moved towards the bookshelf. Upon seeing all of the titles, he had little doubt he was in the right place. Every single book Groaker had written could be seen twice over. Only an author would need more than one copy of his own book: a copy to flip through while he basked in the delusion of his own brilliance, and a second copy to be preserved and never touched, so he would always have a reminder of his past accomplishments. He wasn't too interested in reading Groaker's books. He had read them all already. But other books on the shelf caught his eye, books about forgotten arts and other such things. These books were very rare, the kind that were written centuries ago. There was more truth in these books about how the world truly worked than in their modern-day counterparts, but they were still filled with lies. There were other books, too, mostly fantasy novels, something Mr. Empty had never enjoyed.

However, there was still another group of works that definitely caught his eye. These books dealt with how to perform magician's tricks, cold reading, and other such pseudo-supernatural powers. Their presence only added to the mystery. Perhaps Groaker was truly a fraud, or perhaps he was merely seeing how those without his abilities faked their powers. At random, Mr. Empty picked up another book and was surprised to find it was about alchemy. Though it didn't answer any of his questions, he always found alchemy a fascinating subject. He was so wrapped up in the book that it took him a moment to hear the sound of approaching footsteps.

For a few moments, he had forgotten why he had come here in the first place. If the footsteps he heard were Groaker's, he wasn't alone—it sounded like half a dozen people were hurrying up the stairs. He put the book back on the shelf and casually walked to the bathroom, leaving the door open just enough so he could see who was coming. His guess was correct: there were half a dozen people, two women and four men. He was annoyed that Groaker wasn't amongst them. Each brandished a long knife and seemed eager to stab something. Each wore the same black and white garments, but he could tell they weren't soldiers. They were probably gang members. Had they seen that the door outside had finally been broken? Like flies to a corpse, they had come swarming in. He watched as they looked around the place, with one of the women kneeling down and feeling the carpet. They weren't ransacking or even paying attention to the desk, drawers, and bookshelf. It seemed they weren't here to steal anything.

"Did anyone see him moving through the first level?" one of the men asked.

"No, he should be up here somewhere," one of the women replied.

"I've never seen anyone cut through locks like that before," another man commented.

They all continued to speak in whispers as Mr. Empty figured it all out. These half a dozen weren't here to steal, nor were they here for Groaker. They were here for him—Mr. Empty. He doubted these six would be much of a problem for him. They didn't hold their weapons with much skill. His first guess was they thought he was from the festival and were either going to rob or kill him because of some superstition. He was eager to see them try. From under his coat he took two blades, one for each hand. His weapons were actually the broken-off arms of a pair of garden shears. Once upon a time he had used proper knives, ones he had claimed from a master butcher. But they were too sharp and fine; killing with them was too instantaneous. Murder shouldn't be too quick, and never should it be painless. These rusted, blunt garden-shear blades allowed him to rip at flesh like a monstrous pair of claws, and that was how he liked it.

He found it slightly amusing that this pack hadn't thought of checking the other rooms yet. He didn't want to play hide-and-seek, anyway. He gently allowed the bathroom door to open. The creak it made seemed as loud as thunder. The six now had all turned to face him, their weapons at the ready. The silence that fell was something Mr. Empty had grown used to. Few had been able to look at his mask and trophies while keeping a lucid mind. He raised his weapons. They were dull and rusted, seemingly inferior to the sharp, well-kept blades of the half-dozen people before him. This apparent advantage in weaponry was enough to make the six react. "Get that Sajin!" a man declared. Mr. Empty didn't know what a Sajin was, probably a local slang for something. It didn't matter anyway; it would take a lot more than that to insult him.

He killed the first before the man had a chance to raise his blade; Mr. Empty's impressive height gave him an obvious leverage advantage. He killed the man by jamming the shear straight through his nose, causing a mixture of blood and mucus to vomit forth from the ghastly wound. While the man's body convulsed from the wound, another charged forth, swinging his knife with rage. Mr. Empty tore through his throat using his other shear, loving how the blood bubbled as the man gasped. The cracking of bone could be heard as he removed his first shear in time to decapitate one of the women while gutting the next man. They fought with the clumsiness of thugs, something Mr. Empty became painfully aware of. The last woman rushed towards him, blinded by adrenaline. For her efforts, he stabbed his blade into her heart as though it were a spear. The shear went deep enough that as she gasped her final breath, he was able to lift her off the ground and toss her away. In a mere moment, five gang members were dead, and the once-clean floor was littered by blood, organs, and corpses.

The remaining gang member did nothing to hide his terror. Mr. Empty could see such fear in his eyes as he looked down at the corpses of his companions, no doubt wishing they would get up and help him. But the dead couldn't save him from his own death. In the silence, the dripping of the blood off the shears became dominant, sounding like eerie bells tolling in the distance. The man didn't hold his ground—he turned and ran. He managed only two steps before Mr. Empty launched one of his shears deep into the back of his head. Mr. Empty watched the final body fall before he went over and retrieved his weapon. He would take no trophies from this collection of pitiful victims.

With the distraction of the half-dozen intruders taken care of, his mind returned to the whereabouts of Groaker. If these six were in a robbing mood, why hadn't one of them looked through the drawers for valuables? A place as nice as this stuck out like the only clean spot on a blood-soaked rag. They weren't robbers; they were guarding this place. The question was, why? He doubted they were after him specifically. He had killed many people, but this was the first time he had come to this country. It seemed unlikely a family member of his many victims would be in this place.

He was drawn to a specific spot on the floor, where one of the women had appeared to be checking for something. It was too specific a spot to be random. Why on earth would someone study a piece of the floor without a proper reason?

Not caring if he stepped on the corpses or if their blood stained his boots, he walked over and crouched down, running the tip of one of his blades along the carpet. The carpet had been brushed in a certain direction, hiding the fact that a large piece of it was separate from the rest. Clever, Mr. Empty thought, although it wasn't clever enough. Lifting the piece of carpet, he could see a large trap door underneath. Obviously, something or someone was hiding down there. He could feel another series of locks as he stuck his blade into the slit of the trap door. They broke just as easily as the others. The door creaked loudly as he opened it, reminding him of a certain old man with throat cancer who had tried to scream when Mr. Empty gutted him. He caught a strong whiff of something that wasn't piss or decay, even though the underground region was dank. He could see that a light of some kind was on down there, which meant someone was home and hiding in what was seemingly not much larger than a mere crawl space.

He dropped down and was surprised to find that he could stand at his full height. This was a basement of some kind, but its single lantern left much draped in darkness. The first thing that drew his eyes was a group of objects that obviously didn't belong there. Stacked into a pile were a group of bricks made of dark yellow sand, each individually wrapped. Mr. Empty didn't inspect them more closely, for his eyes were drawn to something on the edge of the light. He could see a number of jars and other powders, along with a brick of the powder that had been ripped open, all displayed upon a desk. Unlike the furniture above, this desk was old and splintered; clearly its appearance had no bearing on its purpose. Had alchemy been performed? Sadly for him, he knew better than that.

Mr. Empty lowered his head as a sharp breath left his body. This was a drug lab. No wonder the six gang members had followed him inside hastily: they were defending their main source of income. Chances were, Groaker was dead. This place was ideal for manufacturing drugs; it would be easy to simply kill Groaker and use his hideout for such a purpose. Yet this didn't explain why Groaker was in this country in the first place, let alone why he would be hiding in such a desolate and dangerous neighborhood. Mr. Empty briefly glanced towards the surrounding darkness, remembering that someone must have switched on the lantern.

It was then that he heard a mechanical click, a sound that snapped in the otherwise silent room. He was fairly impressed by the man with a crossbow. It was rare that someone was able to sneak up on him. Unlike the dozen he had killed upstairs, this one was dressed in green and orange, but again, he didn't appear to be a soldier and was too young to be Groaker. Casually Mr. Empty turned fully to face him, showing no fear of the crossbow he held raised and ready. A flawless mixture of fear and dread consumed the man's eyes; clearly he wasn't expecting Mr. Empty to be here.

"I don't know who you are," the man said, doing his best to stop his hands from trembling. "But you ain't stopping me from killing Groaker."

In response, Mr. Empty tilted his head. So Groaker was still alive, he thought casually, as if the man before him were no more a threat to him than the half a dozen dead that lay above.

"I don't know who sent you, but Groaker has failed to pay the Sajins what he owes them. They paid me to do a job, and I am going to do it." Again Mr. Empty merely stood staring in silence. "I'll let you walk," the man began, his voice still trembling slightly, "considering you killed six Envars." Mr. Empty could tell this man was more afraid than impressed by this accomplishment. "If you try and stand in my way, I'll put a bolt through your eye!" The man reminded Mr. Empty of a tiny dog trying to sound like a wolf and failing miserably.

Mr. Empty wasn't used to people giving so much information willingly. The Envars and Sajins were clearly rival gangs. That's why the doors were so heavily locked: the Sajins were looking to kill Groaker. Judging by the amount of drugs in this place, the Envars must have been offering protection to Groaker in exchange for his stashing their drugs. Mr. Empty enjoyed how this man was telling him everything he needed to know, figuratively spilling his guts. But the idea of making him literally do it was becoming awfully tempting. Mr. Empty took a single step forward, and the man hastily took three back.

"Tell me," Mr. Empty began. "Are you always so terrified when you are holding a crossbow? Can't be much of an assassin if that is the case." His voice was like rusty nails sticking in the man's ears. It only sounded vaguely human, like a morbid mimic of something otherworldly. It was a raspy, raw, and very dark collection of sounds. The man studied the eyes behind the mask. The green of them was terrifyingly light, as though the eyes weren't organic but wooden. Every movement they made was morbid and monstrously mechanical. He tightened his hold on the crossbow.

"I'm not afraid," he replied, an obvious lie. Though he was skilled with the crossbow, he had never seen a single person take on six armed enemies and get the better of them. As he looked down at the blades in Mr. Empty's hands, the masked man followed his gaze. Those wooden eyes were deeply unsettling. Obviously, Mr. Empty was quite good at using his blades, and the man didn't want to go anywhere near him.

The man could have given him one last warning, but he didn't want to give this masked monster any chance of stopping him. Even with trembling hands, his shot was well aimed. It would've pierced deep into the heart of Mr. Empty if it had gotten that far. The man gasped when the ping of metal striking metal haunted the air, before the bolt fell upon the ground. To Mr. Empty it wasn't a big deal: it certainly wasn't the first time his garden shears had stopped an arrow or bolt. The man worked quickly, reaching for another bolt, but Mr. Empty had no further need of him. In two steps he was upon the man, striking his blade deep into the man's stomach before he had a chance to reach another bolt. Mr. Empty watched the life evaporate from his eyes as it was syphoned out of him. He gave the man a relatively quick death, considering all the useful information he had given him.

So—not only was Groaker alive, but judging by the reaction of the six Envars, he was somewhere in this building. But then again, they may have just been checking on their drugs. What other use could Groaker be to them? Unless, of course, they were as superstitious as the festival goers and believed Groaker could keep evil spirits away. The idea was a plausible one. The question remained: where was Groaker? If they had a hidden place for the drug lab, perhaps there was another hiding place for Groaker. He glanced around the surrounding darkness, but couldn't see anything outside the reach of the light.

Just when he was about to return above ground, one loud sniff struck the air. He turned in time to stop an axe from being buried into his head. Mr. Empty forced his attacker to let go of his weapon easily enough. What was in his attacker's other hand seemed far more important to him anyway. "Groaker," Mr. Empty said. It took a second look to recognize him, for this poor excuse for a man had become a grotesque shell of what he once was. By how sunken his eyes had become, how ragged his features were, Mr. Empty knew Groaker had become a drug addict. For a man in his early 40s, he looked more like he was 65. His lips had become incredibly thin, his teeth were on the brink of rotting out of his mouth, his skin was pale and sickly. His pupils were enormous:

clearly he had taken drugs recently and often. With a handful of powder still clenched in his hand, Groaker's eyes were moving all over the place, as if dancing to a tune of drug-induced madness. He had become dependent on the drug to such an extent that he would risk being discovered just so he could have another snort.

Mr. Empty was familiar with this drug: he had seen users ingest, inject, and snort it. Yellow Shit was the nickname Mr. Empty had given it, because it turned everyone who used it into a piece of shit. As Groaker began licking his own lips repeatedly, it all began to make sense to Mr. Empty. Groaker had fled to this country not because gangs were after him, but because of his drug habit. Mr. Empty shook his head at the revelation; he never understood how pitiful most men were. Wasn't fame and money enough for these cretins? Chances were, Groaker was running out of money, and it would be much cheaper in a place like this than in the country he came from. Though he was a now an addict, that didn't necessarily mean he had lost his powers.

"James Groaker," Mr. Empty repeated. Groaker continued licking his lips, trying to get as much leftover powder into his nose as possible. "Groaker!" Mr. Empty yelled, shaking him slightly. For the first time in a very long while, the masked man would have to use restraint. Yellow Shit addicts were often so zonked you could cut off their arms and they would simply smile at you. Mr. Empty knew this from personal experience. In such a state, Groaker only had one weakness, and Mr. Empty quickly exploited it. Using his impressive strength, he forced Groaker's other hand to open.

One would think Groaker was witnessing gold fall from his grasp as he watched the powder descend like a waterfall. Quickly he tried to bring his hand to his mouth, but Mr. Empty wouldn't let him.

"What do you want?" Groaker suddenly screamed, bringing his face an inch away from the mask. Yellow Shit was said to make one fearless; in truth, it just made one incredibly stupid. At least Mr. Empty had his attention now. "Is it true that you can send people to the underworld?" Mr. Empty asked, not amused by the bizarre expressions Groaker was pulling. In response, Groaker began laughing, his once-honeyed voice sounding strained and ravaged. The last time anyone had laughed at Mr. Empty was when he was nine and Jimmy Olan had laughed at a picture he drew. Mr. Empty had made sure Jimmy didn't laugh again—a fork to the throat tended to do that. The masked man grew tired of listening to the laugh and shook him violently.

"Don't tell me you were fooled by it, too? People are so stupid…." Groaker scoffed.

When Groaker tried to laugh again, Mr. Empty squeezed a tight hand over his mouth. With a handful of words, this idiotic drug addict had dashed his hopes.

"What are you talking about?" Mr. Empty asked, his patience becoming thin. Groaker's first few words were muffled, so Mr. Empty released his grasp.

"…. I didn't send the Tenzed Slasher to the underworld, I just found his body, the stupid moron had tripped and fallen on his own axe…All I did was set fire to him. When the villagers came, I just told them I had sent him to the underworld…and they believed me…" The glee in his voice angered Mr. Empty greatly, yet he resisted the urge to skewer him. "What about all of those hauntings?" he asked. To this question, Groaker stopped laughing and began biting his lip. "Oh that," he said, now chewing on his lip. "Easy to fake: a few bumps in the night, and everybody thinks ghosts and monsters are around. All I did was fix a few bad pipes." He began licking his hand again, and Mr. Empty considered feeding it to him.

But something didn't add up—one last very important detail. "If you faked everything," he began slowly, wanting to ensure Groaker heard his question, "how did you know what the underworld looked like?" Groaker began laughing hysterically, his entire body convulsing with the strange amusement. "Answer me!" Mr. Empty demanded, shaking the man violently. Groaker simply continued to laugh, so Mr. Empty threw him across the room. His body hit the wall hard, yet even the pain of impact did nothing to halt his laughter. Mr. Empty quickly picked him up off the ground, again stopping him from licking his hand. He knew it was pointless asking him again—down here, anyway.

Holding him by the scruff of the neck, he forced Groaker to come with him, continuing to stop him from licking his hand. Now Groaker stopped laughing and began fighting, punching, and kicking at the masked man. He wanted more drugs; that's all that mattered to him. Mr. Empty ignored the blows; he had dealt with far worse pain. Showing his impressive strength, he threw Groaker back upstairs through the opened trap doorway, violently grabbing him by the face as he tried to crawl back to the drug lab. He pushed the drug addict far enough away that he too could leave the basement, closing the trap door behind him. Groaker sprang to his feet; the idea of being separated from the drugs was too much to bear.

Groaker ran towards the masked man, diving for the trap door. Mr. Empty forced him to his feet, and Groaker began barking words at him. "No! No!" he screamed, spit flowing from his mouth like he was a diseased dog. "I'm not supposed to be up here! There's no happiness up here! Get out of my way!" Even with the drug-induced adrenaline, he couldn't push his assailant away.

Guessing from his actions that Groaker never did drugs up here, Mr. Empty deduced that the few times he was lucid, he must've been ashamed of what he had become, always leaving the upper floor sparkling clean. The basement was his hidden world, the place where he could commit sins and not be judged. "Answer my question, and you can have all the drugs you want," Mr. Empty said.

"Well, ask then! Hurry up and ask!" Groaker demanded, grasping Mr. Empty's collar. As he had seen before, Yellow Shit made people incredibly stupid. "How did you know what the underworld looked like? Tell me!" he cried, shaking Groaker violently.

"Now!" Groaker replied. "Ask nicely, Alda!" These words were enough to make Mr. Empty let go of him, recoiling as if wounded from the inside. It had been a long time since he had heard that name. "What did you call me?" Mr. Empty said, showing he was still capable of human emotion.

"Alda, now you are not the boss around here. We've been through this a number of times." Groaker was hallucinating, his memories distorting his mind.

"How did you know that name!" Mr. Empty demanded, seizing him by the throat.

"Alda!" Groaker choked out, even though he didn't seem to realize he was being strangled.

"Stop calling me that!" Mr. Empty spat out, his already rusty voice sounding like the growl of a demon. "How did you know my name?"

"The desk told me! The desk! The desk!" Groaker replied, craving Yellow Shit.

Mr. Empty was about to yell again when his mind became clear. He kept a hold on Groaker, finally allowing him to lick his powdered hand. He began opening the drawers of the desk, noticing just how well-organized everything was. "No!" Groaker screamed, in between licks of his hand. "Inside the desk!" Mr. Empty continued to think clearly. He hated riddles, especially those forged by illusion-filled minds. But then he noticed something: the false bottom of the desk.

When he removed the false bottom from the drawer, he let Groaker go, allowing him to fall onto the ground, where he kept licking his hand, curling up like a baby with a bottle. Under the false bottom was a thick folder, its cover worn and discolored with age. The print on the front had faded somewhat, but he could read it clearly. Alda Sate, the name Mr. Empty had been born with. He hadn't seen this file since he was 15, when Dr. Umer had finally given up trying to help him and left the hospital. He flipped through it briefly, seeing the doctor's handwritten notes, as well as various drawings and statements Alda had made all those years ago. The folder contained the notes that spoke in detail about what the underworld looked like.

The notes brought a question to the tip of his tongue. Then a memory flashed in his mind, of the way Groaker had made the bed in his apartment. Groaker must have been an orderly at the hospital when Mr. Empty was living there. Many orderlies were fired for selling information about patients, and Groaker must have been among them. It all came to him now, like acid rain, burning away all hope that he'd once had. Groaker had no more true power than any of the other charlatans that had come before him.

Mr. Empty ripped the folder in half, throwing its contents across the floor, as though adding spice to a disgusting dish of corpses. He was furious; he would never get to the underworld at this rate. He heard Groaker crawl hurriedly across the floor. It seemed he had licked his hand dry. He was too consumed by the drugs to care about the half-dozen bodies, or the blood he was crawling through. He had to get back to that basement, to the Yellow Shit. As high as he was, he had still been able to recognize the light-green eyes of Alda Sate, for they were something that could never be forgotten.

Groaker was no longer of help to him, and Mr. Empty had wasted a lot of time just to figure that out. He could feel his hand grasp the handle of the garden shear; it was time to make an example out of Groaker. He managed to grab him by the ankle as the addict got halfway through the trap door into the basement. Mr. Empty dragged him out kicking and screaming, demanding that he be given more drugs. Mr. Empty liked the way he screamed and hoped he would hear a lot more of it before he was finished.

Mr. Empty was impressed with his own abilities to inflict pain. They were advanced enough that even with the Yellow Shit coursing through his veins, Groaker eventually began screaming in agony. When Mr. Empty was finished with Groaker, he looked like a shucked piece of bloody corn. It would take an expert to discover that the dismembered pieces were once a human being. Killing Groaker brought the masked man little satisfaction; he had been hoping to dine in the underworld on this night. Alas, his search would have to continue.

As he finished cleaning the garden shears of blood and organs, which took some time, he heard something from outside. Even without windows in the building, he could hear the awful chorus of drunken voices and chanting. It seemed the festival was on the move. Looking at his shears, he thought how wouldn't really mind cleaning them again. Besides, the night was still young. Maybe, just maybe, a massacre would lift his spirits.

Bogey
By
Jonathan D. Nichols

Hush, hush, hush, here comes the Bogeyman. Don't let him come too close to you ... he'll catch you if he can.

-Henry Hall

"When he comes, you're going to be sorry," said Trey to his little brother. "The bogeyman likes kids who are naughty."
Casey shook in fear at his brother's stories, especially when he looked at him with such sincerity.

"Shut up!" Casey yelled to his brother.

"He's coming. Halloween is in two days, and the Bogeyman takes kids away if they haven't been good."

"Leave me alone," the young child screamed, running to his room, where he felt safest.

"What's going on?" asked Jessica, the boy's older sister, who happened to walk in the room.

"He's trying to scare me," said Casey. "He keeps saying the bogeyman is going to take me away."

"He carries a sack with him to take away the bad kids," said Trey.

"Shut up," yelled Jessica. "Quit making him upset."

"Here comes the bogeyman," said Trey in an obnoxious spooky voice.

Jessica grabbed Trey and dragged him to his room. She was not the oldest child in the family, but she was used to taking charge in situations where altercations occurred between her two younger siblings. She slammed the bedroom door shut and whispered in a tone of seriousness; no matter how tough Trey acted, he knew when to be afraid.

"I know how long you have been working on that werewolf costume," she said. "I know that you want to go trick-or-treating with your friends. If you don't shut the hell up and stop scaring the crap out of Casey, I'm going to tell mom, and you'll be grounded."

Trey remained silent and stared at his sister. He knew she would not hesitate to follow through with her threats, and the last thing he wanted was to have his Halloween ruined. Anytime she told on him for his behavior, she managed to make the situation sound ten times worse than it actually was. He was always getting grounded. But tomorrow night, he wanted his freedom. He needed his freedom. He hated it when his sister got all bossy and authoritative on him. She was not the mom, and yet she insisted on acting like it. She walked out the door, leaving him in bed with his thoughts.

"I hope the bogeyman gets you," he said to Jessica, but not loud enough for her to hear.

That night, Trey dreamt of a figure entering his room. Not through the door, or even the window, but through the wall. It moved along the floor to his bed and stood over him, watching him sleep. It carried something large and bulky in one hand and leaned forward, inches from the boy's face, breathing heavily, almost growling.

Trey's eyes shot open, and he looked around. There was nothing there; no tall creature looking at him with unknown malicious intentions. He crawled out of bed and ran to the light switch next to his bedroom door and pushed it up. No response came from the bulb. Trey started to panic, hyperventilating. After a few seconds, the room burst with illumination. The boy ran to look under his bed for monsters. He did not find any. He hurried to his closet. Swinging the door open, he found his clothes hanging up, and his shoes lying disorganized on the floor. There was nothing else.

Trey kept the light on and lay in his bed for the remainder of the night. His eyes were wide open as he whispered to himself, staring upat the ceiling…

"Bogeyman."

***

Across the street, a man stepped out of his front door carrying a garbage bag to the trash can on the side of his house. The moon was nearly full, providing light in the midst of the black sky overhead. The man stopped, seeing someone standing beside the garbage can, his back turned to him. Whoever it was faced the corner where the house and the fence met.

"Hello?" the man stuttered out.

The person turned around, his features hidden by a hood pulled over his head. The man narrowed his eyes, trying to focus and see if he could recognize the stranger. Then the person descended upon him and the man was silenced before he could scream, but not before he saw the face of his attacker.

His heart would have stopped from fright had the stranger not killed him first. Seconds later, only one figure remained in the front of the house. The unknown assailant approached the front door and stepped inside.

***

The next day at school, Casey couldn't get the bogeyman out of his head. He asked the other students what their thoughts were on the subject.

"I hear he is a bad man who kills you in your sleep," said one girl.

"My cousin told me he takes bad kids away to torture them," said a young boy.

"Yeah," said Casey. "My stupid brother keeps telling me that he will take me away in a sack."

"The bogeyman is the bag-man," said a girl as she intruded upon their conversation.

She was several grades above Casey and he recognized her. She lived on his street a few houses away. Her name was Sarah.

"There are many legends, but most say that he takes naughty kids away in a sack to his land of evil ... so your brother was kind of right."

"Is he real?" asked Casey.

"Of course not," said the girl. "It is just a scary story to tell in order to make sure that kids behave."

"Are you sure?" Casey asked.

"Of course I am sure," she said. "Monsters aren't real; at least not the kind you are thinking of. Real monsters are evil people who do evil things, not mysterious creatures who serve no purpose, aside from causing you harm."

The bell rang. All students were summoned to their classes and the conversation ceased. Casey's brother was barely a year older than him, and he was a jerk; it was typical for him to tell stories just to scare the crap out of him.

"There is no bogeyman," Casey whispered to himself. He almost believed his words too, but there still remained a hint of doubt in his mind.

***

His mother picked him up from school early that day, and they stopped by the store to pick up some bags of candy for the trick-or-treating neighborhood kids. Over the radio, he heard a song that he did not recognize, but its words seemed to speak directly to him:

Children have you ever met the bogeyman before? No, of course you haven't. For you're much too good, I'm sure...

"There is no bogeyman," he repeated to himself.

When they pulled into the driveway, he looked over at his neighbor's house, where a younger boy named Paul lived. On the ground was a trash bag, torn open and the rubbish spread across the yard. Casey had a bad feeling about it, and despite his self-denial, he thought of the bogeyman again, and his hands began to shake.

He found himself unable to concentrate on his math homework. The entire time, his mind wandered to the mysterious legend of the man who takes kids away in his sack. Every once in a while, he would look out the window and see the leaves blowing in the autumn wind, their orange and red colors reminded him of dancing flames as they twirled and spun on their way to the ground.

The neighbors had put up decorations all over their houses: witches on the patios, spider webs spread across the windows, orange lights lined the roof tops. Casey smiled. It was Halloween, a time when you were supposed to feel at least a little scared. His brother had succeeded in putting him in a fearful mood. But now that he was looking upon the festivity within the decorations and imagining himself soon going to search for candy, he felt better. Bogeyman or not, he would enjoy Halloween.

***

After completing his homework, Casey picked up his handheld game console. He ignored the voices of people walking back and forth in the hallway, as well as his thoughts of the evil bag-man who tried to take away naughty kids.

"Casey, dinner time," said his oldest brother, Henry, at the bedroom door.

"Henry," he started, "Is there such thing as a bad man who takes away kids in a sack?"

"On Christmas?"

"No. I mean, the bogeyman."

"There is the anti-Santa in December," said Henry. "His name is Krampus, and he takes away the naughty kids. He could be the bogeyman, I guess."

"Does he come on Halloween?"

"Why, are you scared?" asked his eldest brother.

"No."

"Krampus is supposed to come on Christmas," said Henry. "But the bogeyman is anytime, so if they are the same thing, then sure. He could come on Halloween, but he probably prefers Christmas."

"What does he look like?"

"Like the devil," said Henry. "With horns and a long snake tongue."

***

That night, Casey entered the backyard after dark and climbed into the tree house. He shook the whole time, thinking about a bogeyman who looked like Satan, but he wanted to prove to himself that he had nothing to fear. He stepped up each gradation of the ladder, listening to the grass in the wind and the crickets in the distance.

Tomorrow night, the tree house would be off limits. Trey used it every year to tell scary stories with his friends before they went trick-or-treating. They called it their "tree house of horror." A title they stole from The Simpsons. And Casey wasn't invited.

He held a flashlight and climbed trembled with each grip he made on the rungs of the ladder. He peered into the entrance of the tree house, pointing the beam of the light inside. Casey gasped at first when he thought he saw a tall creature with horns staring at him, but exhaled a sigh of relief once he recognized it as nothing more than a tree branch at the tree house window.

The wood creaked with each step, making him more nervous. He gazed out into the neighborhood, able to see many of the homes on his street. The lights in the windows across from his house were darkened, and the car rested in the driveway. The garbage remained on the grass, and Casey wondered if anybody was home at all, and why they had left the mess like that.

"Well, bogeyman," said Casey in a loud voice. "Krampus, or whatever your name is, if you are real, come and get me."

He waited for a response, as proof that his fears were unsubstantiated. The wind blew again; there was nothing inside the tree house except for the young boy.

"Come and get me, Krampus," Casey said again, louder this time. He couldn't see anything out of the ordinary with his flashlight. It was dark. It was chilly. But there was no sign of the bogeyman.

"I knew it," said Casey.

He climbed out of the tree house, slightly relieved, but still scared that the evil creature would grab his foot and pull him. Nothing happened. He walked back towards the house; his footsteps on the concrete patio were loud enough to obscure the whispers coming from a figure hiding in the shadows and darkness.

"Not yet."

***

"It's so gross! You're dating a girl with the same name as your sister," said Jessica.

"It's a popular name," retorted Henry. "Better than 'Chuck.'. It sounds like up-chuck."

"Just hurry up and get out of the bathroom so I can put on my makeup."

While they bickered and attempted to get ready for their night out, Trey did his own preparation by dressing as a werewolf in a costume Casey thought was pretty terrifying. He hoped it would frighten his best friend, Jack, who was already sort of a scaredy-cat.

Casey was going as a superhero, and the more he thought about it, the better of a choice he believed it to be. Maybe he would actually gain superpowers tonight if the bogeyman did dare to show his face. He grabbed his small pocketknife out of his drawer and placed it in his pocket, just in case. As he pushed the drawer shut, he hesitated, and reached inside. There was a small container of cardboard matches he had found a while back, half of which were missing. Casey inserted these into his pocket as well.

All members of the family left at the same time. Trey joined his friends in the tree house before going trick-or-treating. Henry left to join his girlfriend and her mother to attend a town wide Halloween festival. Casey joined his friend, John, whose mother would take the two of them door to door on their candy excursion.

At first, Casey didn't feel afraid at all. He laughed and grew excited at the treats accumulating in his bag. It wasn't until they approached the residence across the street—the one with the garbage bag still lying in the grass—that his fears returned. As they approached the house, the porch light conveniently seemed to illuminate as though sensing their presence. John immediately headed for the door.

"Let's skip this house," said Casey.

"Why?"

"I don't know," he said. "Their light was out just a minute ago. They probably don't have any candy."

"Might as well try," John said, continuing forward with Casey and his mother following close behind him.

They rang the doorbell. The porch light went out, and the door opened. Standing inside was the very thing Casey had imagined and feared since his older brother had provided a description of the infamous bag-man. John laughed at the look of what he assumed was an elaborate costume.

The man stepped forward, raised a large burlap sack above his head and swept the opening over the unsuspecting mother. It draped down to the woman's ankles. Placing his hand on her head, he slammed her cranium into the side of the house and silenced her before she could finish her scream. Lifting the woman, he flipped her upside down and began shaking the huge bag so the body would fall inside completely. John shrieked, but not before the man reached down, grabbed the child by his ankle, and lifted him into the air. He opened the bag, which now seemed empty, and stuffed the boy inside, headfirst. The bogeyman slung the sack over his shoulder. John struggled and emitted muffled screams.

Casey shook where he stood. Urine dripped along the side of his leg, creating a puddle around his feet.

The horned man smiled, sliding his long, forked tongue from his mouth as he did so. His grin disappeared as he became annoyed by the struggling child in the bag over his shoulder. He swung the sack hard against the side of the house, making a sickening crack. John stopped moving inside. Casey screamed and fled, so scared he didn't know what to think, or say, or do. He just ran in whatever direction he could move in.

He turned and darted between houses, crashing directly into a firmly planted figure. The bogeyman stood in front of him, blocking his way. The creature grabbed the boy's arm and lifted him into the air.

"Why do you want me?" asked Casey, tears streaking his cheeks. "I am not naughty."

"This is true, young one," he said. "Your two brothers are troublemakers, your sister is something of a whore, and you are very well behaved in comparison."

Casey wailed, so frightened of dying, of being alone with this monster. He repeated the same words over and over between sobs...

"I'm not naughty, I'm good! I'm not naughty, I'm good!"

The bogeyman emitted a breath, which sounded like a sigh. Pressing the child against the side of the house, he held Casey still, not hurting him, but ensuring he couldn't escape.

"In the season of the feast of lights," began Krampus in an eerie, inhuman voice. "I am limited to those children whom Sinter Klass deems unworthy of gifts. On this night, I am known as what you call böggel-mann, and I am free."

"Why me?" said the boy, weeping.

"I merely like fear," Krampus continued. "You believe in me. You are afraid. I like that. I find it ... revitalizing."

The bogeyman began to laugh, and Casey snapped out of his terror that had been hypnotizing him. He might have been against the house with his feet hanging in the air, but his hands were free. He reached into his pocket with a sudden burst of courage, and pulled the knife out. Slashing at Krampus's hand, he noticed that the blade didn't break the skin. It sent sparks flying like it had sliced against flint, but the creature was surprised, despite the lack of injury. He released Casey in his shock, and the boy ran from the house. He ran from the man with horns. He didn't dare to look behind him, but he knew that something was in pursuit.

Overhead street lamps and the full moon lit up the neighborhood that was filled with children who wandering from house to house. It should have been the bogeyman's dream come true. Yet, the horned, bag-carrying bastard was nowhere to be seen. Casey ran through the streets, peering down sidewalks, not even sure what he was looking for. He wanted a sanctuary; he needed a place where he could be safe, but he did not know where this place would be.

Every time he passed a dark corner, he thought he saw a horned figure staring out at him. At first, he wondered if it was his imagination, until he turned up Marshall Street and peered between two houses. Krampus stood in the shadows, holding out a bag in his direction. The creature pointed inside the sack, and smiled. Then, he seemed to dissolve into the darkness.

With his head turned and not looking forward, Casey crashed into someone and knocked her off her feet. When he looked at her, he recognized her after the red cloak and the hood had just fallen off her head.

"Sarah," he said. "He's real. You were wrong. The bogeyman is real."

The older girl's friends who were there giggled at the boy's words.

"It's Casey, right?" asked Sarah as she stood up.

"Stop laughing," the boy shouted through his tears at the other girls. "He killed my friend!"

All laughing ceased.

"Are you serious?" one of the girls asked.

"Who?" asked another girl.

Casey mumbled something.

"What?" asked Sarah.

"His name is Krampus," whispered Casey.

The overhead streetlights began to flicker, and then went black. All the patio lights extinguished themselves as well. Clouds overhead obscured the full moon, and Krampus stepped forth from the shadows. In his left hand was the large brown sack, and his empty right hand kept wiggling its fingers, tauntingly, as though they were ready to grab the first child they could reach. All four of the girls screamed. The bogeyman's mouth opened, and a long tongue protruded. It pointed back and forth at each girl, as if deciding which one would be first. Sarah gasped.

"You were right," she said. "That's not a costume. The tongue is real. It's him."

They took off running. Krampus chased the children, and the slowest one, a fifth grader dressed as a princess, screamed as he grabbed her. Casey glanced back as he ran and saw the bogeyman stuff the girl into his bag. He had seen John's mother disappear. Either that bag dissolved her like acid, or it transported her someplace he didn't even want to think of. And John was gone now too.

"Heather!" screamed Sarah.

Another young boy dressed as a vampire ran past them in the opposite direction.

"Wait," yelled Casey. "Don't go that way."

The boy either didn't notice the tall man, or he did not care. Krampus turned his head, watching the boy run, but then he turned back to Casey. He pointed at him, no longer smiling. There was no distracting this creature. He had one focus this night. If nothing else, he would have Casey.

The children turned a corner onto a street that was still illuminated. Houses were decorated with strings of orange lights, and among them all was a floodlight in someone's driveway, like a white beacon amidst all the orange. As their feet thumped on the concrete while running past houses, Casey noted the absence of feet in pursuit.

"He's gone," the boy called out as he glanced behind them. All four children stopped to catch their breath. One of the girls stood next to a car parked on the side of the curb. No one thought anything of it until they heard a scream and watched her get swept beneath the vehicle, into the darkness and the shadows. The was automobile lifted into the air, falling over on its side, as the bogeyman stood to his feet, out from behind it. He faded away like dark smoke dissipating into the air.

Casey realized something with a start. Despite his fear and his young mind, he had a moment of clarity. The bogeyman likes to hide in the shadows of kid's closets and beneath their beds.

"The light," shouted Casey, pointing at the house with the white floodlight. "Get to that house. Stand in the light."

The orange bulbs on the strings of lights streaming along the edges of the roofs began to burst; one at a time. It started at the furthest house and moved quickly to the next. A canopy of darkness traveled towards them.

On the opposite end of the street, the same thing happened. Lights burst and small shards of glass fell to the ground from each bulb. Other children who walked the streets screamed in surprise. None of them had a clue what was happening or the cause of it, but Casey knew. They were being cornered, trapped.

He kept running with the two girls, until they stood in the brightened yard. Casey stared at the large floodlight. He watched it shudder and shake. With all the other lights gone, this was the one thing keeping Krampus from getting to them. Then the huge bulb above them exploded and they were in darkness once again.

Krampus materialized before them. He reached for Sarah.

"Stop!" shouted Casey. "Let them go. Take me. I'm the one you want."

Krampus laughed loudly, his booming voice rattling the windows of cars in nearby driveways.

"Run," said Casey to the two girls. They darted away, and Casey remained stationary in front of the evil bogeyman who looked like the Devil himself. Krampus gripped the front of the boy's shirt and lifted him so the two of them were eye level. He stared into Casey's eyes.

"You little fool," he said. "You cannot stop me from taking them, too."

Casey felt himself falling as he was dropped into the bogey-man's sack. But Casey knew something was terribly wrong. Searing pain started at his feet. Casey ran his fingers along the side of the bag. While the material felt like cloth, it was as hard as concrete. Casey reached down to his legs, where the pain had reached his knees. Nothing was there, but he was fading away, like Krampus had done in the light.

Where would he end up? He did not want to know.

In a last ditch attempt, Casey grabbed the matches from his pocket, and tore one from the package. Swiping the end of the stick along the rough strip, it burst into flame. He held the burning stick to the ends of the other matches, and the entire cardboard pack lit up like a small torch. Casey dropped them and felt the burning catch onto the sides of the bag, onto his clothes and his costume. In the horrifying pain of the fire, the boy knew he was going to die.

***

Heather screamed as she turned back and watched the flaming bag in the bogeyman's hand. The fire caught onto the beast's arm and quickly spread to its torso, legs, and head. The bogeyman roared as he stood in her yard like a flaming wicker man. The ground began to shake, and then, in what looked like a dark surge of energy shooting into the sky, the bogeyman disappeared. On the ground, lying in a fetal position lay Casey, his clothes singed, but his body completely unscathed.

***

The white snow fell to the ground in light flakes. It was the first snow of the season. The day was December 4th, a few weeks until the traditional date of Christmas, but only a couple of days before Saint Nicholas Day. Casey hid in the shadows, watching.

What he wanted, what he truly wanted, was forbidden. His life was changed and no longer what he had imagined it to be. Casey wanted revenge, and he would never be able to have this.

Casey wondered if anybody in his family ever noticed the difference in him, and if so, how had they reacted? As he stared into the window, he saw his old face, sleeping peacefully.

The boy would never be afraid of Krampus. He knew he was safe. With a sigh, Casey stood to his feet, the weight from the horns on his head still an adjustment he was not used to.

Another holiday was finally almost upon him. In two nights, he would begin his work. He would capture the naughty kids and place them in his sack. While this was a task he had not wished to perform at first, he was now feeling more excited about it.

Something unexpected happened with the flames when he was in that sack. The bag was Krampus's source of power. With its destruction came his defeat, or his freedom. But there has to be a Krampus. Somebody had to take the job, whether they wanted to or not.

Casey faded into the darkness with a smile on his face. The small bits of his humanity still tried to fight their way through sometimes. But he knew that over time, the feelings of remorse and sympathy for others would disappear completely. He was adopting his new role as the bogeyman, and the closer his night came, the more excited he grew.

***

Fear grows in darkness; if you think there's a bogeyman around, turn on the light.

-Dorothy Thompson

Domenica
By
Kay Brooks

Spoken words in December of 1813:

"Don't go too far ahead. Remember the little girl who didn't hold her mummy's hand when she was asked? She was about your age when she disappeared..."

..."This is the worst mutilation case I have ever seen. Whoever did this was a monster!"

..."Where are my daughter's eyes? What have they done to her eyes?"

..."I just can't seem to take it in. All I ever wanted was for her to go to school and grow up like any other girl..."

December 2013:

"Who does she think she is, wearing sunglasses inside? Some kind of celebrity or something? She isn't even pretty for God's sake."

"Maybe she's blind, Carly! Or she could be one of those albino people. You know? The ones with red eyes."

"She has black hair, Gemma. Albinos have white hair and if she's blind, where's her white stick? Where's her guide dog? And what kind of name is Domenica anyway? Her mother probably made it up. A freak name to match her freak daughter."

***

Domenica didn't want to return to high school again. It was all her mother had wanted for her though. So she kept trying, hoping the result would be different. Was that not the very definition of madness? Domenica knew her name may be different and the walls may be painted a different colour, but all high schools were intrinsically the same. They all had cliques to which she would not be invited. They all had a group of popular girls who entertained themselves by destroying the self-esteem of others, and they all had the unbelievably good-looking boys who lusted after them. These said boys were now swaggering past Domenica's table, picking up chairs without asking, regardless of whether there was food sat before the chair or not, and sliding over to join Carly's glamorous gaggle.

"Hi, Scott," crooned Carly.

"Ladies!" he greeted. "What are you talking about?"

Carly nodded deliberately and indiscreetly towards Domenica, who stared right back.

"Freak," he spat. "She was in our math class this morning. What are the glasses all about? Can she actually see?"

The girls shrugged in response.

"Scott," another boy at the table nudged him, his face displaying a sly smile. "Let's have some fun with her."

"What've you got in mind, Martin?"

"I think it's time to make friends with the freak."

The girls all shrieked and clapped their hands with glee, exactly the reaction Martin had been hoping for. This was what they lived for: other people's misery. It was how a person got into the popular circle. By being cruel and creating fear.

"Go on then," Scott nudged Martin.

"What? No, I thought you..."

"It was your idea, genius," Carly said, fluttering her eyelashes at him. "Why not take credit for it?"

Martin turned around to look at Domenica, who stubbornly remained facing in the same direction. He took in her black jumper with a lace collar, her gold locket that may or may not be a genuine antique, the drawn, colourless cheekbones and lastly, the pitch black lenses that covered her eyes. He found himself wondering what colour they were behind the shades and what she would look like if she sat in the sun for a while. Or maybe smiled. He realized her face had tilted, and though he didn't know for sure, it felt like she was looking right at him, almost daring him to approach.

"What if she's deaf as well as blind?" Martin whispered, desperate to break the connection with her.

"She's not deaf, you idiot. If she was deaf, she'd use sign language like Gwendolyn in the year below. Are you chicken, Marty?"

The thought of taking Carly's ridicule until she tired of it was far more worrisome than speaking to a creepy girl with sunglasses on.

As he walked over to her table, her head followed his movement. Whatever the glasses were for, they weren't to cover unseeing eyes. He slid onto the one stool that remained at her table and gave her what he hoped was his most genuine, winning grin. She remained impassive.

"Hi. On behalf of Rigley High, I wanted to welcome you to our glorious school. My name is Martin Cross and I hope that you will be very, very happy here." Titters erupted from the table behind him. They filled him with courage and he extended his hand for her to shake.

Domenica slid her plate to one side and leaned slightly forward, as though examining him.

"Is there something wrong with your hearing as well as your eyes?" he asked. The titters grew into laughter, spurring him on. "Or are you just fucking rude?"

Slowly, Domenica lifted one hand. Martin stared at the slender, white fingers as though hypnotised. The nails, which were the same colour as her pallid skin, were shaped into a point, reminding him of the Tennyson poem they had been reading in English about an eagle's talons. One extended and motioned for him to move forwards. He was aware that he had the full attention of Carly and the rest of his peers who he aimed to impress on a daily basis.

"The freak wants to get cosy, Marty!" Carly shrieked.

He noticed that the girl before him didn't respond to Carly's taunt. Instead, she moved her finger as though pulling him towards her more urgently.

"Hey, everyone wants a bit of Marty!" He leaned in, moving closer until there was less than a centimetre between them.

Domenica then drew even nearer, so he could feel her moist breath on his face. The smell reminded him of fallen autumn leaves. She lifted one of her hands to her sunglasses and gently pulled them down close to the end of her nose.

It all happened within seconds. Domenica got up from the table, picked up her satchel and walked away. The dining students leapt from their seats and formed a noisy, inquisitive circle around Martin Cross, who lay on the floor, his eyes wide open, his chest convulsing, completely unresponsive. Teaching staff on duty hurried over to assist. One staff member had seen most of the bullying aimed at Domenica, but had chosen out of laziness and a hatred for filling in incident forms to turn a blind eye. Martin began to regurgitate and choke on his lunch. The canteen was emptied. An ambulance was called.

Reluctantly returning to school the next day, Domenica was greeted with stares as usual, but now they were filled with fear.

Carly was surrounded by her usual admirers and a couple of extra hangers-on who were desperate to hear her retell the story about Martin.

"He had a fit, right there on the floor in front of us and there..." Her voice trailed off as she saw Domenica walking towards the doors. Carly had always felt braver when there was a crowd around her. She had carefully engineered it so that being surrounded was the norm; she was rarely alone. Even at night, her bedroom door remained open and she still used the same plug-in nightlight she had been given as a young girl when the night terrors that continued to torment her began.

Last night had been worse than usual. Carly had awoken to her father wrestling her arms on to the mattress as she tore at her own face to stop a masked man from taking her eyes. Her parents had been told she would grow out of the night terrors. Stress made them far worse.

The memory of last night's terrors only made her angrier as she elbowed her way to the front of her audience, blocking Domenica from entering the building.

"Hey, bitch, what did you do to Martin?"

Domenica stopped impassively before her as though she was simply joining a queue in a supermarket.

"Do you know he could have died? He nearly choked on his tongue. Mrs Farrier had to pull it out of his throat." She stepped back and looked Domenica up and down.

Rumours going around said that Carly had a punch as powerful as any man, but the truth was, she had never been tried. Girls were intimidated by her beauty and bravado. They naturally allowed her the spot at the top of the pecking order. Now, she was unsure. This girl did not appear to be afraid of her at all. She appeared completely unflustered. The crowd that gathered exchanged unsure glances.

"Mr. Walters is coming," a voice whispered.

Everyone, including Carly, started to dissipate, clearing Domenica's path. Mr. Walter, the strict and proud headmaster of Rigley High, would not tolerate any form of drama. He held the belief that children were there to be educated first and socialisation was second. He enforced his code by a strict punishment system. They were the only school in the entire county that had full day detentions take place on a Saturday. As such, the behaviour was good and the reputation outstanding. Carly knew that Mr. Walters would do anything to keep it that way. Having a swipe at some bitch was not worth keeping her away from the nail salon that weekend. Her acrylics were chipping.

Recognizing the painfully shy girl who had attempted to sit with her the previous day, the one who had whispered the warning, Domenica muttered a thank you as she walked past. Erin Platt debated over whether to catch up to the new girl and try again to make friendly contact but, though it had indeed been Erin who whispered of Mr. Walters' fictional approach, she could not help but be afraid of the icily aloof girl.

Domenica didn't make an appearance in the canteen that day or the next. She attended classes as normal, but made no attempt to join the other students during break or lunch times. Instead, she found a corner in the library where she sat completing homework tasks and studying. Nobody questioned her sight capabilities now, but everyone talked about what lay behind the dark lenses. Although there were many rumours ranging from her being capable of hypnotising a person into a state of medical distress to her having laser-eye powers like Superman. One thing everyone agreed on was that Domenica Sable was abnormal.

Being used to marginalisation, Domenica was not surprised when a curious teacher approached her under the guise of being concerned. The middle-aged woman, who clearly needed to learn how to dress appropriately for her age, tottered over in her three inch heels and short pencil skirt.

"Miss Sable, I wondered whether I could have a word?"

Domenica kicked the opposite chair out from under the table and nodded for the teacher to take a seat. She wondered whether it would be appropriate to tell her she had red lipstick on her yellow-from-too-many-cigarette-breaks teeth.

"I was just wondering how you were settling in?"

"Fine, Miss Shore." Domenica's voice was raspy and quiet.

"It's just, you don't seem to be making many friends. I mean, after the Martin Cross incident, it must be difficult—"

Domenica held her hand up to stop the woman speaking and shook her head.

"No, hear me out." Miss Shore said.

Domenica's hands rose to her glasses, holding the arms firmly.

"Epilepsy can strike at any age, my dear." She reached out and touched Domenica's raised hand softly. "I know it must have been scary for you, but Martin will be fine. He should be back at school next week." The teacher withdrew her hand and smiled softly before continuing. "I just wanted you to know I'm here for you, should you want to talk, ok?"

Domenica looked at Miss Shore's face, taking in the heavily rouged cheeks and extended eyelashes, reassessing the teacher's motives.

"Thank you," she rasped and looked back down at her science journal.

Miss Shore tottered away, her concerns far from allayed. The girl was strange, there was no doubt about it, but there was something vulnerable about her. Miss Shore had heard the cruel comments made in the corridors by both the students and the teaching staff, who should know better but didn't. Miss Shore was no stranger to verbal cruelty, having overheard the "mutton dressed as lamb" and "old slapper" comments one too many times while walking into the lady's toilets. She knew it was difficult to be the different one. It was far too challenging to be accepting and far too easy to hate. She stalked down the corridor and stepped into the airless staffroom, took a seat in the corner and pulled out her lunch to eat alone, again.

***

The morning Martin Cross was due to arrive back at school, students gathered on the front field, waiting for him to arrive. They wanted him to put an end to the speculation and tell them what was truly behind Domenica Sable's dark sunglasses.

Carly was the first one to accost him, determined to do maximum damage to any shred of reputation that Domenica had left. She linked her arm through his as he climbed weakly from the passenger seat of his mother's car.

"Don't worry, Mrs Cross, I'll look after Marty," she assured the nervous looking woman, who sunk back into her seat and drove away. "Wow, Marty, you look like shit."

He smiled faintly.

Crowds of students moved out of their way as she led him up to the doors of Rigley High. Once there was a large enough gap between them and the other students, she leaned in and asked, "What did Domenica do to you?"

"Nothing," he stammered, pulling his arm free from hers. "I had a fit, Carly. An epileptic fit. That's all. Leave me alone."

She stood incredulous as he walked away, joining the others heading into classrooms. Nobody spoke to Carly that way and got away with it. She took a deep breath and turned, grateful that nobody had seen her get snubbed by a worm like Martin Cross.

A moving shadow caught her eye. Domenica moved forward and circled around her. A small smile danced on her pale lips and Carly felt a shiver a fear down her spine. "Move!" she squawked, unable to hide her nerves.

Where was Gemma and the rest of her back up?

"If you want to know the truth, Carly, ask me."

Carly winced at the sound of her voice, reminding her of metal scraping against metal. Her breath smelt of damp ground and made Carly want to heave. She maneuvered around the ashen girl, making sure she didn't make contact, and scurried off down the corridor.

***

The canteen was packed as usual. Strangely, there were two tables only occupied by one person now. Domenica Sable and Martin Cross. Martin rebuffed all attempts from his peers to join them. Domenica sat in silence, taking in the action around her.

"What's the matter with you, Carly? You're acting strange," Gemma said. "Is it to do with Martin coming back?"

"Do you think epilepsy can change someone's personality?" Carly asked.

Scott laughed and received a glare for it.

"My Aunt Judy has epilepsy and my mum said she used to get really anxious when she was little. Is that what you mean?" Gemma added.

Carly wasn't listening. She staring at Martin. The notion that she was being monitored just as intently overwhelmed her and she turned to find Domenica's hidden gaze facing her. She got up from the table and left the canteen, leaving behind an untouched salad and sealed can of Pepsi.

Five minutes before the end of school bell was due to sound, Carly covered her mouth with one hand and raised the other.

"Problem, Carly?" Mr. Rowe asked.

"I feel sick," she cried. "Please can I go to the toilet?" He looked unconvinced but, just as Carly had hoped, he simply couldn't be bothered with any aggro.

"Yes, you may go. Take your things with you, in case you don't make it back before the bell."

Carly left the classroom, walked past the toilets, out of the unsecured front doors and sat down behind the steps where she could not be seen. She waited for the loud bell and for Domenica to leave the building.

At least ten minutes after all the students left for the day, Martin Cross walked down the steps and wandered towards the school crossing. He got into his mother's car parked across the street, and then drove off.

Carly glanced at her watch. Maybe Domenica had gotten detention. Unlikely though, Carly thought. The girl didn't speak enough to get herself into any bother. Just as she was about to give up and head home, Domenica descended the steps. Carly saw the pale green socks underneath her bulky, black shoes. She was the biggest freak Carly had ever come across and she was determined to find out what her game was.

After waiting for Domenica to cross the street, she followed at a safe distance. There were no more cars waiting to pick students up; Martin's understandably protective mother had been the last. Carly followed Domenica past the huge Georgian properties lining Rigley Street, past the smaller, semi-detached abodes, through the council estate, where she normally wouldn't tread for fear of being seen by some of Rigley's poorer students, and towards the woods at the bottom. The houses became more unkempt as they neared the woods.

Carly had been told stories about children going missing there when she was little. Her mother always said, "There was a little girl your age who went missing because she didn't hold on to her mummy's hand tight enough!"

Back then, it had put the fear of God in to her, but now she recognised it as a mother's tactic to keep her child from straying. Everyone she knew had been told the same story to keep them close by. Still, the sight of the tree, now bare from leaves in winter, made her wrap her coat around her chest tighter. She watched as Domenica opened the rusty gate and stepped through, continuing without a care in to the forest.

Carly's feet sunk into the mud as she stepped after the freaky girl. She looked down to judge how far her shoes had sunken. But when she looked up, Domenica had disappeared.

"What a waste of time!" Carly grumbled then, took a few steps further into the midst of trees, but the immediate woodland was deserted. Turning around, intending to head back, Carly was met with a shock.

The gate had disappeared, as had the dilapidated housing.

All that laid before her was trees. All behind her was trees. She twirled around, trying to get her bearing, but there were just trees with branches so close together they blocked out the bright winter sun.

Panicking, Carly pulled out her phone and dialled her home number. She waited for it to ring. It didn't. She looked at the screen and found no signal. Surely, she thought trying to be rational, if I head backwards, I will reach the gate again. This couldn't really be happening. She must've walked further than I'd imagined!

Though she knew that was impossible, there were no other explanations.

***

Half an hour passed. The air was chilled and Carly's feet were wet from the deep, damp mud. Goose-bumps covered her body and she was no closer to finding her way out.

Putting aside her pride, she shouted, "Hello? Anyone there? I'm lost."

A few birds flew from the branches, startled by her cry. Then there was silence. Carly looked up. A gloomy grey sky poked through the sparse, high branches. Had it really gone so dark in such a short span of time?

She pulled out her phone again, praying for a signal. Still none. Though the time caught her eye, causing her to a double-take. She left school at a quarter to four, and yet her phone stated it was half past eleven.

That couldn't be. She struggled to swallow the frantic feeling overtaking her body and lost the fight. Throwing her head back, she screamed as loud as she could. Nothing for a while and then there was the sound of a twig snapping.

"Domenica? Domenica, is that you?" she whispered. "Please, if it's you, help me."

"Why did you follow me?" The dry rasp seemed to come from above, in the branches of the trees. Carly looked up but saw no-one.

"I'm sorry, okay? Where are you?"

She saw the bare feet first, mottled green and brown, padding against the damp mud. Then spindly calves, bruised skin clinging to the barely concealed bone. One knee had split open, revealing grey hardness beneath. The other knee reminded Carly of a golf ball. The naked thighs were no wider than Carly's own wrists, seemingly incapable of supporting the weight of a teenage girl.

Carly looked away, afraid of what she might see if she looked higher.

"What's wrong, Carly? I thought you wanted to know."

Carly squeezed her eyes shut tighter. "What's wrong with you, Domenica? What's happened to you?"

There came a throaty laugh. Carly pinched herself hard and blinked. The skeletal girl still stood before her, naked and unashamed. Where the girl's breasts should have been were two gaping holes. Carly gagged and threw up bile from her stomach.

"Come on, Carly. There's more to see yet. Don't you want to see for yourself?"

"No," Carly cried. "I just want to go home." Tears of fear and humiliation at acknowledging how pathetic she sounded rolled down her cheek bones. She jerked sideways as she was hit by a pair of sunglasses. Picking them up, she stared at them. "Domenica, I'm sorry. Just, please leave me alone now."

"Are you sure that's what you want? I thought you wanted to look behind the glasses."

Rather than look at her, Carly squeezed her eyes shut. The sound of her heart beating was like thunder in her ears. She shook with fear, realizing that whatever Domenica was, she wasn't human.

"Maybe I can help you," she suggested in desperation.

Domenica laughed.

"I had one year to go," she growled. "You could have helped me by leaving me alone!"

Carly felt Domenica move closer to her. No warmth came off her but her presence was overwhelming. Terror filled Carly at the thought of being touched by the ghastly girl and instinctively opened her eyes to see where she was and was met by her stare.

Two dark caverns faced Carly. Rotten stringy flesh that once held the eyes in position dangled over the green-rimmed edges. Carly fell to the cold, dank ground and stayed there for what felt like an eternity, too afraid to open her eyes for fear of what else she might see, but Domenica taunted her no more.

The freezing night air overtook Carly's senses.

***

"She's here!" came a shout, breaking into the black swirls of hair, surrounding dark sunglasses.

Carly opened her eyes. White sky was above her and then the concerned face of a man she didn't recognise peered down at her.

"This is the girl from the picture!" he shouted behind him. The man took his coat off and put it over the shivering girl lying before him. "It's ok, Carly. Help is on the way." He tucked the coat beneath her and pushed the hair away from her face. He was sure she had been blonde on the photo passed around in a growing fit of hysteria last evening.

Right now, it was so muddy he couldn't tell what colour it was. Shouts came from behind him. The voices seemed jumbled and Carly couldn't separate the words to make any sense from them.

"Ambulance…"

"Parents…"

"Disappearance…"

"Murder…"

It would be a while before anything made any sense to Carly again.

***

When Carly returned to Rigley High, she was different. The other students that crowded around to welcome the school's princess knew how different she was as soon as she stepped out of her mother's car.

The girl who had been known for her good-looks and confidence was gone. In her place, was a hunched-shouldered mute with grey hair, wearing a gold locket that may, or may not, be a genuine antique.

How the changes happened, nobody knew. Nobody had seen her journey down to the woods, and she hadn't told anybody that she was going there. Some people speculated about what had happened to her. Perhaps she had been going to meet an older boy who she knew her parents wouldn't approve of and he had attacked her, or maybe she had got hold of some illegal drugs and gone to experiment.

Her close friends knew differently. Carly couldn't have kept her mouth shut about an older boyfriend and she was anti-drugs, allowing her to look down on the students that did experiment. Gemma, Scott, and her other admirers were as desperate to find out the truth as she had been when Martin returned.

***

Carly wasn't surprised when her friends gave up pursuing gossip from her. They soon ditched her when they realised she wasn't "fun" anymore. Carly had seen several different therapists over her time recovering at home; none had been able to reach her.

Since being found in the woods, Carly spent her time staring at whatever was in front of her and being forced to eat soup by her mother. It was only when she had overheard her parents speaking that she moved without insistence from others.

Her mother said, "I just want her to go to school and grow up like any other girl."

The words had echoed in Carly's head several times before she stood and went to find her Rigley High uniform. Life would never be the same, but at least she had one. Some weren't that lucky.

Carly spent most of her lunchtimes sitting with Erin Pratt at a corner table, away from the hustle of student life. Erin was surprisingly soothing company and a loyal friend too. Just what the new Carly needed.

Soon Martin joined their small group. He didn't need to say anything. Carly knew by looking at him the knowledge they shared tied them together.

***

Domenica didn't return to Rigley High, and when the teachers were asked by their students, they had no explanation. The girl had vanished. The school office sent letters to the address given to them when Domenica Sable enrolled; all were sent back with "return to sender" stamped on them.

The Family Liaison Officer attempted to visit the house but found that it didn't exist. He was later informed by the Land Registry Office the address hadn't existed for over two hundred years. The street had once existed alongside the woodlands, down by the council estate, but after a young girl had gone missing and her body found horrifically mutilated, they determined that their own offspring should not meet the same tragic fate. People moved. Though a huge manhunt had been initiated, with all of the surrounding land scoured with fervour, no culprit was ever found.

Whoever had murdered the young girl had gotten away with it, and no-one was above suspicion. Eventually, the feeling of safety in numbers and the value of community disintegrated. People no longer trusted their neighbours. The houses were demolished, and the forest spread over the land.

For many years, no-one spoke the girl's name for fear their own daughters might be cursed to the same fate. By the time the legends about the murdered girl started to circulate, her name had been forgotten. All that remained were stories of a girl who was found mutilated with gouged voids where her eyes had once been. Rumour was that every so often, the girl would rise and attempt to repent for not holding her mother's hand tight enough by going to school and growing up like any normal girl should.

Queen Zombie
By
Elenore Audley

Levi Colton tapped his keyboard impatiently, each time striking the delete key with more force. Another error message blinked in his face. He felt his temperature rising. His neck tie suddenly felt too tight. He rubbed the back of his tense neck, glaring at the dull screen in front of him.

Years ago, Levi worked as an undercover cop, specializing in inner city drug and prostitution crime busts. It was bloody business. When he found himself in the crossfire one chilly December night with three shots to his side in a close scrape with death, Nancy insisted he find another profession. A desk job never felt right to him, but it kept him coming home to his family every night.

"Levi?" a female voice startled him out of his thoughts. It was just Susan, the secretary. "Mr. Salinas wants to see you in his office."

Almost grateful for the reprieve, Levi swiveled around in his chair and walked briskly through the maze of cubicles across the office floor and knocked on the manager's door. A voice from within said, "Come in."

"Ah, Levi," Mr. Salinas rose from his glass-top, cherry wood desk. He was a Latino man, about thirty years old. Deep down, Levi always resented him for being six years his junior and head of the department. "So soon … please, have a seat."

The mood in the room was not what Levi expected, and he awkwardly sat down in front of Mr. Salinas. His flat screen TV was mounted on the wall, silently displaying the news about the number of bizarre hospital deaths mysteriously rising in the area.

"As you know," Mr. Salinas began, folding his hands in front of him diplomatically. "The bid for Regent and Company did not fare well, and we lost that opportunity. It was supposed to be the deal that would, in a lot of ways, save our proverbial ship. The recession hasn't been kind to us."

A knot tightened in Levi's stomach and he could feel his toes inside his tasseled dress shoes begin to curl.

"As a result of this loss, in order to maintain high standards to our clientele, we'll have to make some changes and cutbacks to the department."

"Anything I can do to help." Levi forced a stiff nod and a cooperative smile that seemed to freeze when he saw Mr. Salinas' hand reach for a drawer to his left.

"I've always appreciated your team player attitude Levi. I don't know how to say this. Unfortunately, your position here must be eliminated."

He slid a white envelope towards Levi, bearing the printed company logo. Mr. Salinas gave a few brief words about its contents, but Levi heard very little because his mind was racing. There was something about a severance offer and more appreciative talk. Without saying a word, Levi snatched up the envelope and took his leave.

"You take care, Levi." Mr. Salinas called out behind him. "The flu season is a killer this year."

Levi found himself at his cubicle, trying to decide what to do first. He heard something to his left and turned to see Susan standing there, holding a white empty box with a lid. She wore a tight-lipped, empathetic smile.

"Thought you might need something like this." She set it down then shrugged uncomfortably as her perfectly golden, wavy hair bounced on her shoulders. She tried to smile reassuringly again, and then walked away.

As Levi carried his professional remains to his car, his cell phone chimed in his coat pocket. Slamming the box down on the trunk of his burgundy sedan, he checked his messages.

"Don't forget."

"Dammit!" Levi seethed. It was their anniversary. He had remembered that morning, but after getting laid off, he'd completely forgotten all about it, and now remained the question of when and how to tell Nancy that he lost his job. Surely, not on their anniversary dinner date.

Levi had made reservations weeks ago at Le Pigeon. Nancy arranged for her parents to watch five year old Luke and seven year old Shawna. For once, everything came together perfectly. Now, all he'd be able to think about was finances. Would they lose the house? Would they have to move and the kids switch to lesser schools? Would they have to downsize to one vehicle for a while? File for bankruptcy?

"Levi, you're early!" Nancy called from upstairs when she heard him come through the front door. "I'm so relieved. My mother actually canceled on us but I just found us a babysitter, thank god!"

"What…" Levi moaned, dropping his keys on the table by the stairs. He'd left the box in the trunk of his car. "Nan, you know the last thing I want to think about at dinner is some gum-chewing teenager taking care of Luke and Shawna."

"Oh come on. She's babysat for Mike and Diane … it won't be that bad. They said she's very mature and responsible. They highly recommended her."

Levi protested further, but only silently in his mind as he marched upstairs to get changed. He heard his children playing in Luke's room.

After a while, the doorbell rang, and Levi made it downstairs just as Nancy welcomed the babysitter inside.

"Are you Cassie?" Nancy asked cheerfully.

"Yes ma'am, good to meet you." Cassie smiled. Her red hair was woven in two braids that went a little past her shoulder blades.

Levi caught her more than once blowing soft, pink bubbles with her gum while Nancy showed her around the house. He managed to mutter quietly in his wife's ear as she passed by, "Mature and responsible, huh?" Nancy merely rolled her eyes at him and continued on her way with Cassie upstairs.

Minutes later, they were finally in Nancy's silver SUV and ready to pull out of the driveway. Nancy touched her hand to her forehead as if she was in pain.

"You okay?" Levi inquired, looking intently at her face. It looked clammy, despite her make up.

"Oh, I'll be fine." Nancy replied. "Just been feeling a little under the weather today."

"How are things at the hospital?" Levi asked, putting the car in reverse and backing out of the driveway. "I saw the uh … the flu is hitting people pretty hard this year. Old folks, mostly?"

"That's just the thing," She answered, dropping her hand to her lap and she seemed to stare off into the distance in front of them. "It seems to be hitting younger people the hardest. Strange symptoms … fevers like I've never seen."

"Scary stuff. I'm sure glad we got our flu shots this year."

Studying the menu at the restaurant, all Levi could think about was how expensive everything was. He was tempted to order a salad and leave it at that. Especially when he heard she wanted to order the duck and an eighty dollar bottle of merlot. He wasn't very hungry anyway.

"Honey, are you alright?" Nancy asked, looking up from her menu with her large, brown eyes. "You seem a little agitated tonight."

"No, no, Nan." Levi forced an affectionate smile. "I'm fine." He saw her rubbing her forehead again, closing her eyes with a wince. "Maybe I'm just feeling under the weather too."

As the evening went on, Nancy's illness became more and more obvious to Levi. He watched beads of sweat form on her forehead. She shivered occasionally, as if chilled. She was becoming oddly distracted by movements around her and her breathing slowly changed. It was raspy and irregular. He touched her hand with concern.

"Nancy, you're burning up!" he said with dismay, but as quietly as he politely could in a fine restaurant. "We've got to get you home."

At once, he dropped his napkin on the table and nervously signaled for the waiter across the room. When he turned back to his wife, her skin had gone pale and her eyes dim and glazed over. Her hands viciously clutched the tablecloth. Saliva ran down her chin, and she stood up from her seat.

"Nancy!" Levi said, also rising from his seat. "Help! We need help here, someone call an ambu-"

Before he could finish his request, she lunged at him savagely. He instinctively clobbered her in the head with his elbow, then immediately felt horrible for doing so. This deterred her for a moment, but she was on him again. He was barely able to keep her at arm's length. Her hands clawed at his body unnaturally and her frothy mouth and jaw snapped open and shut in the direction of his face, like a rabid animal.

People in the restaurant shrieked and moved away. Two waiters came to restrain Nancy, and she quickly turned on them, biting one in the neck and ripping the flesh away with her now bloodstained teeth. He cried out in agony and fell to his knees, clutching the flesh of his neck that sprayed blood all over her navy blue dress. That's when the second waiter took the eighty dollar bottle of wine and smashed it over her head.

"Don't!" Levi screamed desperately. The sight of seeing his love drenched in blood and merlot, with glass shards sticking out of her hair, was too much for him to take.

Alarmingly, this still did not stop her. She pounced on her new assailant and tried to bite him. The large, dark man grabbed her head in both hands and, in the process of keeping her at bay, snapped her neck. She fell lifeless to the floor in a pool of blood.

"Oh my god..." Levi cried out, afraid to come near his wife's body. He looked to the left at the waiter, who had been bitten moments ago, and his eyes had already glazed over, his breathing was turning raspy, and in a matter of seconds, he was attacking nearby customers, biting and tearing at them in a frenzy.

Levi had no choice but to get out of there, along with the terrified mob of customers. His first thought was to get home to the kids. Nancy had been with them all afternoon, what if they had taken ill? What if Cassie had?

Driving down the strip of bars and boutiques, all seemed normal at first, until Levi reached the corner of Milwaukie Avenue and Ninth Street. There he saw a man, staggering about in torn clothes drenched in blood, stumbling after people, growling and reaching with his arms. Several minutes after this, he saw another, this time a woman. He nearly smashed his car into the curb in horror when he saw that she was walking along chewing on someone's arm.

His heart raced frantically as he sped into his driveway. He decided to use the garage this time, in case there might be trouble in the neighborhood later that night. Everything felt so unreal. He could barely get his keys together and get out of his car without fumbling in adrenaline.

He entered the house through the kitchen door that was connected to the garage. The lights were all out. He paused, listening for any sounds. After several seconds, he heard crying.

"Mr. Colton, is that you?" Cassie's voice squeaked.

"It's me," he answered, trying to sound calm. "Where are you? Why are the lights out?"

"I was scared … I didn't want anyone to know we were home." She sobbed. "I turned all the lights off and locked the doors."

"Good … you did good Cassie." He felt his way to the kitchen island. Using his cell phone as a light, he found her there, sitting on the floor, hugging her knees. "Where are Luke and Shawna?"

"Upstairs sleeping…"

Levi immediately darted upstairs to check on them. They were both asleep in Shawna's bed. He touched each of their foreheads. They felt cool.

The sound of a car alarm startled him. He went to the window and peered through the blinds. There were several deranged figures out there. Stumbling, moaning and growling.

"What's happening?" Cassie's voice whispered behind him. "Where's Mrs. Colton?"

"She took ill."

"Stay here with them. Do not leave this room."

Levi raced downstairs and opened the door underneath that led further down to the basement. Luke was three years old when he developed an obsession with the gun cabinet, so they had decided to put them away until he was older. Levi found the key sitting on the top ledge of the doorframe inside. When he flicked the light on, the light bulb blew.

"Shit!" He hissed. At least there was enough light being streaming through the small, high windows from an outside flood lamp. He could easily see the safe. It was unusually damp and cold down there. He grabbed everything he could. He retrieved two lever action shot guns and three hand guns with holsters. He quickly loaded everything to the max with ammunition and strapped the rest to his body. He turned to head back upstairs, but stopped dead in his tracks when he heard that same, raspy breathing.

Unable to move or breath, he tried to detect where it was coming from. He tossed one rifle that had been slung over his back around his shoulder and made himself ready. And he waited.

His eye caught sight of one of the windows, and he noticed it was broken. Someone had gotten in, and they couldn't be very large. It seemed that only a child could fit through that window.

That's about when he saw the dreadful child. She crept out from behind a concrete pillar in the middle of the room, with blood dripping from her mouth, holding the mutilated remains of the neighbor's cat in her hands. Bloody bits of flesh oozed from between her teeth when she suddenly hissed at him in dim light. He raised his rifle, aimed it at her head, and fired. No hesitation. Her body fell in a broken, messy heap.

He had no time to think or feel after that, because as soon as the shot was fired, he heard Cassie screaming upstairs. He bounded upstairs and slammed the basement door shut, then slid the cherry wood table in front of it and ran up to the next floor.

"What? What happened?" He asked frantically.

"What was that? Did you shoot someone?" Cassie said, then pointed at his guns, wild eyed.

"There was one downstairs," Levi answered. He was relieved to see Luke and Shawna were still asleep. "We can't stay here."

"Wh-wha-where are we supposed to go?" she stuttered with fright. "We can't leave. We can't go outside! You've seen what's out there…"

"They can easily get in the house and we'd be trapped. I'm running this show, and if you want to live and not get sick, just do what I say, okay?"

Cassie squelched a sob and began chewing her gum even more furiously. She nodded her assent.

"We need to get the kids up and load them in the car. You're going to do that, and act like nothing is wrong. I'm going to gather supplies."

Before heading downstairs, he stopped in his bedroom for a change of clothes. He nearly lost it when he saw the dozens of dresses and skirts strewn on the bed. She'd tried on so many, just for him. Pushing through his emotion, he ripped his dress shirt off. He didn't even know when it had become blood splattered. Was it hers?

He paused in front of the mirror and saw the three scars on his abdomen. He remembered the pain that night and the horror of lying face down in a puddle of rain and street sludge that stung his wounds, moments before his partner had raced to his side. As he threw a black muscle shirt on and army green cargos, he wondered where Colin was right now and how he was holding up in this chaos.

Once he was downstairs, Levi piled canned goods, non-perishables and any snack foods he could find into a cooler. He heard Cassie coming down with the kids who were now dressed, trying to calmly address or avoid their groggy questions about what was going on. While Cassie got them buckled in, Levi tossed the cooler into the back of the SUV and shoved a case of bottled water on top.

Where are we going?" She asked Levi as he got in, chewing her gum loud and hard.

Levi couldn't take any more of this. He grabbed her jaw and reached into her mouth to pull it out, with Cassie struggling and looking at him like he was crazy. He stuck it to the dashboard and started up the engine.

"What the hell?" she yelled at him, rubbing her jaw and mouth with her hands.

"Hey-" Levi snapped. "There are kids in this car." His hands gripped the steering wheel as he waited for the slowest garage door on the planet to open. As soon as he had enough clearance, he threw it into reverse and backed out onto the street. Three sickly figures caught sight of their rapid movement and began coming towards the vehicle. One of them nearly got right in his path. He swerved not to hit it.

Levi zoomed down the street, dodging anything in his path with professional accuracy. Cassie could only grip the dash and stare ahead as if she was car sick, occasionally looking over at Levi with astonishment. He looked over and saw Cassie tightening her seatbelt across her hips.

"A radio report, thank god!" Levi said, turning up the speakers. A jittery woman's voice was heard, reporting a virus that had severely mutated in the last twenty-four hours. She said it began with flu-like symptoms and ended in death that would seize control of the victim's brainstem. Not much more was known about it. Then she started to give a list of safe places that had been set up. Levi ordered everyone in the car to be quiet so he could hear the nearest haven. Rockfield High School.

"Is that where we're going?" Cassie asked. "Maybe my parents went there."

The high school was fairly organized by local police. A task force was set along the road leading to the front gates, in order to take out any of the sick ones who approached unloading vehicles. There was nowhere to park anymore, however. After unloading Cassie and the kids, security gladly took the food supplies.

Levi had to park many blocks away and abandon his SUV there. He ran hard and fast to get back to his children. He took out a sick man who had somehow lost his legs. Perhaps it was a waste of bullets, since he couldn't really hurt anyone anyway, but it just didn't seem right to leave him there like that.

Inside the facility, he was taken to the gymnasium where his children ran up to him and hugged him. It was crowded there, full of adults with stunned faces and crying children. Cassie was still hanging around; she was upset. She hadn't found her parents.

"I'm sure they're safe somewhere, Cassie." Levi tried to reassure her. "There are a number of safe places they could have gone to and they are probably there wondering about you too."

"Daddy, why do you have all your guns?" Shawna asked, tugging on his arm.

"They've been asking questions, non-stop." Cassie told him.

Levi didn't know what answers to give his children as their innocent faces stared up at him. "Will you stay here with them?"

Cassie nodded and made a small smile. Levi left and headed down the hallway. The police were centralized in the ad- ministrative offices. When he entered the room, he was instantly recognized by several officers.

"Levi!" Chief Moon rang out. He was leaning over a table with several others, looking at a map of the city.

"What's the scoop?" Levi asked, approaching his old co- worker. "I was glad to hear you were chosen for chief last year."

"If you'd stayed, it would have been you." Chief Moon replied, shaking his hand warmly.

After a brief exchange with a few others, Levi was shown where the safe havens were and where specific forces were at work, trying to secure more areas.

"Some areas are worse than others," Lt. Harvey explained, pointing to areas they'd circled in red and others circled in yellow or blue. "You can see the sicklies are more concentrated down- town, and as you move farther out, there are less of them."

"They must be concentrated at the hospital, then," Levi speculated.

"That's what we thought too," came another officer. "But that hospital has been locked down and we know that isn't where they are concentrated at. We think it's the train yard."

"Strange. Why would they be so heavily concentrated there?" he wondered out loud. His eyes scanned the entire map. "You're right though. They're fixated here, but as you go farther and farther out, they are fewer in number."

"We're in touch with the other safe havens and we're all just trying to understand why," Chief Moon said, brushing his Asian salt and peppered hair away from his forehead. "And that's not all that we don't get. Hacksoff, you want to tell him?"

Lt. Hacksoff cleared his throat nervously. "Once the virus has taken the brain, it drives the body to feed on living flesh. This much is obvious. But we have seen some of them actually appearing to be taking hostages. I've seen men, women and children being dragged off and we couldn't save them … god knows where they took them to and why."

"Holy shit," Levi exclaimed. "Can you map out these instances?"

"They're happening everywhere," Lt. Harvey shrugged. "Probably about a tenth of the attacks are hostage situations. Only a few we were able to save."

"This could be why the train yard has such a higher concentration of sicklies. They might be dragging people off over there and infecting them, breeding some kind of army."

"Then we've got to get in there," Levi said without hesitation. "We've got to cut off whatever operation they have down there."

Chief Moon and the others exchanged glances around the room. "That's what we're planning to do. We're going to need every able bodied person and our team. Can I count on your help?"

Levi thought for only a moment, before saying, "Of course."

"Excellent," Moon answered, sounding relieved. "Then we'll all try and get some rest tonight and meet in room 24C at o' six hundred."

Levi slept on the floor that night between his children. Cassie slept on the other side of Shawna. Levi found himself watching Cassie sleep, and noticing the delicate curve of her waist that sloped back up to her hip. Maybe he'd been unfair to her. He could spy just a little bit of soft skin between the top of her jeans and the bottom of her disheveled shirt as she lay on her side. Feeling slightly guilty, he did his best to put his thoughts aside, and soon after fell asleep.

Bad news came in the morning. During the night, two of the safe havens had been taken by sicklies. Their own force outside had taken a beating and had had to retreat behind the gates. They couldn't take in anymore survivors.

"Why didn't someone come get me up?" Levi asked, irritatedly.

"It was bad, Levi." Chief Moon explained to him, stirring his coffee. "Once we retreated behind the gates, the danger was past. We needed our very best men well rested for today."

There was also new information on the viral war. Another task force had been to the train yard and brought back horrifying news. There were now identified different kinds of sicklies. Most of them were what was stumbling around on the streets, mindlessly feeding and stealing bodies. Inside the train yard was a more disturbing breed of sickly. These particular sicklies were more capable of thought and could work things out, almost like a higher species of animal. Witnesses said that some hostages were trapped inside empty train cars, bitten, and left there to turn ill. They turned into the cunning sicklies that they had been bitten by. Those sicklies would eat other live hostages, and others they would lead away deeper into the train yard where no one had gone to yet.

"The situation is darkening by the hour. We're starting to see more cunning, faster sicklies moving out onto the streets now. We've got to get in there," Lt. Hacksoff uttered with restrained fear in his voice.

Levi went back to his children and hugged them tightly for a long time. Cassie stood by, awkwardly. Levi gave her a thankful nod and then walked out to the empty hallway afterwards to leave, but Cassie had followed close behind and threw her arms around him, crying on his neck. He hesitated, but at last put his hands on her and found himself touching that same soft skin he'd been staring at the night before.

"I'll watch them as best I can," Cassie sobbed. "I won't leave them."

"You're running up quite the bill for me," Levi answered softly, trying to be funny. "I don't think I can afford you."

With that, she pulled away from him and gave him a much unexpected kiss on his mouth and then went back to the gymnasium. Levi wasn't sure what had happened just then as he stood there frozen, watching her walk away. When he turned to leave, he saw that they hadn't been alone. Lt. Hacksoff had seen.

"Teenagers," Lt. Hacksoff smirked. "I could smell the hormones all the way over here."

Levi chuckled nervously, as if to coolly shake it off and forget about it. He wouldn't though. Those lips had been too soft and sweet.

About ten police cars were waiting outside and everyone piled in. The gates were opened, creating frenzy between police and the hissing, growling sicklies. Heads were pulverized by shots and flying clubs as the vehicles made their quick getaway to the red zone. Blood ran down the window beside Levi, who was riding with Chief Moon at the wheel. Two more officers sat in the back seat.

"Are we going to take Waters Rd. to the train yard?" Levi asked, rolling down his window and back up again. He had hoped to clean it somewhat, but it mostly just smeared.

"Waters is packed with sicklies because it's so close to the hospital. We better take First Avenue."

They parked their cars just outside the train yard. It was immediate chaos. A thick web of sicklies surrounded them and they had to fight their way out of their own vehicles, pumping them with lead and smashing the sickly faces in with the butts of their rifles if they got too close. It was getting bad. He saw several officers being bitten and gorged upon by the other sicklies as their screams echoed in the yard. Tragic, but distracting and it gave some relief to the rest of them.

Soon, another task force arrived and they were able to join forces. They dispersed into groups of four. Levi was teamed with the chief, Lt. Hacksoff and Officer Houston.

Presently, the sicklies were swarming an entire team that had fallen and were being eaten alive. Levi and his team moved forward along a group of multiple tracks running parallel and broke off in different directions at the gate. They approached two long trains sitting parallel on the tracks and walked silently between them towards the rail barn.

Slowly, they made their way across the ballast between the two trains with no sicklies in sight for the time being. Officer Houston made a bad turn with his foot and he stumbled hard, jostling rocks loudly. One rock flew and hit the wheel of a train car, sounding a loud metal, PING!

Immediately, all of the train cars around them erupted with the sound of metal and wood clanging loudly together, and hands beating against the walls of their confines. Then came the eerie roaring sounds of the dead and not the living. With dozens of cars around them, the commotion was deafening, so they picked up their pace, bolting down the right of way.

"Dammit, Houston," Chief Moon seethed between deep breathes. "If we get caught here, we're sitting ducks!"

Sure enough, up ahead at the coupler between two train cars, a sickly poked his head out and spotted them. It turned away and roared, as if to summon others. This was definitely the higher class of sicklies. Five of them poured out and met the team head on. Levi took out two with his Beretta 92, while the others handled the rest.

Only moments later, a dozen more sicklies appeared. Levi popped off as many as he could, while still on a dead run in the midst of the clamoring train cars. This class of sickly was indeed more terrifying. They made eye contact with their pale, yellow eyes, and unlike the other sicklies who moved rather slowly, these were almost capable of running.

"Colton!" Chief Moon shouted, pointing his handgun at Levi. He instinctively ducked down to the ground, a second before the chief fired, stopping one of the sicklies that was about to have him. It's body tumbled over the top of Levi and he got up and continued running. They were almost to the barn.

Just then, Officer Houston was taken. Not eaten, nor bitten. He was hauled away, crying out for help. His teammates stopped and turned around. Levi and Lt. Hacksoff were covering Chief Moon, who was trying to get a clear shot to free Houston. He fired twice, but failed to hit his target. Houston was gone.

"Come on!" Levi called, leading them on towards the barn. The doors were open, but all that could be seen was darkness inside.

As he ran, Levi loaded a fresh magazine in his Beretta, then reached for his flashlight and clicked it on, preparing to jump the three foot ledge into the barn in three…two…one.

He nearly miscalculated the ledge and lost his balance for a half second. When he recovered, he shined his light forward and his heart nearly stopped at the sight of an army of yellow, angry eyes turning towards him. His two remaining comrades had jumped up with him now, and they froze for a moment in fear as the sicklies realized they were intruders and began coming towards them.

Levi's eyes darted around and his mind worked quickly. He spied a steel ladder on the side of a parked train car inside the barn to their right, and motioned for the chief and Lt. Hacksoff to follow him. He climbed with all his fury, followed by Chief Moon. Lt. Hacksoff was last, and just as he nearly had gotten himself to the top, a sickly grabbed his leg and was pulling him down. He dropped his flashlight, which had been in his mouth.

Chief Moon and Levi came to his immediate rescue and fired on the sicklies that they could make out in the darkness. Levi yanked Lt. Hacksoff up onto the roof of the train car, and shined light on his foot.

"Thank god," Chief Moon exclaimed. "The bastards didn't bite you!"

"Let's hope they can't climb," Levi cautioned, peering over the edge.

The sicklies were clamoring below, but none seemed to be able to climb.

"Let's move in, then." Levi called to his partners. They ran the length of the train, hopping from car to car. Swarms of sicklies surrounded them on both sides of the train, becoming more bellicose by the moment. At times, they piled on top of each other so thickly that they nearly could have climbed on top, if they'd thought enough about it.

Up ahead was a high cement wall that led to a loading platform, high enough that the sicklies couldn't follow them there. On the platform there were a few sicklies, nothing Levi and his team couldn't handle.

Blood and guts spilled all over the concrete as they took out the small group on the loading bay. Once that was taken care of, they stopped to catch their breath.

"Where to now, boss?" Lt. Hacksoff panted, bent over with his wrists resting on his knees, Glock still in hand.

"Let's just..." Chief Moon wheezed, finding his words. He was much less out of shape than the other two. "Let's just get our bearings."

Levi scanned the area with his flashlight as he regained control of his own heavy breathing. Behind them was the train. In front of the loading platform was a huge warehouse that appeared to be full of lumber. He could hear the sicklies below the platform snarling and clawing at the walls on their left, and to their right was a doorway that led down a hallway. He pointed his flashlight up and saw a second floor with broken, bloody glass windows that overlooked the bay.

Suddenly, they saw a movement of flickering light down that hallway, and they positioned themselves with their weapons and waited. It was another police team of four officers. Relief filled the air as they greeted one another, only to be cut short by a hoard of sicklies coming over the wall of the loading platform from below. Enough of a mass had collected there that they were able to climb up to the platform.

"Let's check out the manager's office and dispatch center!" said one of the other officers. "We passed the stairs down that hallway there and it has a steel door."

The team of seven headed for the hallway, but not before having to spill more blood as the sicklies gathered one by one onto the platform and attacked with ferocity. Levi ran out of ammunition for his Beretta and began popping off rounds with his rifle, moving backwards towards the corridor. It was harder to hold his flashlight while firing the rifle.

They made it to the stairs and flew like the wind to the top before the sicklies could figure a way to get up, and they slammed the metal door shut at the top and breathed once more in the dark. They'd gone in so deeply now, Levi wondered how they would ever get out again.

The manager's office had several workspaces, and a wall that didn't reach quite to the top of the ceiling separated the office from the lunch room and restroom area.

There in the dark, he thought of a young and lithe teenage girl who was probably waiting for him to return. He felt the shame of dishonoring Nancy's memory with thoughts like this, but couldn't bring himself to stop. Nancy had been good to him, but their marriage had become so stale the past few years. She'd gone from being an exciting cheerleader for his college football team to a professional, working woman with little time for him and nothing to talk about besides deadlines and expense reports and changing hospital policies.

Meanwhile, he'd given up what he loved most: his career and service to the public. He traded that for menial keystrokes on a computer and staring at a screen that couldn't save him from the emptiness he felt inside. It couldn't save anyone at all. It was an utter futility that only subsided when he could defend and protect the weak. But since this morning, he hadn't felt that emptiness or futility at all. Whatever might happen between him and Cassie was just a fantasy. But this feeling of fulfillment was real and he never wanted to lose it again.

"Colton," came Chief Moon's voice in the blackness. "We've secured the room; its empty."

"Wait, boss…" Lt. Hacksoff interrupted. "I didn't notice this before."

He shined his light on the floor, starting at a door on the other end of the room with a green, lit up EXIT sign above it. From the bottom of that door, on the floor, was a trail of thick, gory blood and entrails, leading somewhere they could not yet tell. As they came nearer, they covered their noses because of the horrid stench of rotting flesh filling their nostrils.

One of the officers pushed that door open and they discovered a wheelchair accessible ramp leading up to the offices. Streaks of blood and carnage went all the way down to the warehouse below. They closed the door and began to follow the trail through the lunchroom. At the back of the room was an open door with a glass window that read, "Dispatch & Admin" on it.

Just as they were about to go through it, Levi could hear screams coming from the handicap entrance behind them. They ducked down and hid behind tables and counters. In the light of the emergency signs, they saw one of the sicklies dragging a live hostage, a woman in her thirties. Through her strained screams she tried her hardest to get away, but the sickly was a large, strong male with a death grip on her throat as it dragged her along.

Chief Moon, crouched underneath a round table, had positioned his rifle to take down the sickly, but Levi put his hand on the barrel and shook his head. He waited for the sickly and it's captive to disappear, then he signaled for the others to follow him in pursuit.

Silently they crept behind it, keeping a sensible distance, hoping to go unnoticed. There were a number of rooms they walked past, but the room at the end of the hall was the one the sickly disappeared into, even slamming the door behind it. Soon after, the woman's screams ceased and they all knew they couldn't help her.

They stood there for a few moments outside the door, guns poised. Levi knew in his gut they'd found the hub, whatever it was.

This was the main operation. Behind this door was the real threat that needed to be taken out. Then people could be safe again. His children could be safe again.

He counted down from three with his fingers for the others. At one, he lead them through the door, slipping inside, two by two.

The room was buzzing like a beehive with both kinds of sicklies. Levi and the others skulked along the walls, unseen in the shadows for now, taking in what they could see. The sicklies were all clustered around and reaching up towards one solitary creature sitting on top of a chair that sat on a work desk in the middle of the room. She was backlit by windows that spanned the wall behind her, looking out over the yard.

She was appalling to look at, with peeling dead flesh that hung from her face and arms, some in large chunks and others in long, slimy strands. Blood and pus were weeping from the raw skin under her eyes, and her lips were marred from biting herself with her broken, jagged teeth as she ate. Her arms and hands were so badly decayed that they could hardly be used.

She hissed and snarled at her subjects in the dimly lit room, as if communicating to them her will. They fed her by hand the bleeding remains of the dismembered hostage, tearing flesh from the body and putting it directly into her mouth. Others just seemed to brush their filthy hands all over her, pulling at the hanging bits of flesh that had deadened enough to come lose, tugging strands of her hair out, doing strange things with her tattered clothing. They attended to her like a savage queen bee of death. Sometimes she would sink her teeth into one of them, should their hand or arm get very close to her face. When she did this, they appeared to become stronger and more alert. They wanted her to bite them. It seemed to Levi that she carried the mutating virus that could change them all.

Suddenly, she stopped eating, with flesh still between her teeth. She spit it out onto the floor, the other sicklies stared at it in their dumb confusion, then looked back up at her. Then, she opened her mouth and said with a hoarse roar, "INTRUDERS!"

All eyes now turned to their direction and fell on them. Levi held his breath, and then he saw Chief Moon slowly reach for his vest pocket and draw out a black grenade. Levi's eyes lit up, just as the mob of sicklies began making their way in their direction.

Levi and Lt. Hacksoff began furiously shooting at the sicklies, which only lasted moments because the hoard of the rank creatures were practically on top of them. Levi drew his police knife for close combat, stabbing the sicklies through the eyes or in their mouth, going up through the roof of their mouths into their sinuses and brains. He heard Chief Moon cry out in agony, and he quickly retreated back out to the hallway, slamming the wooden door shut on a number of gnarly, waving arms. Three other men had to assist him to finally get the door fully closed. Levi held the door knob tightly in place as he pressed himself hard against the with the others.

"Alright, we've got a scant chance of blowing this beehive to hell!" Shouted the chief, who stood back away from the door, limping. "I'm going to count to three, and you're going to open that door and run past me. I'll throw it…"

"Sir, that's not going to work!" Levi yelled back as he struggled against the door with the others. "They're piled up behind this door; you'll never get that grenade through at this point. We should have thrown it while we were in there!"

"I was going to," Chief Moon replied remorsefully. "But I was attacked and we had to get out of there.

"What's wrong with your leg?," Lt. Hacksoff asked, pointing at the one that Chief Moon had little weigh on.

Reluctantly, Chief Moon lifted his pant leg and exposed a nasty bite that oozed green. He was infected. Already, his brow was developing beads of sweat.

"Well," the chief said almost to himself. "There's nothing for it then. I'll take care of this myself."

He crouched down on the floor in front of the door, already feeling weak. There wasn't much time. Levi went to help him up. He couldn't stand the idea of losing the chief now, after they'd come so far.

"No, I'll get farther in if I can crawl." Chief Moon gave the signal, and everyone released the door at once and fled down the hallway. Instantly, the door blew open as a riot of rotting sicklies charged out. Levi turned to look behind him and watched Chief Moon bulldoze through their legs and disappear inside. He was in.

Levi, Lt. Hacksoff and the other team sprinted through the lunchroom and dashed down the stairs that lead back to the loading platform. Only a few stragglers were left there, which they slaughtered with their knives or merely shoved them out of the way, leaping for the train car and taking refuge on the rooftop. That's when they felt the explosion. They ducked as part of the roof vibrated severely over their heads and thick dust fell on them. Other parts of the barn, like the warehouse, were completely caved in. Light shined again. They'd been lucky.

The nightmare was over. More police forces arrived and re-took the train yard. Several of the train cars were found to have live, uninfected people inside, probably being reserved for food later. They were safe now. Slowly, the city regained control of the virus, which was eventually banned and completely contained by a high security lab for testing. As for Levi, he returned to the service and was promoted to Chief Colton several years later.

Put down the book and run. Please…it will be more…fun. No reason to bloody a good book. It'll be quick and painful. Turn out your light if you don't want to watch. Mr Empty is coming…

Printed in Great Britain
by Amazon

12084042R00171